TULKU

Attack in the dark, screams, the thatched huts blazing: the Boxer rebellion reaches Theodore's once peaceful mission settlement in remote China. Though Theodore manages to escape, his father lies dead and the life he has known is in ruins.

On the run, he falls in with Mrs Jones, an ageing quick-witted plant-collector, and together they flee to the forbidden country of Tibet. Or are they really fleeing? Are they not being drawn to a destiny beyond their imagining?

In the great gold-domed monastery of Dong Pe, they meet great dangers. With his narrow upbringing, how can Theodore face them? And how can he and Mrs Jones and their Chinese courier escape from the mountains, when the old Lama who rules the monastery insists that they hold the clue to the birth of the long-awaited Tulku?

This rich and exciting novel achieved the unique distinction of winning both the Library Association's Carnegie Medal and also the Whitbread Award.

PETER DICKINSON

PUFFIN BOOKS

Puffin Books, Penguin Books Ltd, Harmondsworth, Middlesex, England
Penguin Books, 625 Madison Avenue, New York, New York 10022, U.S.A.
Penguin Books Australia Ltd, Ringwood, Victoria, Australia
Penguin Books Canada Ltd, 2801 John Street, Markham, Ontario, Canada L3R 1B4
Penguin Books (N.Z.) Ltd, 182–190 Wairau Road, Auckland 10, New Zealand

First published by Victor Gollancz Ltd 1979
Published in Puffin Books 1981

Reproduced, printed and bound in Great Britain by
Hazell Watson & Viney Ltd, Aylesbury, Bucks
Set in Bembo

Chapter 1

Theodore woke in the dark, sucked harshly out of the pit of sleep by a hand shaking his shoulder and a voice hissing in his ear. Before he could groan a question the hand covered his mouth. He jerked himself free and sat up, making the straps of his bed creak with the strain, but by now he had recognised the voice, and guessed at the urgency.

"Fu T'iao! What? Why?" he whispered.

"Dress. Be quick. Your father says . . ."

No more questions, then. As Theodore reached for his clothes where they hung from a peg in the beam above his head he saw Fu T'iao moving across the room, and knew by the fact that he could see at all that there was more light than there should be, a pinkish flicker of moving flame through the window. And there were more noises in the night than the usual faint water-rattle from the ravine and wind-hiss from the woods beyond—there was a grumbling murmur, which suddenly clacked into recognisably human shouts, and now there was Father's voice riding above the racket, slow, heavy and confident, with the unmistakable mid-Western honk only half-modulated into the tones of the local dialect, Miao. (A visiting Baptist had once told Father that he spoke Chinese languages as though he was wearing native clothes but had forgotten to remove his tall hat.)

Theodore pulled on his trousers, then stood and wriggled

into his long over-shirt, automatically twitching his pigtail clear of the collar as his head poked into the open. Father's voice was half-drowned now by the shouting, but he spoke on as steadily as if he had been arguing a point of doctrine. In the moment of stillness after putting on his clothes Theodore was appalled with sudden terror—not ordinary alarm, but a feeling which seemed to rush up through his body from the floor, like water surging up one of the bamboo irrigation pipes on the terraces. It was as much shock as fear, the shock of uncertainty rushing into a life whose every detail was fixed and known. Slowly he sat back onto his bed. Unwilled, his hand slid under his pillow and grasped his Bible. He was still sitting there, shivering, listening to the yells—to Father trying to speak still, and his voice stopping with a grunt in mid-sentence—when Fu T'iao came scuttling in from the living-room with a bundle in his arms.

"Come now. Quick. By the back way. Carry this."

Shivering, Theodore rose and took what seemed to be one of the satchels which they all used for carrying their midday meals up into the further fields. He slid the strap across his shoulders and followed Fu T'iao through the living-room, moving without a stumble among the unseen furniture because it stood where it always had. In the kitchen beyond, the air smelt of the remains of supper—beans flavoured with fennel and enlivened by a few small lumps of fatty pork. Fu T'iao took several seconds to open the monkey-proof catch on the outer door, but made no attempt to shut it once they were through, scuttling off at once across the gardens, crouching into the shadows of the huts. Theodore followed without question, though his path took him straight across a fresh-sown seed-bed. It was Father's orders.

There was more light in the Settlement than he'd ever seen at night—far more, surely, than torches could throw. Through a gap between huts he saw three elders walking along the road towards the centre of the hubbub, their hands folded into their sleeves, as though they were going to Church. In a sudden patch of silence Mrs Teng's voice ran on, clacking like a night bird, asking Teng how he could permit this disturbance to happen. A wild shout rose further off and a yellow light flared high and sudden, making even the trees beyond the ravine stand sharp-leaved, where before there had been dark vaguenesses. Shouts became screams.

"Hurry!" panted Fu T'iao. "Hurry!"

When they reached the last of the huts he twisted away from the road and into the orchard, crouching even lower now to duck beneath blossom-laden boughs, but moving more and more carefully until they reached the ancient cypress that stood like a landmark on the edge of the cliff above the ravine. They halted in the blackness beneath it. Several huts were burning now, and the smoke drifted in black hummocks towards the orange-tinted clouds. Fu T'iao peered round the cypress along the line of the ravine, paying no attention to a scream, a woman's, that rose above the hubbub and snapped short.

"Men guard the bridge," he whispered. "The old path."

Without waiting for him Theodore turned and ran, crouching low, along the lip of the ravine. Voices were singing now—"Rock of Ages" in Father's translation—interrupted by savage yells but rising unfaltering into the flame-lit dark. Only Theodore and Fu T'iao seemed to be running away. It was Father's order, but still there was a strangeness in it, for normally the order would have been to come forward and face the cause of fear. At the ruined heathen shrine Theodore turned and led the way down the slanting pathway into the dark, feeling for each footstep. The cliff soon blanketed the clamour among the huts, but the rattle of water grew louder and the streaky glitter of foam shone sixty feet below. He probably knew the path better than Fu T'iao, because no one but children used it since Father had built the bridge. It was littered with loose stones, which clattered away as their feet displaced them. He reached the bottom and at once poised to jump to the first stepping-stone.

The rains had barely begun, so the water was not knee-deep, except in hollows, but it still ran fast enough to knock a man over if he wasn't careful. The stepping-stones stood like pillars amid the silver onrush. Theodore jumped, using the momentum of each stride to carry him into the next, and at the sixth stride onto the further shore. Fu T'iao followed more sedately.

"Now, Theodore, you must go on alone."

"Why? What are you going to do? What's happening?"

"Your father says you must hide in the forest. I have put food in your bag, and money, and here is a blanket. When day comes be very careful. Trust no stranger. Look from far off to see what is happening in the Settlement. Perhaps these people will only burn a few huts, and then your father will persuade them to go away. Then, as soon as you have seen any of our people moving freely, you can return, but speak and act like a peasant boy until you are certain. If you think it is not safe to return, your father says you must find your way to Doctor Goertler at Taho."

"But what are you going to do?"

"I have obeyed your father's order to take you beyond the ravine. Now my place is with the Congregation of Christ. After the manner of men I must fight with beasts at Ephesus.

May Christ watch over you, Theodore. There is cash in the bag, but remember the roads are full of robbers."

"My place is with the Congregation too."

"Your father gave the order. He had little time, but he was very certain. Listen! Someone on the path! Hurry, before men come from the bridge along this cliff! God guard you!"

Fu T'iao's voice had none of the slow confidence with which the adult members of the Congregation usually spoke. He pushed the blanket-roll into Theodore's arms, turned and leaped for the first stepping-stone. Theodore began to climb as quickly as he could, listening through the gasping of his own breath and the thud of his heart for any sound of movement at the top. The trees, he knew, grew thickly along this cliff and the path wound away from the ravine to reach the road further along. But his alertness was only on the surface, for all his inner mind was taken up with what Fu T'iao had said. *If, after the manner of men, I have fought with beasts at Ephesus, what advantageth it me, if the dead rise not?* Members of the Congregation knew their New Testament almost by heart, and often used its words when they were making a serious decision. Now, stumbling and panting up the cliff path, Theodore worked out what Fu T'iao had meant. The Settlement was being attacked and burnt because the people in it were Christians, and just as Saint Paul had been made to face the lions in one of the Roman circuses, so he was returning to confront these attackers. To do otherwise would be to deny his faith.

But Theodore was running away. Father's order, Fu T'iao had said. Father had ordered him to deny his faith, to hide in the wood and then look for Doctor Goertler. Had Father really given the order? Or had Fu T'iao, driven by loyalty to save his master's child, acted on his own?

The sudden pang of doubt stopped Theodore in his tracks, and as his panting eased he heard voices on the far path. Fu T'iao, climbing, must have met somebody coming down, so others were running away—on Father's orders? Because their faith had failed? There was yelling now at the bridge; along the edge of the ravine, silhouetted against the glare from the Settlement, people were streaming towards the old path, some cowering as they ran, others pursuing. They were like devils, sharp against the blaze of hell—one had a hoe raised to strike. The cypress was a warning pillar, the hard-pruned trees of the orchard were gestures of pain, all black against orange. The enemies on the bridge would see that there was an escape route here and send men to block it. Theodore scurried up the last few yards of cliff and ran between the trees. No special shouts rose, as if someone near at hand had spotted escaping prey. Instead a new noise started, the unmistakable tock of an axe. Another joined it.

Theodore ran on. Where the path forked he chose the arm that led away from the road. About fifty yards along it he stopped and looked back. A few streaks of orange showed between the smooth trunks, and the voices and the uproar were softened by the nearer leaf-noise. The axes were striking now with a steady rhythm. There were voices in the wood. I must hide, he thought, climb a tree, find a hole or a thick bush. He knew from many games that it was not a good wood for that, the trunks too straight to climb, the leaf-cover too thick for undergrowth to flourish. Even so he was about to turn off the path when a fresh idea struck him—there was one place where no heathen Chinese would come till daylight, at least. He walked on, calmer now, until he came to the clearing.

The glow reflected from the clouds gave just enough light for him to see the double row of mounds, all close-mown and kept clear of coarse weeds, but otherwise unmarked. Clearly, even in the dark, to anybody of any faith, this was a burial place; to the heathen Chinese it would be a haunt of ghosts, unappeased by ancestral rites, roaming for prey. To Theodore it was almost as familiar and comfortable as home. As he stepped from under the trees he whispered the customary words, just as if Father had been there beside him.

"To live is Christ, and to die is gain."

Deliberately he chose the gap between the fifth and sixth mounds of the nearer rank. When he had spread his blanket out, lain down and rolled it round him he became just another mound in the dimness. He sighed, and the sigh set up a shudder he was unable to stop. The nights in South West China are warm at that time of year, but Theodore felt as though a heavy, chill liquid was flowing through all his veins, which the shuddering did nothing to warm. At the same time his mind was filled with nightmare imaginings about the Settlement, though as soon as he tried to think coherently about what had happened, or might have happened, his brain refused to function. He found his lips moving, repeating over and over the last words he had spoken, "To live is Christ, and to die is gain." They didn't seem to mean anything. Twice he tried to rise and make his way back across the ravine, but his muscles wouldn't stop shuddering long enough to obey him. He was still in this state when he slid suddenly into the pit of sleep.

A slow, warm rain began before dawn. In his sleep Theodore imagined that he was awake, dozing on the floor of his own

room, from which somebody had stolen the roof. It seemed to
him that nothing could be done about this till Father came back.
It was a miserable sort of dream with no centre or focus to the
misery to turn it into a proper nightmare. His sleeping body
tried to huddle further into the roll of blanket, whose coarse,
oily, close-packed wool took a long time to let the wet through.
He was properly woken at last by a little river that had formed
where the rain runnelled off the mound on either side of
him and flowed along the hollow in which he lay; at first
the fold of blanket under his head had dammed its path,
but when he groaned and shifted the tiny torrent rushed
through.

He sat up violently, trying to shake the rain out of his hair.
The memory of last night swept through him like a storm-gust,
making him huddle back instantly into his soggy hiding-place
and then twist, taut-muscled and slow, until he lay on his
stomach and could inch his head up to peer around. The low
gravestone of the right-hand mound confronted him. "Con-
stance Halliday Tewker. Born in darkness. Died in Grace.
April 17 1891, aged 32." Theodore could barely remember his
mother, except as a vague and silent presence, far back. She was
more real to him dead than alive, a grave-mound to be mown
and weeded, a source of warmth and cheerfulness in Father's
voice, a saint known to be at the side of Chris* in heaven. The
message on the stone struck him with no new force; he was
aware of it, but more aware of the stone itself as some cover for
his raised head as he peered through the veils of dawn-grey rain
into the dripping shadows under the trees.

Nothing but rain moved. No hunting cry told that he had
been seen. No far voices called. A low roll of thunder trundled
its way among the clouds, emphasising the absence of man-

made noises. He wriggled out of his squelching blanket, picked it up, and his food-bag, and walked steadily towards the nearest trees. There, after a little searching, he found a drip-free area and knelt down on the soft leaf-litter to pray.

It was impossible to concentrate. As soon as he closed his eyes the wood was full of creeping presences, their movements muffled by the rattling streamlets shed from the leafage far above; but when he opened them and looked round he saw nothing but the smooth, reddish trunks and the glistening thin threads of falling water. He would start again, but inside his mind the memories of last night nudged and jostled for attention, Father's voice, the shouts, the flames, the dwindling hymn, Fu T'iao in the ravine, the demon-figures running along the cliff-top. "When you speak to God you may be sure that He will hear, but you must not assume that He will answer." That was one of Father's favourite sayings, but now Theodore felt for the first time in his life that his attempts to speak were being cut short, were not going out of him towards any hearer, but instead were scurrying round in his skull like mice in a box.

He tried several times, even finding a fresh dry place to pray in in case that made a difference, but it was no good. Something enormous had changed, inside him as well as outside, and slowly, achingly, he realised what it was. Suppose he were to go back to the Settlement and find out that all was well there, that nobody had been really hurt and only a few huts burnt, and that Father had persuaded the attackers to go away—even then things could not be the same. He had run away. He was cast out from the Congregation.

As this certainty dawned he stopped trying to pray, rose to his feet and walked round towards the cemetery path. By the

time he was on it he was running, but where it branched into
the path that led from the road to the cliff he stopped again. If
he was cast out it was because he had obeyed Father's orders,
or thought he had. At least he could continue to obey. To be
both cast out and disobedient. . . . He must look from far off
to see what was happening in the Settlement, Fu T'iao had said.
There was only one place this side of the ravine where he
could do that.

He walked cautiously along the path that led to the road,
looked left and right through the drizzle, then darted across
into the trees beyond. The wood was younger here, and the
leaf-cover not thick enough to suppress all the undergrowth, so
the people from the Settlement did not come here much, but
there was a place some way down where the whole Settlement
was visible, tilted on its small plateau towards the west with its
fields and terraces rising behind it. Theodore knew this because
there was a painting by Mother of the Settlement from the
place; it hung—had hung—on the wall beside Father's desk.
He took a chunk of bread from his bag, blessed it automatically
as he broke it, and munched untasting as he picked his way
south.

Twenty minutes later he stood at the edge of the ravine once
more; the rain had let up for the moment and the low cloud-
roof was ridged with pink and gold where the rising sun,
almost straight in front of him, shot its horizontal rays through
some gap out of sight behind the hill. The Settlement was still
in shadow. Slant in the south wind the streams of smoke rose
thinly from the huts until they reached the sunlight, where they
changed from grey to gold. Each hut sent up its wisp, though
only memory and longing told Theodore that those shaggy

piles had once been dwelling-places. No one moved between the charred heaps. The roof-tree of the Church was down, but its end-frames still stood, draped with smouldering thatch. Someone had left a brass cooking-pot upside down on a door-post. One or two of the smoking piles showed a patch of colour where a cloth or blanket had not burnt completely. There was nothing else. Where were the pigs, the cats, the ploughs, the rakes and hoes, the water-buckets, the beehives, the looms and spinning-wheels? Where were the people?

A movement below the terraces caught his eye, but it was only three monkeys sidling with waving tails to and fro along an invisible boundary, peering at the changed scene with inquisitive wariness; having looked that way Theodore now saw that the pipe-line was gone—the cunning structure of giant bamboo-stems, raised on stilts, that carried water from the spring to the terraces. It was not just pulled down; it was gone. He could see no sign of the pieces. Somewhere among the smoking heaps lay the ashes of those pipes, which Father had been so proud of. Their disappearance seemed final proof that the Settlement was wiped out, burnt, or looted, or slaughtered and thrown into the ravine.

All gone! It was as if a child had been playing in the sand, building its toy village with detailed passion, when the wheel of a passing cart had rolled across and demolished it into mere sand.

He couldn't tell how long he stood there, staring, trembling, gasping as if he had a fever, shaking his head to and fro. It was no use praying. Even God, the strong, unchanging presence who had filled every second of sleep and waking in the life of the Settlement, creator, judge, friend—he too had been driven away by that heedless wheel.

A fresh downpour from the uncaring clouds broke the trance, and because there was nothing else to do Theodore picked his way back towards the road, careless of whether he was seen. His mind was numb, but his body had decided it was going back to explore the ruins of the Settlement.

Chapter 2

Out on the open road the rain was a fine drizzle. Theodore's feet walked his body along the grassy edge, still obeying Fu T'iao's advice to be wary—in this case to leave no tracks on the slithery bare clay at the road's centre. When he reached the ravine he halted. The bridge was gone.

His mind, which seemed for a while to have been wandering somewhere outside his body, came back and stared at the wreckage, unsurprised. He remembered the hammer of the axe-strokes in the night. He remembered Father fondling the hand-rail and saying, "With God's will, that'll stay put for a hundred years." The bridge was somehow part of Father, of his belief that man must worship with his hands as much as his mind, of his ingenuity in combining Chinese techniques with American knowledge to produce structures which were both light and strong and always managed to look as though they belonged where he put them, of his seeing that if he built the bridge then the road would take the short-cut and bring trade to nourish the Settlement. And now, for the very reasons that Father had built it, the people who had come in the night had smashed it down. Sure. But the old path would still be there— they wouldn't trouble to destroy that because it was not Father's work.

Theodore turned heavily, and felt his eyes widen at the sight of the people who had appeared behind him in the road, their coming muffled by the swish and whisper of rain. He gazed at them, too exhausted and uncaring to bolt for the cover of the trees. About ten people, and four horses. A slim young man, bedraggled despite the brown umbrella he carried, walked in front. His clothes were those of a peasant but he wore a neat little embroidered cap and moved in a manner which declared that he was not accustomed to trudging along sodden upland tracks. Behind him came the first of the horses, a creature so strikingly noble in its bearing—its coat a glossy brown, with a white blaze, its neck arched and ears pricked despite the drenching morning—that it took Theodore a moment to observe that its rider was almost equally out of place in this setting. The rider, who carried a dark green umbrella and sat sideways in the saddle, was clearly a woman and not Chinese, though her long reddy-brown cloak concealed her figure and her face was hidden by a veil which hung from the brim of her hat and was knotted under her chin.

The others were nothing unusual, ponies and peasants, hired to carry burdens—in the ponies' case a pair of long wicker baskets slung on either side of their saddles and covered with green canvas, and in the men's case a pair of smaller baskets slung fore and aft on a coolie-pole, which each man carried on his shoulder. All, except the noble horse and its veiled rider, trudged with a sullen and despairing air, as if they could hope for no end to their journey or to the rain. None paid any attention to Theodore, who was also a normal enough sight, a sodden peasant boy carrying a blanket and a satchel. The woman rode to the edge of the ravine and stared at the wreckage of Father's bridge.

"Oh, Jesus!" she said. "Why did I ever leave Battersea?" She spoke good English but with a curious, clipped whine.

Theodore winced at the blasphemy but couldn't stop staring. The men put down their loads and muttered.

"Ah, for Christ's sake!" she said. "There's got to be another way across. Ask the men, Lung. Ask them how far it is to this here mission."

The young man with the cap and brown umbrella turned to the porters.

"How far is to foreign village?" he said in bad Miao.

The men shrugged and looked away. One muttered something inaudible. The young man turned back to the woman.

"No way cross," he said in English as bad as his Miao. "Mission place very far."

"Come off it," said the woman. "That bloke don't know nothing and what's more he didn't tell you nothing. Ask that kid there."

The young man turned to Theodore.

"Do you speak Mandarin?" he asked despairingly.

Theodore nodded.

"Why is there no bridge?" said the young man. "This foreign princess is hideously dishonoured by the inadequacy of these roads. Can this appalling chasm be crossed elsewhere? How far is it to the Christian village? Is the missionary rich and charitable?"

"Mission is burnt," said Theodore, wary now with human contact and trying to speak as though Mandarin didn't come naturally to him and also as though the news meant nothing to him. "Men came in night. Break bridge. Burn mission. Is another path cross river."

"Men burnt the Mission?" said Lung, disappointment shading into alarm. He took a couple of paces to the woman's side and began to whisper to her in English, voluble and frightened. Theodore, as he had turned to point the way to the path, had noticed some of the porters listening and had guessed that they spoke more Mandarin than they'd admitted. Now they drew back behind the horses in a close group, the Mandarin-speakers clearly explaining to the others what had happened.

"It is begun," said one of them in Miao.

Lung and the woman were at the edge of the ravine now, peering across the gorge and no doubt seeing for the first time the wisps of smoke that still drifted above the blossoming orchard. The group of porters opened out and came forward in a stealthy line, one with a stubby knife in his hand and two others with clubs.

"Miss! Watch out! Behind you!" shouted Theodore.

His yell made the men hesitate, but the woman moved with extraordinary speed, dropping her umbrella, kicking her horse round and reining him back as he half-reared, and at the same time snatching a stocky-barrelled rifle from the holster by her saddle. She dropped the reins but remained steady in the saddle as the horse fidgeted back into stillness, and the gun swung along the line of porters, who fell back a pace, glancing at each other out of the corner of their eyes, waiting for someone else to start the attack.

"Slimy bunch of bastards," she said. "Knew it the minute we hired them. Where've you skived off to, Lung, you yellow bleeder?"

There was no answer. The young man had vanished.

"Show your face or I'll leave you here," she said calmly. "And you won't get no wages, neither."

Lung emerged creepingly from behind a tree on the other side of the road.

"Jesus, what a cock-up!" said the woman. "Have we hired a bunch of bleeding Boxers, then?"

"Not honourable Boxers, Missy. This men robbers, pirates. Think rob Missy, kill Missy, say they honourable Boxers."

"Spect you're right," she muttered. "Don't make no odds. Tell 'em this gun here's a twelve-shot repeater—that's one bullet each and a few to spare. Tell 'em to drop their knives and turn round. I'll count three and then I'll shoot—I'll start with that beggar with the club."

Tremblingly Lung managed to put the sentences together. Nobody moved. The woman raised the gun to her shoulder, aiming at a squat, angry-looking man near the centre of the line.

"One," she said. "Two."

The club fell and the man turned. She swung the gun along the line, pivoting the others by force of will. Three knives and another club fell.

"Fair enough," she said. "Now tell 'em to put their hands over their heads. Right. Now, Lung, pick up a knife and slit the back of each man's trousers, from his belt to arse. Ah, get on with it, you yellow bleeder. I want 'em so they can walk, but not without holding their breeches up, see? Keep yourself bent low, so as I got a good sight of the bloke you're doing."

Still Lung stood twitching by his tree. The woman began to swear, without raising her voice but somehow flooding it with energy. Theodore had heard people swearing before—donkey-drivers and such, using the Settlement road because of the new bridge—but never in English. Some of the words he knew from the Bible, others were strange; but he knew that only a soul, man or woman, hopelessly lost to Christ could have spoken them in this manner.

Lung's nerve broke. He darted forward, grabbed up a knife

and bent behind the right-hand man, then moved down the
line like a gardener performing some rapid piece of pruning on
a row of fruit-trees. As he left each man a dramatic change
took place, the shabby but serviceable pantaloons tumbling
down to ankle-level, leaving some with bare buttocks and
some with a twist of loin-cloth.

"Fair enough," said the woman. "Now tell the bleeders to
grab their trousies and march. Straight along the road, see?
First feller to stop, I'll shoot him dead, right? Same if he tries to
scarper for the woods."

Lung, strutting now with a sort of confidence, strung the
order into his smattered Miao. The men clutched their trousers
by the waist-bands and shambled off down the road. One or
two glanced over their shoulders and saw the gun levelled
steady as ever. The woman clicked her tongue and her horse,
with no further command, walked forward behind the retreating porters. Half-hypnotised Theodore followed the procession
to the first bend in the road, where she stopped the horse with
another muttered order. Beyond the bend the road lay straight
for more than a hundred yards, so when the men began to
glance over their shoulders again they saw her still sitting
there, motionless and ready. Slowly the group lost cohesion.
Heads turned in argument, free hands gesticulated; another few
seconds and they would break for the cover of the trees.
Sensing that instant, the woman raised her gun to her shoulder
and fired two shots above their heads. Yelling like parakeets
they broke into a run, straight on down the road. Two of them
tripped—over their trousers, perhaps, or each other—but
picked themselves out of the mud and raced on round the
further bend. Theodore heard the woman chuckle and turned
to see the gun now pointing at him.

"Scuse the liberty, young man," she said. "Just I can't afford to lose you. You speak English?"

"Velly little English," said Theodore.

"Fair enough. I shan't hurt you. I want you to show me this here path. You're from the mission, I expect? Poor little bleeder. What's your name?"

Theodore hesitated. Father despised all liars, godly or pagan. "Christian name Theodore," he said.

Her face was a shadowed vagueness behind her veil, but from the way she cocked her head he had the impression that she was looking at him with sudden sharpness.

"That'll have to do," she said. "Hullo, Theo. I'm Mrs Jones. This here's Lung. Hi! Grab that pony, one of you!"

She had slid the gun into its holster while she was speaking and was turning back towards the bridge when one of the pack-ponies came round the bend at a nervous tittup, almost knocking Theodore over. More by luck than skill he caught its halter and led it back to where Mrs Jones and Lung were gazing at the baskets which the porters had left behind. She slid from her horse and handed its reins to Lung while she went to catch another of the ponies which was wandering off between the trees. Her skirt was so long that she had to hold it clear of the ground with her left hand, but she seemed to find this no impediment and cornered and caught the pony with no fuss at all. The third pony, a grey, was grazing placidly by the edge of the ravine, so Theodore handed his halter to Lung and caught it and led it back.

"There's a young man what's got his head screwed on," said Mrs Jones. "Tie her to that there branch, and we'll see what we can chuck out. Heave my bath off Rollo for a start, Lung, and all that lot of empty specimen boxes—that's the ticket..."

Mrs Jones and Theodore did most of the sorting, because Lung was fastidious, even in this mud and danger, about handling objects or carrying weights, so in the end he took the gun and stood sentry. Mrs Jones was quick and decisive, knowing what every basket held and making up her mind at once what she could spare and what there would be room for. Theodore piled the discarded stuff at the edge of the road.

"Leave 'em good and obvious," she said, "so as if any of them bastards come back after us they'll stop here and see what they can nick."

Everything seemed very well made, though most of it had seen a lot of wear. A spare tent bore the label "Army & Navy Stores, London. Invincible Weatherproof Size 3." The collecting boxes were of dark oiled wood with brass corners. There seemed to be a surprising number of stoves.

"That'll have to do," she said at last. "We're not a bleeding Chinese charity—it'll cost me a couple of hundred quid to replace that lot, I daresay. You take Bessie and lead the way, Theo. She's lazy but she's quiet. Then you, Lung, with Rollo. I'll take Albert, who's a right bastard, and Sir Nigel can tag along behind. I better take me rifle, Lung, if you've finished playing soldiers."

Lung, who had indeed been acting out the role of sentry in a slightly exaggerated way, handed over the weapon and Theodore started between the trees, heading left-handed until he reached the footpath. Looking back over his shoulder he saw the line of horses winding between the trunks, with the one which the woman had been riding coming steadily along in the rear. Drenched and mud-spattered though it was it moved in a quite different style from the dispirited trudge of the pack-ponies, with its head held in a manner that seemed aware and interested as it followed Mrs Jones. She strode along, holding her skirt in a graceful fashion with her left hand and Albert's bridle with her right. She was short—no taller than the Chinese women in the Congregation, many of whom stood barely as high as Father's elbow—and under her shape-muffling cloak she looked decidedly plump; but she moved with a sway and ease that made it seem as if she weighed very little, and though Albert—a lean-headed, liver-coloured brute—tugged and wrestled at the bridle she controlled him without apparent effort. She saw Theodore looking round and raised the hand that held the skirt a little further, at the same time cocking her wrist, a gesture no doubt meant only to tell him that he was doing well, but somehow full of liveliness and also vaguely teasing.

The effect was sharp enough to pierce through the trance of shock in which Theodore was once more moving, and to make him wonder what sort of person she was. English, he thought, though she spoke differently from the few English missionaries he had met, with her tinny vowels and lack of aitches. She seemed to be rich. She was wicked—a blasphemer, who had also laughed at the exposed buttocks of her porters. Shameless. But the few words she had spoken to Theodore, like the gesture he had just observed, gave him a sense of somebody full of life and intelligence and friendliness.

Pack ponies in hill country are used to awkward tracks, and Bessie followed Theodore down into the ravine easily enough, without interrupting his confused musings. He reached the flat rock by the stepping stones and waited till Lung reached the rock and stood beside him, staring at the stepping-stones where they stood black amid the white rush of foam.

"Horses cannot cross here," Lung said angrily in Mandarin.

"Why have you brought us here? What have I done that I must perish in this place of uncivilised demons?"

"Horses used to cross here before the bridge was built," said Theodore, "provided the river was low."

"Where is the Princess? Why does she take so long? If she falls in the river, who will pay my wages? Did I join the robbers when they attacked her? No, I fought for her with my bare hands!"

A loose stone clattered on the rock beside them, and they turned and saw that Mrs Jones had managed to blindfold Albert and was forcing him to feel his way down. Her voice, swearing steadily, rose above the river-noise.

"No cross here, Missy," called Lung. "Water very bad."

"Oh, go and fry your face," she shouted, as with a furious heave she managed to rush the pony the last few yards down to the rock.

"Jesus!" she said, "I wouldn't do that again for a thousand quid. What are you on about, Lung? I've taken horses through worse than that. Theo, you nip across them stones and get ready to hold them. I'll ride Sir Nigel through and lead the others, one at a time. I'll take Albert first and get him done with. Right?"

She managed it, though twice she nearly lost her seat when a horse missed its footing in the tearing waters. Lung crossed last of all, teetering on each stone as he nerved himself for the next leap.

"Don't you look so smug, young man," muttered Mrs Jones as she and Theodore stood watching him. "It takes a lot more nerve to do things what you don't fancy than it does with things what you do. You could start taking Bessie up that path now."

The climb was easier than the descent had been; the path was better and in any case the horses found it more natural to pick their way up hill. Theodore had time to look about. Further down the ravine, held by the river against a jut of rock, was a bundle of green-blue cloth half-hidden by foam. Mrs Teng had an overshirt of just that colour. Theodore peered at it until he realised that he would rather not know for sure whether it was Mrs Teng's body or just some bundle dropped in flight, and as he looked away his eye was caught by a movement on the further cliff. Three men were beginning to scramble down the path on the further cliff.

"Look! Ma'am!" he shouted, throwing out an arm to point.

Mrs Jones glanced across the gap and nodded. She slid her gun from where it was slung across Albert's back and gave the animal a slap on the rump to send him on up the path. Her own horse halted and waited while she steadied herself against the rock wall and raised the rifle to her shoulder. A shot snapped out almost instantly, and then another. Theodore hurried on, watching the pursuers over his shoulder. They had hesitated at the first shot, and at the second the leading man flinched back; all three paused, staring across the ravine. Another shot, and the leading man leaped and staggered, stood for an instant staring at his fore-arm, and then all three were scrambling back up the path. They reached the top and disappeared into the wood just before Theodore himself came out into the open. He handed Bessie's halter to Lung and turned to catch the unpredictable Albert the moment he reached open ground.

"Well done, young man," panted Mrs Jones as she came over the top.

"Did you hit him?" said Theodore, forgetting to speak with an accent.

"Not bloody likely," she said with a laugh. "I was aiming at the rock a foot past him. A splinter must of caught him. He didn't half jump, did he?"

On the ridge to the west of the terraces stood a grove of wild fig-trees which Father would not let be cleared because of the parable Christ spoke in *Luke* 21, xxix. From here one could see the whole slope of the Settlement on one side, and then the orchard, and then on the other side of the ridge the ravine and the ruined shrine where the old path rose. Close against the grove the tethered ponies champed at feed-bags. Lung, with the rifle under his arm, stood sentry just beyond the sky-line in case the porters recovered their courage and crossed the ravine. Theodore waited with the ponies and watched Mrs Jones riding among the smouldering huts.

The rain had stopped and the cloud-layer was rising and thinning. Soon it would vanish and the day would half-clear to the steamy brilliance usual at this season. The smoke from the huts, which had dwindled to nothing under the steady rain, revived and slanted up in wispy parallels. Mrs Jones rode very straight-backed, glancing from side to side like a sight-seer, but with a shot-gun ready across her knees. She moved at a steady pace between the huts, pausing only by the wreck of the church, where she reined to a standstill and gazed for some time before starting back up the slope.

"Well, that's not much cop," she said in a sombre voice, then gave a deep sigh and swung herself to the ground. She turned away from Theodore and set about giving her horse its feed, but continued to speak while she was working. Theodore got the impression that she was using the process as a way of not looking at him directly.

"No, 'elp there," she said. "Jesus! You'd of thought they'd . . ."

"Who these men?" lisped Theodore, wary once more. "Why they burn Settlement?"

"Must have been Boxers, I bet," said Mrs Jones.

"Boxers? Please?"

"Jesus! Don't you know? Ah, I 'spect your missionary fellow kept quiet about it—didn't want all his converts scarpering off . . . there's bands of young thugs wandering all over China, trying to kick the foreigners out, burning and murdering. They call themselves Boxers. The Empress don't do anything to stop them—ask me, she's pleased they're at it . . . Anyway, you're going to have to stick with us, young man. There's nothing for you down there. Not any more."

"Stick with you? Please?"

"What else can you do? I'm not having you going down there, seeing what I seen. It's all over and done with, see?"

"Then I must go to mission of Doctor Goertler."

"Where might that be?"

"About hundled miles," said Theodore, pointing north-east.

"Then we'll come along of you, and let's bleeding well hope the same's not happened there."

Theodore drew a deep breath.

"Solly," he muttered. "I cannot come along by you."

"Why in hell not?" she said, turning and straightening. He shook his head.

"Ah, come off it, Theo. We're much best off, all together. There's more to our friend Lung than meets the eye, but he only speaks pukka Chinee. You know the lingo in these parts, and you know where we're going, and I can manage the horses and the rifle. What's biting you?"

Theodore found himself unable to speak. He stood dumb while she stared at him, her expression invisible behind the thick veil, until she took a pace towards him, lifting her arms in a gesture of appeal.

"What's up, Theo?" she said in the gentlest of voices. "Is it something I done? Spit it out, then. I got to know, ain't I, or how can I do anything about it?"

It would have been easier if she'd stayed in the saddle and cursed him as she did Lung and the horses. He could have borne that in silence. Now, he didn't know how, she forced him to speak.

"Thou shalt not take the name of the Lord thy God in vain," he said in a toneless mutter.

"Je . . ." she began, and bit the word short. "Is *that* it?"

She stood for a moment in silence, then slowly raised both hands and unpinned the large green brooch that held the veil in place beneath her chin, continuing the movement to lift the filmy stuff aside and settle it behind her shoulders.

Her eyes were large, round, blue—not sky-blue, but the colour of still water on a cloudless noon. Strong black eyebrows made them seem bluer still. The skin of her plump cheeks was white and flaky, so that for a moment Theodore thought she wore the veil to hide a disfiguring skin-disease, but then he saw that the flakes were a mixture of powder and sweat, concealing innumerable tiny wrinkles. Her wide mouth was painted poppy-red, and its emphasis made her chin seem absurdly small, just the first of a series of receding folds that eventually became her neck. Her nose was small and snub, like an afterthought.

"I bet I don't half look a picture," she said, turning her head slightly and watching him a little sideways, as if suddenly shy.

"Now, listen here, duck. You can't stay in these here parts—
it's dangerous, and there ain't nothing to eat, and I'm not
having you go down in the village, not if I have to tie you up
and carry you along of me. Lung and me could do that easy—
he's ever so handy with knots. But I want you to come willing,
so let's start all over again, shall we? I'll mind my lip and you'll
forget as you ever heard me cussing. It won't half do me good
—I been letting myself get out of hand in these heathen parts.
So is it a deal, young man?"

Theodore hesitated. Whether she cursed or not she was
certainly a wicked woman—the paint on her face only confirmed that. But the eyes in the painted face were earnest and
pleading, and her voice, though still faintly mocking, seemed
to be mocking only herself and was as gentle as the contented
chucking of a mother hen.

"Oh, I can do it," she said suddenly in a quite different
accent. "I've had to mind my tongue before. I've passed
myself off in swell houses, taking tea with Lady This and the
Duchess of That, and not one of them spotted I didn't
belong."

She giggled and dropped back to her normal voice.

"You'll come along of us, won't you, Theo? Didn't Jesus
himself go along of harlots and sinners?"

She was still looking at him with her head tilted a little away,
and now her eyes were half-closed. He noticed that her eye-
lashes were enormously long and paler than her eyebrows,
glinting here and there with gold. His lips seemed to make up
his mind for him.

"I guess I'll go along with you," he said. "Are they all dead
in the Settlement?"

"I didn't see anyone as wasn't," she said, beginning to

refasten her veil. "Looks like they herded them into that big building and . . ."

"The church. Did you . . . did you see the missionary?"

"Big feller in a night-shirt? 'Fraid so. What was his name?"

"The Reverend Simeon Tewker."

She nodded, turning towards the horses, then slowly swinging back.

"'Scuse my asking," she said, "but you're speaking English pretty nice all of a sudden. American, I should say. Been faking it, have you?"

The danger and action of the morning, the vigour and warmth of her company, had faded in the instant that she told him for certain that Father was dead, and now he was settling again into the numbness of shock. The question barely broke through his consciousness but once more his lips answered for him.

"He was my father."

Chapter 3

They travelled north along the forested foothills, taking the old track that had barely been used since Father had built the bridge. It would have been easier to go east, but that would have taken them to Shiacheng, where the men who had attacked the Settlement must have come from; so the best chance was to make a detour and hope to strike another road to Taho. All the first day Theodore rode, sitting sideways, peasant-fashion, across the rump of his pony, slumped into the trance of shock. He barely noticed where they went, what they ate or how they camped. They met no one. The woods, the whole of China, the world—they were as empty as his soul.

In the middle of next morning Mrs Jones dragged him out of his stupor to talk to a couple of hunters who spoke a rough version of Miao which he could just understand. They insisted that the best way to Taho was back, through Shiacheng, but agreed that it was possible to travel on north. They seemed to know nothing of any Boxer uprisings, or anything that happened beyond the valleys they hunted. As soon as the talk was over Theodore slid back into numbness. The usual morning rain drizzled on. It took an age to climb each rise and to plod down into the next valley, where the usual stream, steeper and angrier each time, had to be somehow forded.

Around midday the clouds lifted and the rains died. They

halted on a rounded upland of grass and stunted scrub, where they fed the horses and then ate their own meal; but barely had they moved off again when Mrs Jones reined in, dismounted and peered at something growing beside the track. Then to Lung's obvious disgust she opened one of the baskets, brought out a folding stool and some equipment, and settled to painting a little flower, mauve and hairy, which she had found. Lung made a parade of taking the rifle and standing sentry, scowling down the path they had travelled; the horses grazed; and Theodore, somehow unsettled from scurrying round the endlessly repeated maze of his despair, looked around him. East and south the hills were veiled with heat-haze, but west and north a chain of larger hills stood clear. He realised that the landscape had indeed been changing as they travelled, and the seeming steepness and weariness had not simply been products of his own misery. He shrugged, and was about to retreat into the maze when Mrs Jones closed the paint-box with a deliberate snap and pointed.

"See there? That's where I'm going, some day."

Theodore gazed along the line of her arm and saw, through a notch in the hill-range, a glimmer of silver and purple— snow-peaks, clearer each instant as the clouds thinned, a hundred miles away or more, but even at that distance making the hills among which he stood seem like little more than dimples in the earth's crust.

"Tibet," he said dully. "You can't go there. They don't let you in."

"That's as may be, young man, but I'm going there before I die. I bet there's things in them valleys like what nobody's never seen."

"Things?"

"Plants," she said, strapping her kit together. "What else do you fancy I'm doing in these heathen parts? I'm a plant-collector, see? One day there'll be a flower what everybody grows in their garden and it'll have my name on it. *Something or-other Jonesii*. Won't that be grand?"

She laughed, self-mocking, as Lung helped her into the saddle, but she had been talking with a sudden intensity, enough to draw Theodore's whole attention. Now, as they rode on across the upland, she continued to chatter away.

"Mind you, I have got a rose called after me, Daisy Dancer, but it ain't a proper wild species and it ain't my real name. I was born Daisy Snuggett, see, but you could hardly put that at the top of a bill, could you? I'm not saying as Daisy Dancer ain't a pretty little rose, pinky with hundreds of curly petals, though it's turned out a devil for mildew, I hear . . . oh, I beg your pardon, young man. Does that count?"

"I don't know," said Theodore. In fact he knew quite well— Satan counted. But Mrs Jones was already chattering on and he had no urge to stop her though often he had little idea what she was talking about. She had made a break in the monotony of his grief, and he was grateful, though without any conscious awareness of gratitude. Only when he knew her better did he guess that she had deliberately chosen the moment, had understood his needs, first for privacy and now for interruption. At one point she tried to involve Lung in the talk, but to Theodore's surprise he held up a reproving hand, though he smiled with sudden charm as he did so, then reined his pony in and fell behind.

"Making up one of his poems," muttered Mrs Jones. "Didn't I say there's more to him than what meets the eye?"

After that she gossiped on all day, unwearied as one of the mountain streams.

Two evenings later they waited, half-hidden by a wattle fence that had been built as a shelter for young vines, and watched an old woman hoeing her garden. The flies, which had swarmed and settled and stung all the weary afternoon as they worked their way round through the hill-scrub above the fields, had gone. To the west the sky was palest yellow, streaked with pink along the mountain rims. The thin moon that floated in the darkening edge of night seemed to be nearer than those snow-peaks. Quarter of a mile ahead lay the river, a network of shallows and gravel banks. They knew it could be crossed here because from the hillside they had seen small herds of cattle fording it, and had decided that it was safer to make this circuit than to risk using the bridge in the middle of the town that lay at the head of this sudden fertile valley. The last peasant they had met up in the hills had seemed dangerously sullen. They had discussed concealing Mrs Jones somehow among the baggage and letting Lung and Theodore take the horses through; but even so there would be a good chance that someone would want to see the strangers' travel papers, and the baggage would be searched, if only for loot. Then they had seen the ford.

"Ah, get on with it, you old besom," whispered Mrs Jones.

She stood as straight as ever, but Theodore could hear the exhaustion in her voice. He himself was ready to lie down and sleep where they stood. The horses could smell the river and were restless with thirst. Beyond the river a good road ran due east, but between them and the river, less than a quarter of a mile away now, lay this last lone cottage, with the old woman hoeing and hoeing. It seemed a pity, now they had come so far without being seen, to let this one person witness their passing. At last she straightened her back and hobbled away. Mrs Jones waited another minute and started down the path. The cottage was in darkness, but just as Theodore came level with its gate a voice spoke from the vine-shrouded porch.

"*A peach-blossom sky—*
Men lead horses to the ford . . ."

Even to Theodore, whose sole reading was his Bible, the tone was unmistakable—an old man's voice, detached and amused, quoting poetry and ending on a note of question. The horse-hooves padded on the soft track for a few paces, then another voice spoke, whispering but clear.

"*A boat-shaped moon—*
I fetch rice-wine for a friend."

Before Theodore had fully grasped that this second voice was Lung's, a cackle of pleasure rose from the porch.

"My flagon is already half-empty, Traveller, but anyone who can quote Tu Fu in this wilderness must stay and help me finish it, that we may start on another."

Lung hesitated. The hoof-sounds of his pony had ceased.

"Weng," he called suddenly in an authoritative voice, "run ahead and ask the Captain to wait."

Theodore dropped Bessie's reins and trotted down the path. He found Mrs Jones had already halted.

"What's the bleeder up to now?" she muttered. "We got to get across while it's still light enough to see."

"He wants us to wait. He's being careful. He called me Weng

and you the Captain. Maybe he's getting news, or faking a story so the man won't guess he's seen foreigners."

"Let's hope," she sighed.

They waited for several minutes, listening to the murmur of voices. At last a gate creaked and Lung appeared from the loom of the cottage.

"Missy, we sleep here this night," he whispered.

"Here! You think we can trust this bloke? What have you done with the horses?"

"This fellow not a bloke, Missy. He very OK gentleman. He official long time in yamen at Pekin, but not in favour now, so he live here. He say put horses in shed, eat here, sleep here, maybe cross river before sun rise."

"Oh, fair enough. I'm that fagged . . . What did you tell him about me?"

"I say you English Princess."

"Oh, Lor! I'm going to have to mind my manners, ain't I?"

Mrs Jones insisted on seeing that the horses were properly groomed and fed and watered before she would come into the house. She and Theodore did the work while Lung held the lantern and talked to their host, a fat little man with a bald head and a leathery face puckered into a million wrinkles. His name was P'iu-Chun. He needed a crutch to walk, and wore clothes like any peasant's, but Lung was very respectful to him. He was polite to Lung, if a bit grand, but he watched Mrs Jones all the time with bright-eyed amusement.

As P'iu-Chun led the way into the house at last Lung said in English, "Is not custom for woman to eat along by man, but honoured P'iu-Chun say this night forget custom."

"That's very good of him," said Mrs Jones in her grandest

voice. "Tell him that my gratitude for his hospitality is exceeded only by my pleasure at the prospect of his company. Oh, and you might ask if there's anywhere I can give myself a bit of a wash."

Mrs Jones's idea of "a bit of a wash" turned out to be rather more than that. Theodore was sitting on a low stool in P'iu-Chun's living room and half listening while Lung and the old man discussed a poem by somebody called Li Po, who seemed to have died more than a thousand years ago. He guessed that P'iu-Chun also had only half his mind on the talk, and was fidgety for Mrs Jones's return. This no doubt was one reason why he was prepared to break with custom—another was that there was only one proper room in the house, so there was nowhere else for her to eat. Theodore had no idea where the old peasant woman had vanished to. The room was not large, but the few pieces of furniture had a look of quality about them; there were two glowing dark blue vases on a chest, and one wall was covered with large brush drawings, hanging on scrolls.

"Enter!" called P'iu-Chun suddenly, though Theodore had barely noticed the light scratching on the inner door. At once he found himself wide awake and staring.

Mrs Jones had re-applied her make-up, twice as thick. In the dim lantern-light her face was like a china doll's—scarlet lips, clay-white skin, a rosy circle on each cheek, black brows over those exaggerated eyes. She had piled her hair high on her head, and put on a long red skirt and a filmy pink blouse whose lace-work frothed up her neck to her chin-line. On each hand she wore several rings over white gloves that ran to her elbows. A triple row of pearls ringed the pink lace, and a large brooch rode on the big curve of her bosom like a boat on a wave.

As she came through the door she drooped, so that for a moment Theodore thought she was fainting until he saw that she was moving into a slow, full curtsey, finishing with her head not six inches from the floor. It was astounding that she could bend her plump body to this posture, but she came up out of it, effortless and smiling.

P'iu-Chun was on his feet and bowing stiffly from the waist, and so was Lung. Theodore, who had risen automatically (Father had always insisted he should stand even for the poorest peasant-woman, and had done so himself), copied them awkwardly.

"Honoured Princess, my poor cottage is yours," said P'iu-Chun.

"The hospitality of the renowned What's-is-name makes any house a palace," fluted Mrs Jones when Lung had translated. "Got that out of a panto, when I was principal boy in Aladdin. Don't put that bit in."

Deftly Lung added a few courteous twiddles to account for the extra sentence. The exchange might have gone on for some time, but just as P'iu-Chun was bowing himself into a fresh compliment Mrs Jones gave a little cry and ran with fluttering steps towards the pictures on the wall.

"Why, these are lovely," she cried, still in her grand voice but somehow no longer acting. "That's *Rhododendron megeratum*—I've seen that in Nepal . . . and *Paeonia lutea*—we all grow that now . . . what's this primula—I've never seen that? Lung, ask him where he got these perfectly adorable things, and who painted them."

"The Princess is a great lover of plants and admires the

drawings," said Lung. "She names each plant in her own tongue. She asks who painted the pictures."

"My own poor hand made these scrawls," said P'iu-Chun, purring. Theodore fancied he could see a tear of pleasure in the corner of the dark little eyes. Mrs Jones understood what he was saying before Lung could translate, and once more darted across the room, seized his hand and patted it softly. P'iu-Chun was obviously amazed by this behaviour, but too happy to resist.

"Oh, it wasn't you!" she cried. "Oh, how I wish I could draw like that. I have to paint, to make a record of what I've found, and I get them accurate—I mean you can see every petal and how it goes—but what I can't do is that . . . that . . ."

Despairing of words she gestured towards the drawings again with a single sweeping movement that exactly expressed the few flowing strokes with which P'iu-Chun had brought the flowers out of the paper.

"Theo," she said. "Be an angel. The saddle-basket with the patched cover, near the top, my sketch-books. Please bring me the red one with my initials on it . . ."

When Theodore came back he found that P'iu-Chun had fetched more scrolls and was spreading them in turn on the chest, shaking his old head from time to time over one which was not as perfect as he'd hoped.

"You found it?" cooed Mrs Jones. "Lovely. Now come and help me talk to Mr What's-is-name—poor Lung's having trouble keeping up with me. Oh, look at this bamboo! That's as common as daisies, but look how he's drawn it just like it mattered as much as this gentian here, which I've never seen and I doubt if anyone in Europe has."

Lung coughed a warning, but P'iu-Chun seemed to take it

for granted that the Chinese boy travelling with this extra-ordinary woman should speak good English. He smiled as Theodore spoke, and reached a long-nailed hand for the sketch-book.

"You'll tell him I don't think they're very good, won't you?" pleaded Mrs Jones. "They're accurate, but they're not *art*."

This was difficult to say in Mandarin without making it sound like another polite expression of humility. P'iu-Chun began to turn the pages, holding the book at arm's length and straining his neck away.

"My old eyes no longer see what is near," he said. "Ah, this detail! The Princess paints the outwardness—every leaf, every hair—while I do my poor best to paint the inwardness. We walk on opposite sides of the way. Now, compare these . . ."

He held the book open at a particular painting and with his other hand pulled from his scrolls his own version of the same plant, a curving, grass-like stem from which dangled a line of little yellow bells. Theodore could see that Mrs Jones had used several different colours and dozens of brush-strokes to paint each bell, whereas P'iu-Chun seemed simply to have dipped a brush in ink and blobbed it once onto the page, and yet the bell was there. You knew how it would move in the wind. You could even, somehow, guess its colour from the nature of the dark grey blob.

"If I hadn't just done my face I'd burst into tears," said Mrs Jones gravely. "I shall never, never, learn to paint like that. I wonder where he found that one—ask him, Theo. It's got to be in the mountains somewhere, but I've only see it one place, right over the other side of the Himalayas."

"For much of my life I was a government official in Pekin,"

explained P'iu Chun. "Unworthy though I am, I held posts that were not without honour. But then I fell from favour and was sent to this province with orders to survey the frontier with Tibet and to seek new routes of access, I who had been . . . but never mind that. My report was returned to me with its seal unbroken, to show me how little I was now regarded. I was employed no more. But in my journeyings among the mountains I made these pictures, choosing especially plants that were strange to me. This one I found in vast numbers growing on the ledges of a gorge beyond Tehko. Ah, never again shall I see those peaks, those thundering waters!"

"Tibet!" said Mrs Jones. "I don't see as we shouldn't try and get to Tibet. If Mr What's-is-name knows the way . . ."

"We go to Taho," said Lung firmly.

"Tibet'd be just as good."

"Taho."

"Tibet."

"Taho."

They laughed together, like children playing a secret game. It was so surprising that despite the trance of tiredness Theodore looked at Lung and saw him as a person in his own right, and not just an animated bit of Mrs Jones's baggage. He showed his teeth as he laughed, and his dark eyes flashed. It was as though a spring of inner happiness had suddenly sparkled on a dull hillside, giving a whole landscape life and focus.

As if the laughter had been a signal the old woman came hobbling in with food—all very plain, boiled vegetables from the garden, dark bread, cheese, water for Theodore and rice wine for the others. Theodore must have fallen asleep in the middle of the meal, because the next thing he was conscious of was waking up and finding that he had been laid on a rough

mattress against a wall and covered with a blanket. The meal
had been cleared, but the rice-wine flagons were still there,
more of them than before. The other three were sitting in a
row, on cushions, with Mrs Jones in the middle. The lantern-
wick was smoking, and cast a dull, bronze light across their
faces. The two men were listening with rapt attention to Mrs
Jones, who was singing in a rich, sweet voice:

> *"Wotcher, 'Ria! 'Ria's on the job.*
> *Wotcher, 'Ria! Did you speculate a bob?*
>   *O, 'Ria she's a toff*
>   *and she looks immensikoff*
> *And they all shouted Wotcher, 'Ria!"*

Dazedly Theodore stared at this scene of debauchery, until Mrs
Jones noticed him watching them, and winked. He closed his
eyes, achingly aware of the huge weight of fatigue that prevented him from rising up and declaring their wickedness. He
remembered that he had had a chance to bear witness to his
faith, and had run away, so who was he to denounce anyone
else? All he could do was pray. His lips moved automatically
into the familiar words.

"Our Father . . ."

He was asleep again before he had whispered a dozen
syllables.

Chapter 4

Often, during the journey to the mountain, Theodore would remember the argument in P'iu-Chun's house and the laughter that had ended it. Lung had lost the argument, but now he was behaving as though he had won. Theodore would look ahead and see above the bobbing hats of the line of porters, the yellow umbrella, the little round embroidered cap and the blue quilted surcoat, all enhancing Lung's air of dignified swagger as he rode Sir Nigel at the head of the procession.

P'iu-Chun had apparently settled the argument while Theodore slept. It was quite simple—there was no point in going east, because the rage against foreigners was sweeping through the province like a brush fire. The Governor was trying to suppress the Boxers, but this only had the effect of driving the young fanatics outwards and spreading the blaze. A week ago they had reached Taho and burnt the mission. Dr Goertler was either fled or dead. Nor did P'iu-Chun dare to hide the travellers for more than another day and a night—he was rumoured to be a rich man, and the local townsmen would be delighted to ransack his house. But to the west lay the great barrier of the Yangtze, and if Mrs Jones and her party could only cross that they might be safe, because the authorities would use the river to prevent the Boxer madness spreading that way. But for the time being Mrs Jones must travel in disguise.

So next morning Lung had ridden into the town and bribed

the local magistrate to supply him with papers authorising a rich widow to cross the river and journey to the Plain of Shrines, where she could burn incense at the tomb of her husband's ancestors. P'iu Chun himself had provided the disguise—clothes and a litter belonging to his dead wife, Lung's uniform, a similar jacket for Theodore, a Chinese-style saddle for Sir Nigel. He had insisted that all these were gifts, but he had had no hesitation in accepting a gift of gold coins from Mrs Jones, in fact the two of them had conducted the exchange with complete understanding, and Theodore had needed to do very little translation. When it was over P'iu Chun had added one genuine gift, the map from his rejected survey.

So now here they were, doing what Mrs Jones longed to do, heading towards the mountains where she might find flowers no botanist had ever seen. Three days earlier they had crossed the Yangtze with no trouble at all, and now were travelling almost due west along a steep-sided valley; below them rushed a tumbling tributary, green with melted snows. As they climbed the climate changed, the rain ceasing earlier each day until by now it had ended before they were moving. But the forests that clothed the valley's flanks were ancient and reeking with decay, and though the air grew steadily cooler, the valley still breathed out a heavy, sodden odour which seemed as oppressive as the heat in the lower hills. Only sometimes, brought into view by a curve of the track or the crest of a ridge, was there a glimpse of anything beyond this prisoning cleft—far off, blue against blue, the snow peaks of the Himalaya. No day's journey, however long, seemed to bring them nearer.

They hired porters at the villages, each sourer and poorer than the last, a huddle of ramshackle huts spilt down the hillside like a rubbish-tip. The poorer each village seemed, the more sullen were its inhabitants, though they must have needed the money they were paid. Lung conducted all the negotiations with great lordliness while Mrs Jones encouraged him with fierce mutters from behind the closed curtains of her litter.

On this third morning the track narrowed and began to climb erratically away from the river. Mostly the party was forced into single file, with Lung at the head, followed by half a dozen porters carrying their burdens slung fore and aft on coolie poles and jogging up the track with an apparently tireless shuffle. Next came Theodore, leading Bessie, who carried the front end of the litter; its rear end was carried by Albert, because the litter-poles prevented him from straying and Mrs Jones was close enough to coax or bully him into tolerable behaviour. Then came two more porters with coolie poles, and finally Rollo, led by an elderly, tiny man who carried no load but had a huge old pistol stuck in his belt to show he was guarding the party against bandits and so was worth his extra copper coin a day. He spoke a little Mandarin and Miao, beside his native Lolo. He wore a long wisp of grey beard, so Mrs Jones called him Uncle Sam.

"Come and look here," called Mrs Jones after they had been travelling for a couple of hours. "Path's wide enough for two, and old Bessie'll jog along without you. I been looking at these here hangings."

Theodore hitched Bessie's reins to a basket and dropped back. Mrs Jones had drawn the litter curtains and was looking around for something to amuse her. The litter was a gaudy affair, like a miniature pavilion with gold tassels dangling at the corners; its curtains were scarlet, embroidered with green trees through which swooped blue and yellow birds. At the foot of each tree sat a man and a woman, fully clothed and not touching each other, but with something about their poses and expressions which produced in Theodore a flicker of unease.

Mrs Jones was dressed in much the same style as the women in the pictures, with her hair piled up into a bun, stuck through with great wooden pins, and her face painted white and scarlet like a doll's. Her small hands fluttered inside the huge sleeves as she spoke.

"Isn't it perfectly marvellous needlework?" she fluted in her upper-crust accent. "I can't help wondering what they're up to. What do you imagine the story is, Theo?"

"There's got to be a story?"

"Oh, yes, please. I wouldn't trust this gentleman here one inch. Why's he giving her that lily—*lilium tigrinum*, I'd say? He's just the type to deceive an innocent young girl. Would you say she looked innocent?"

"The rain has spoilt them."

"I don't know," she cooed. "These vegetable dyes don't run and wool stands a lot of wetting . . . Now is this the same lady? Ooh, fancy, she's got a knife! Is it for herself or for him? It's a different gentleman, I think . . ."

Theodore knew quite well what she was doing, deliberately steering the conversation as close as she could to the frontiers of indecency, to see how he would take it. At first she had been amused simply to play the mourning widow, a figure of mystery behind her curtains—to peep out at the fabulous Yangtze and the busy ferry-towns, or to wait with her gun cocked beneath the litter-rugs while Lung bargained with porters or officials. She had positively enjoyed the danger, and the triumph of using that danger to force both Lung and Theodore in the direction she wanted to go, towards the forbidden mountains. But now she was bored—bored with the slow jog of the porters, and with her role as a female, mere baggage, not allowed to ride her own horse, let alone to halt the procession and botanise in the teeming woods. She had spent twenty minutes swearing at Albert, pitching her voice just below the level at which Theodore could pick out definite blasphemies, and now she was bored of that too and had found a subtler way of teasing him. He looked at the embroidered picture, and smiled.

"I guess she's going to cook him dinner," he said. "Isn't that a turnip?"

"Oh! Men!" she said. "You ain't got no souls, none of you!"

Theodore smiled again. Even the careless phrase gave him barely a twinge. Since the decision to travel west, the break with Father's last definite order, he had felt an odd sense of freedom from anything in his old life. The inner numbness was still there. He prayed morning and evening, but not as if anyone was listening to his prayers. He was cast out from the Congregation. But for most of the time he hardly thought about any of this, and was happy to play his part in the journey and let Mrs Jones tease him if she wished.

Before she could start again he had to trot forward and lead Bessie down a sudden slope. In front of him the porters used the incline to swing into a faster trot which opened a gap between them and the litter ponies. They were wizened little men, dressed in layer on layer of rags all bound to their limbs with leather thongs. They were the first Chinese Theodore had seen who didn't wear the pig-tail, but whose hair stood out in shaggy plaits beneath little grey fur caps with tight-rolled brims.

The path swung right between close-packed trunks and

emerged into a clearing of lush, fine grass patched with pink flowers. The morning's rain twinkled off the grass-blades and dripped all round from forest leaves. The earth seemed to whisper to itself as it sucked the moisture in.

"Might be a plant or two worth looking at here," said Mrs Jones. "Time for a halt anyway. Give Lung a yell, Theo."

Theodore put a hand to his mouth and shouted. Lung, almost at the far trees now, reined and swung Sir Nigel up the slope to circle back towards the litter.

"Hey! Look out!" shouted Mrs Jones, grabbing suddenly beneath her litter-rug.

Her voice was answered by yells from the wood, and a shot. From the trees ahead, a little above the path, sprang a group of men as wild as animals, brandishing short curved swords or rough clubs. The porters dropped their loads and stampeded down the slope into the trees. Bewildered, Theodore looked to see what their guard, Uncle Sam, was doing. The old man had drawn his pistol and was pointing it roughly level with the tree-tops; with his head turned well away he pressed the trigger; there was a far louder explosion than any normal shot, and a lot of black smoke. The last coherent thing Theodore saw for a while was Uncle Sam running for the trees, screaming and nursing his arm.

By this time Albert was rearing and twisting sideways between the shafts and Bessie was trying to bolt down the path. The litter was empty. Theodore wrestled with the bridle, dragging Bessie's head down. Under her neck he glimpsed Lung toppling from his saddle and still beating down with his umbrella at a wild man swinging a sword. Three sharp bangs. The shriek of a bamboo litter-pole twisting into shredded splinters, but still not breaking. A scream of pain from Albert, and a lunge that rushed Bessie forward, with Theodore tumbling under hooves, and then somehow up, still holding the bridle, with a bandit rushing down at him, club swung high two-handed. A fresh lunge from Bessie, dragging him off his feet, letting him slither somehow round to her far side. He struggled up, still gripping the plunging halter and twisting to face the attacker, but as he rose he saw the bandit topple, all of a piece like a falling tree, with his mouth wide open. He remembered hearing the shot as another banged out, and another, close by. Mrs Jones was kneeling in her Chinese clothes, with her doll-face cradled to the stock of her rifle and her left elbow steadied on a fallen basket. Her finger tightened on the trigger, and before the snap of the shot ended she was working the bolt again. The triple click of metal seemed to create new silence. Even Albert stopped rearing and stood between the broken shafts, twitching and foamy with sweat. Mrs Jones got to her feet. Theodore could hear that she was swearing to herself. She turned to him biting her scarlet lip.

"Give me that horse," she said in a shaky voice. "Go and see what's happened with Lung. Don't get near any of them others."

On his way up the clearing Theodore found that his left upper arm and the ribs beside it seemed very sore and guessed that a hoof had caught them. He passed Sir Nigel, who was nervously edging down towards his mistress, head high and alert, tail swishing. A little above the path a bandit lay face down, arms spread wide. All the porters had vanished, but a heavy erratic rustling came from the trees below the clearing.

Two bodies lay close to each other in the grass. One was a

bandit, huddled sideways, the rags round his chest stained with blood. The other, lying on his back, was Lung. A sword lay between them, its hilt hidden in one of the patches of pink flowers.

"Lung?" whispered Theodore.

The young man groaned and sat slowly up. His right hand felt the back of his head and then patted around among the grass until it touched his little cap. He put it on and stood up.

"The Princess is not hurt?" he said, staring down the glade to where Mrs Jones, bridle in one hand and gun in the other, had moved up the slope to look at a third body.

"She shot them," said Theodore.

"She is a soldier," exclaimed Lung.

He prodded the dead bandit with his foot, then stooped and picked up the sword. They went slowly back down the twinkling turf, glancing from side to side among the trees but seeing no movement. Mrs Jones turned towards them as they came and Theodore saw that her make-up was runnelled with tears which still flowed helplessly down.

"Never thought as how I'd have to do that," she whispered. "Always thought just pointing a gun would be enough ... Theo, see if you can catch that Rollo—he's got the shot-gun in his left-hand basket. Then Lung can hold that and look danger-ous while I re-load this one—I'll have to get the fresh rounds out of my saddle-bags, and Rollo's got that too. I don't want the bastards rushing us while I'm mucking around."

"Not many live," said Lung. "Missy shoot three."

"Them porters is in it too," said Mrs Jones. "They knew as it was coming—look how quick they scarpered."

"The old man shot at the top of the trees," said Theodore. "His pistol blew up. He wasn't aiming anywhere near them."

"That shows," said Mrs Jones. "Fair enough, we'll get along like we was before we reached Mr What's-is-name's. If we don't have the litter there'll be two horses spare . . ."

It must have been more than an hour before they were ready to move again. Mrs Jones was unusually sharp and bossy about the details of packing. All round them the rotting woods seemed to watch them move, and Theodore's nape prickled at every crackle and whisper from the shadows, but even while Lung and Theodore held the guns so that Mrs Jones could change into her riding-habit, no sign of attack came. The ponies grazed. Sir Nigel champed at his feed-bag. Lung and Mrs Jones mimed an elaborate argument about whether to go on up the track or back to the porter's village and pretended to settle on the latter. At last, shivery with nerves, they were ready.

"Now Missy foreign woman again," said Lung, with a touch of sadness in his voice which rang strangely in this scene of danger and urgency. Theodore guessed he felt that somehow he had been demoted—there was a difference between leading a ritual procession for an important Chinese woman and being guide and factotum for a foreign plant-hunter.

"Looks like you're as foreign as I am round these parts," snapped Mrs Jones. "Tuck that sword you found away and take the shot-gun. Ride with your thumb on the safety-catch, too, and keep your eyes skinned. With a bit of luck they've guessed we're going back, but then again they might of split up, ready to have a go at us either way, once we're in among the trees. You first, Lung. Theo, you'll have to ride Bessie and lead Albert—don't stand no nonsense from him. I'll be rear-guard. Off we go."

Lung started towards the dark chasm between the trees. Theodore coaxed Bessie into movement and Albert followed, nervous but subdued. As they reached the trees a voice called in the wood below, but some way back.

"Don't hang about, Lung," shouted Mrs Jones. "We got to get well ahead."

Lung slapped his pony into a bouncy trot, and Bessie followed the example. One more alarm, Theodore, guessed, and she'd try to bolt again. He was tense with readiness when, just before he reached the first bend in the track, a weird wailing rose behind him, shrill and throbbing, like a dog baying. He glanced back and saw that Mrs Jones did the same. Beyond her, framed in the arch of light where the path opened into the glade, Uncle Sam was kneeling by one of the bodies. He looked up to the sky and raised his arms, one swathed in blood-soaked rags. Still wailing, he bowed over the body and covered his face with his hands. His fingers tore at his tangled grey hair.

"Move along," called Mrs Jones. "I can't stomach no more of this. Looks like it might of been his son."

Chapter 5

In the rest of that day, though the track became steadily narrower and steeper, they travelled further than they had done in any two previous days. They heard and saw no sign of pursuit, but Mrs Jones would rest no more than the horses needed. She was unusually silent, riding close behind Albert so that at the slightest sign of jibbing she could flick him across the haunches with a long withy she had cut—but indeed she seemed to drive them all on, horses and humans, as though she had funnelled her swirling energies into a single blast before which they were nothing but wind-borne seed, blown steadily up the track. It wasn't that she was scared, Theodore guessed. It was something else.

The map which P'iu-Chun had given them looked like an illustration to a fairy-tale, with a curly dragon blowing the prevailing wind from the south-east corner and delicate drawings crowding the blank spaces; but it was surprisingly accurate, marking every fork in the track, and at last the endless series of zig-zags which brought them up into the Plain of Shrines. For more than an hour they had climbed this last section, with the tree-tops below the path not reaching high enough to obscure the view across to the opposite side of the valley, just as steep and now astonishingly near. And then they were in the open.

The trees ended as though a line had been shaved along the rim of the valley and they came out wearily onto a vast, undulating, grassy plateau which seemed to reach right to where the wall of the true mountains shot towards the sky. Scattered all across this plain were strange rock outcrops, carved by wind and water into pinnacles and pillars and shapes like fortresses, and pocked with caves. Sometimes a fuzz of twisted trees crowned these outcrops, and nearly always there was a shrine or tomb, mostly in ruins but once or twice looking almost new.

To Theodore's eye the path vanished—you could roam where you wished over the measureless grassland—but Mrs Jones seemed to see where it lay. The grass itself was deceptive, shimmering green in the distance but underfoot only tufts and sparse blades protruding through shaly soil. The air was almost painfully sharp and clear after the muggy heat of the valley. At first their path took them back to the line of the river, which now ran a thousand feet below them, cutting its way through a gorge which made the ravine at the Settlement seem no more than a trivial crack. Even from this height, though, they could hear the mutter of rock-torn water. Then the river curled away south and for three hours they rode through the weird plateau, with no landmarks except the rock formations, which often looked completely different from different angles. It became steadily colder, and Theodore was grateful for another of P'iu-Chun's "gifts", a hip-length jacket of coarse-woven wool, with a breast-pocket he could fill with bread to munch as he rode.

Towards dusk they came to a pillar crowned by a shrine and a single, leaning birch-tree. A flight of steps had been cut in the sheer side. Mrs Jones reined and looked at it.

"This'll do," she said. "You two give the horses a feed, and I'll nip up with the glasses and see if I can spot if we're being followed. If we ain't, then we'll camp here—if we are, then we'll have to plug on."

She dismounted, took a pair of binoculars from her saddle-bag and started to climb the steps. Lung seemed even more absent-minded than usual, so Theodore saw to the horses single-handed. When he had finished he found Lung staring up at the rock-pillar and followed his gaze. Mrs Jones was there, standing on a slant of rock stair forty feet up, her back braced against the cliff and the binoculars to her eyes.

"She has a great head for heights," said Theodore.

"She is the osprey on the crag," said Lung. "She is the song men sing when they march under banners. Her heart beats with the blood of dragons."

"Yes, she doesn't seemed scared of anything."

"But she is the duck on the nest. She is flute music heard under willows in the evening. Her eyes shine with lamplight from old gardens."

"Is that your own poem?"

"A beginning. You have fed the horses?"

"Yes. Do you . . ."

"Look, she has seen us."

Mrs Jones's voice floated down through the evening stillness.

"Cooee! I can't see nothing, and that's right to the forest. We'll camp here. And I've found a nice cave a little up the cliff."

The cave was dry and surprisingly clean. Lung said it had probably been used by a hermit. They made no fire, but cooked hot stew from a can using Mrs Jones's patent stove, whose white tablets of solid fuel reeked vilely in the clean air. They ate their food in the dark, by feel and smell, and watched a storm build itself against the mountain wall far to the north.

Lightning whipped and blinked, too distant for them to hear the thunder, but overhead the sky was full of stars.

"Going to be a moon," said Mrs Jones. "We better keep watch, I suppose. Don't feel like sleeping, myself, so you go and kip down, Lung, and I'll wake you when it's your turn . . . No, you stay along of me, young Theo, and I'll tell you my life history. I need a bit of company, stop me thinking. You're not too fagged?"

"No, not at all," said Theodore with automatic politeness, though his eyes were sticky with needed sleep and his whole body chilled through.

"That's the ticket. Here, wrap yourself in a couple of blankets. Off you go, Lung, and don't lie awake half the night making up poetry—I can see you're in the mood. You'll have the other half for that, when you're doing sentry."

Lung mumbled his goodnights absent-mindedly and felt his way down the stair to the single tent they had pitched for him and Theodore. Mrs Jones had decided to sleep in the cave.

"He's all right," said Mrs Jones. "Matter of fact he's a sight better-mannered than some of the poets I've known—he can hold his liquor, for a start. You think I'm a wicked old woman, don't you, young man?"

Theodore was too surprised to answer.

"I'll lay you do, though, don't you?" insisted Mrs Jones.

"Let him that is without sin cast the first stone."

"Jesus said that, didn't he? 'Bout a harlot, what's more. I was never that, not really. Wouldn't do me much good in any case, would it, young man? You've not had the time to do much by way of sinning, nor the opportunity neither. Do you want to chuck any stones?"

Behind the flippant words there was an urgency which cut

through exhaustion, cut through the carelessness of the past few days, and woke the numb centre.

"I am worse than anyone," muttered Theodore. "I have betrayed my faith."

"Ah, come off it! You couldn't help that—you did what you had to! Now see here . . . it ain't no good, though, just having to. I suppose I had to shoot those blokes this morning—'nother second and Lung would of been a goner if I hadn't got that feller what was swiping at him with his sword . . . but it's shook me up a lot worse than a lot of other things I done what you'd call wickedness I daresay . . . Do you like me, young man? Spite of it all, do you like me?"

Her voice had dropped to a throaty mutter, but all her energies lay behind the question, compelling an answer.

"Yes," said Theodore, "I like you all right. And my father says . . . used to say . . . it's no odds what a man's done in his past life. It's what you're going to do in your future life—that's what counts."

"Good for him, then—not that I'd stake much on me becoming a holy body for the rest of my born days . . ."

She was silent for a while, as if brooding on the possibility. Theodore became aware that he could see her now, sitting at the mouth of the cave, surrounded by an irregular glow, a mere paling of the blackness. For a while he thought that he was imagining the effect in his weariness, that his mind was playing tricks, making him see the invisible forces that beamed out from her. Then, rather to his relief, he realised that the moon must be rising.

"Do you want to know why I'm here?" said Mrs Jones suddenly.

"So you can watch and see if we're being attacked."

"That ain't what I meant. Here I am, bundling round these heathen parts, looking for odds and bobs of plants, running for my life now, 'cause of a young man whose family paid me to stay out of England for ten years."

"Was that Mr Jones?"

"Lord no. I give *him* the push years before. He was a wrong 'un, if ever. Like to hear about this other bloke?"

"If you want to tell me," said Theodore.

"He's a nice young man," said Mrs Jones. "Least, he was when I met him. I suppose he must be around thirty-five now. That's right, he's four years younger than what I am . . . rich as crazes . . . you see, he's the one and only white-headed boy of one of them old Jewish banking families. He never took me home, of course, but he told me about it. There's his Dad, what ran the bank and could of bought up the Prince of Wales twice over, and his Mum, come from just the same kind of family only in Paris, dripping with diamonds, handsome, full of brains, sharp as a green lemon, and all his sisters and his aunts, them as nobody's managed to marry off into other banks, all sitting around of an evening in this great big house north of the Park; and in the middle of them, all in black, deaf as a post but still missing nothing, is his Gran—his Dad's Mum, and what she says goes. Even my Monty's Dad, with his hunting-lodge in Scotland and his yacht at Cowes and his pack of hounds in the Midlands—even he's scared stiff of her. Now, I don't think any of them minded a straw when Monty hit it off with me— only an actress, my dear, keep him out of trouble till we choose a wife for him. What they didn't realise was it was going to get serious between Monty and me . . .

"I suppose I better explain about that. I told you I wasn't a harlot, 'cause I've never been with a gentleman what I didn't fancy a bit, and I let them give me jewels and things, but it wasn't serious, not more than once or twice ... anyway, I was too young then to know what I was doing, almost. But Monty and me ...

"When his family saw what was going on, they done their best to break it up, but it didn't work 'cause Monty upped sticks and took me to Africa. Funny, ain't it, how a rich Jew-boy, brought up in the middle of London, should want more than anything else in the world to have a great big garden full of foreign plants ... two years we spent at it, fossicking round after roots and bulbs and things. We done Africa. We done Inja. We done South America. I used to tell Monty, teasing him like, as I was only his excuse for getting away from his bank and going plant-hunting. Course, it wasn't true ... he was gone on me and I was gone on him ... mercy, yes! Not that he's much to look at, a little bloke, trim, going a bit bald even when I first met him, something about him made him look like he's just been polished, even in the middle of a jungle, know what I mean? Oh, they was good times ...

"Funny how things work out. We was in Mexico, and I started having a baby. I'd always managed to miss that before, but now it seemed like the best thing of all, and Monty took it into his head that he was going to bring me back to London, where I could have good doctors—and spite of his family he was going to marry me. Me, I didn't care what happened, I was that happy for him. So we come home.

"We found a nice little house, up in Swiss Cottage, and Monty set about arranging everything. He would of married me if they'd cut him off with a shilling, but he was used to being rich, and there ain't no point in being poor if you can help it, is there? So he had a bit of argy-bargy to do, took him out a lot. And we hadn't been settled even a week when I was sitting alone one morning and a lady come calling, and it was Monty's Mum.

"Surprising how we hit it off, despite we was on opposite sides. She didn't say so right out, but I got it into my head something must of happened to her, back in Paris, like what was happening to Monty now, and she'd come and married Monty's Dad when she was stuck on someone else. She didn't come the grand lady with me, nor lay down the law, neither. But she told me straight out that if I married Monty he wasn't getting a penny. They'd chosen a wife for him, and what's more she wasn't one of themselves—she was the daughter of an English Marquess. I can't hope to explain to you what that meant to them—all these years the Jews being shovelled aside by the English nobs, not being let into their clubs, not being allowed to meet their wives, being treated like dirt, really, despite lending them all the money they needed . . . Monty'd told me how it hurt. And then Monty's Mum explained how they'd set him up if he married this girl, with everything he wanted. I remember I asked if the girl was interested in garden-ing, and Monty's Mum just smiled and nodded. She'd taken care of that! She even knew the bit of ground we'd chosen for Monty's garden—Monty'd come home the day before a bit down in the mouth, because he thought it was all settled and then he'd found it had been sold all of a sudden to someone else. Guess who had the title deeds in her handbag!

"I didn't tell Monty she'd been. I got him to take me down a couple of days later, pretending I wanted to look for another bit of ground in the same part of the world, but while we was there I said we might as well have a wander round this bit what we'd missed, as I'd never even seen it. Raining stair-rods it was when we get out of the carriage, but we walked all round under Monty's big black brolly, arms round each other's waists so as to keep out of the rain, and even so my shoes was falling apart and my skirt was sopping up to my knees by the time we'd been round—and my heart was breaking, too, 'cause I knew he had to have it. Seventy-three acres, running slant along a ridge looking out south-east. You couldn't see fifty yards that day, but Monty said in decent weather you could see clear across to the Downs, twenty-five mile away—nothing much of a view round these parts, I suppose, but it's a long way in England. *I* couldn't see what made it so different from any other bit of farm on a hill-side, 'cept there was a huge old grove of sweet chestnut near the top and a long wood sweeping down half sideways, not too thick, just right for his lilies ... Ah, he's such a one for lilies. Me too ... And as we went round he told me where he was going to put all his plants what we'd been collecting those two years, and what his gardening friends had been looking after for him, his clematis and his peonies and his eucryphias—you never seen a eucryphia in flower, I dare say, young man ..."

"I don't know," said Theodore. The urgency with which she told her story, though she seemed to be talking as much to herself as to him, had somehow buoyed him out of sleep; but even so it was difficult to bring his wits together to answer the sudden question.

"I suppose there were quite a lot of flowers round the Settlement, but I only got to know a few of their Chinese names," he explained.

"No, there wouldn't be a eucryphia round there," said Mrs Jones. "I wonder how he's been getting his through the winter—they're not that hardy ..."

She sat brooding again, framed in the silver moonlight.

"What did you say to Mr Monty?" asked Theodore.

"Nothing. Not straight off. I had to see his Mum again. Fix up about my income, fix up about the baby. You know, till she died last winter she wrote me a huge long letter, twice a year, telling me how the kid was doing; and when the doctors told her she hadn't much time left she wrote again, saying she'd sent him down to live with Monty, giving out he belonged to one of Monty's sisters what had died in France. I never seen him since he was two weeks old, and I was that sick having him, what with all the heart-break and the rows with Monty, that honest I hardly remember him. Monty guessed, you see. First off I told him I wasn't going to marry him 'cause I wanted to go on fossicking round the world and I could see he wanted to settle down, but soon as that bit of land come back on the market he guessed we'd been going behind his back. He was that angry! Honest, I didn't know he had it in him to get so stirred, him such a gentle bloke. It was me getting together with his Mum as done it . . . Whole evenings I was down on my knees beside his chair, begging him to see he'd be happier in the end . . . I wore him down, poor man, and in the end he went off and proposed to this girl and she said yes, and then he took her down to Sussex and showed her his piece of ground— I remember lying on my sofa, huge as a beer-barrel, I was that near my time, and looking out of the window and thinking they had a lovely sunny day for it.

"Next time Monty come to see me—he wasn't living in my house no longer, of course—I asked him what the girl had made of it and he smiled like a pawn-broker and said she had the right ideas. And then I knew they'd make a go of it, and there was nothing more for me to do except have my baby and clear out. I only seen him twice more, once when the doctors thought I was dying, after the baby, and once very formal when his Mum took me along, pretending I was just a pal of hers, to meet his new wife, what I never seen. Funny how stuffy he was about that—didn't like it at all. *I* could tell, of course. Never seen him again."

"But you still send him the plants you find?" asked Theodore, after a pause.

"No. Course not. Couple of times, when I've got something special, I thought of asking Mr Hillier—he's the bloke I send things to, big commercial gardener near Winchester, I know he'll do right by my plants if anyone will—I've thought of asking him to send a rooted cutting or some seed on to Monty, not telling who it really come from, but it wouldn't be right, would it? What do you think? What do you think about the whole thing? I've never told anyone all this before, but I'd like your opinion, young man."

Her tone was odd, suddenly mocking but still somehow earnest. Theodore hesitated. There was an easy way out. *Matthew* 7.1—"Judge not that ye be not judged." But he guessed that if he simply quoted that it would bring out her full mockery. She needed something from him, but he wasn't sure what. He had understood most of her story, in the sense that he had followed the events in it; but why these things had happened, what force had driven her and this man together, and what other force, or set of forces, had then prised them apart, he could not comprehend.

"Spit it out!" said Mrs Jones. "I'm past praying for, ain't I?"

"I don't know," said Theodore. "Honest, I don't know enough."

Perhaps she chose to misunderstand him.

"You want the story of my life, eh?" she said. "So you can see how I come to set up with Monty in the first place? Fair enough, though I warn you it's a lot different from anything you've known. Eight children, we were, the ones what lived past weaning, all in a couple of rooms in Battersea. Dad, he wasn't a drunk, and he never hit my Mum, far as I know. No, they were decent people, but dead poor. Dad was a docker, but he'd gone and ruptured himself lifting weights too heavy, so all he could do was sweeping kinds of jobs and there ain't much of a living in that, even when the work's there. And all those kids. Mum must have starved herself, often as not, see we got a bite, and even so three of us popped off afore they was eight, and that left me third eldest, what had been fifth . . ."

She was talking in a low, even voice, almost a whisper. The memories seemed to drag her back to those sooty, slime-paved alleys and dank, tiny rooms so that her accent became more marked and harder to follow than Theodore had ever heard it. *Pay* became *pie*, *with* became *wiv*, *getting* became *ge'in'* as she relived that tatterdemalion strange childhood, as full of dangers as the wildest forest, with Saturday night stabbings as common as church-going, and the wheels of the always-drunk carters grinding along the cobbles—a life for the quick and the lucky to escape from and the rest to be submerged like rubbish tossed into the greasy Thames. Theodore was not aware of falling asleep.

He woke alone in the tent at dawn. Goodness knows how she had got him down there—woken Lung, perhaps, and between them carried him down the narrow steep steps in the moonlight. It was strange that she had not simply rolled him up in his blankets and left him to sleep in the cave. Her voice was still vivid in his mind, as if it had become part of his dreams. *I'm past praying for, ain't I?*

He crawled out of his blankets, stiff with travel, and stood up outside the tent. Far up the rock pinnacle a dove was calling; the rock spired into an almost white sky, but the air was so clear he felt he could see the individual grass-blades all the way to the mountains. Mrs Jones was presumably asleep in the cave, and Lung was nowhere to be seen. The hobbled horses grazed near by.

Theodore stood for a while, feeling very strange. The cleanness of the upland air, the whiteness of the sky, the ache of muscles and nerves remade in sleep, the dew and the one dawn bird—these combined to make the world seem not merely clean but new. They had come out of the ancient, stifling, ever-decaying forest into this austere arena and here they had found a new beginning. He started to climb the stairs, moving with extra caution so as not to break the spell of newness by speaking to anyone before he had first tried to speak to God. It was colder than he had realised. His breath hung in white puffs before him and the air rasped in his throat, but at last he reached the top.

The shrine was in good repair, a little, square wooden hut, with a pointy, tiled roof which ended in up-turned eaves, all painted gaudy red and green and streaked with bird-droppings. To the south-east lay the tumble of infolded forested hills through which they had journeyed; to the north east, more hills, ringing a vast shadowy basin; and to the west the enormous wall of the Himalaya. For days these mountains had been retreating as the travellers had trudged towards them. Now, seen from this height, they had rushed in.

Theodore had forgotten about the little heathen shrine when he had decided to climb up here to pray; he chose a smooth patch of rock the other side of the single birch tree and knelt, closing his eyes and waiting for the last beating of his heart to quieten. Then, as always, he started with the Lord's Prayer.

"Our Father . . ."

He moved his lips through the familiar words and held his mind to their meaning, but they were still no more than words. He was talking to a white sky and a huge, clean, empty plateau, neither of which could hear him. Nothing had changed. Nothing had been born anew. The world was the same stale, mindless place in which Father had been murdered by the Boxers and the Settlement wiped out, and the old man in the forest had wailed over the body of his bandit son, shot by Mrs Jones . . .

I'm past praying for, ain't I?

No words formed in Theodore's mind, but for a moment while he was considering how to begin he sensed that some-where in the unlistening emptiness around him a crack had opened and that his thought, his image of Mrs Jones, was being perceived and received. The feeling lasted only an instant, and then the blankness walled him round. For some time he tried to recapture the feeling, but it didn't come again. He was about to return to the routine of familiar prayer when the silence was broken by a suppressed cough.

He opened his eyes and looked round. Mrs Jones was standing in front of the shrine with her binoculars in her hand.

"Sorry to interrupt, young man," she said. "I hope you popped one in for me."

"Yes."

"So you don't think I'm past praying for, then? Though I'm a wicked old woman in all conscience."

She smiled at him teasingly, as though she pitied him and was thoroughly pleased with herself. A cooing note in her voice echoed the call of the dove that had woken him at dawn. Theodore felt he wanted to shake her, to shock her, to take water and soap and harsh flannel and scrub away the make-up that plastered her wrinkled skin; and at the same time he wanted her to smile at him without mockery, to speak as she had last night when she had seemed to need him for more than his ability to speak Miao and Mandarin and to manage a packhorse. He looked away, but was still aware enough of the tension between them to know the moment when her stance changed and her plump and pliant body stiffened into concentration.

"Come and look here," she said. "See if you can spot what I think I just seen."

He moved across and took the heavy binoculars.

"See that tall lump with the pines atop?" she said. "Line up on that, so you can find it in the glasses. Right? Now go up from there . . ."

The binoculars seemed to make mist, faint layers of quivering grey which were not there to the naked eye. The image jumped at the slightest tremor in his hands . . . now, there, a little blurred in the mottled grey and fawn, spots of darker matter, clumped at the centre but with a few outliers on either side. Deer? The clump changed shape. An outlier moved inwards, and for a second the blur of distance sharpened and the spot was a man.

"People," he said.

"That's what I make 'em. What are they carrying?"

"Not much. Not coolie-poles."

"Then they ain't traders. And you see how they ain't all sticking to the one path? Only time I seen men moving like that—in Africa, mostly—was when they was following a trail. Tracker in the middle, main party following him, couple of blokes out each side case he misses where the trail jinks."

"Boxers? The men from the forest?"

"Well, they might be hunting some kind of animal, but my guess is it's us."

"You mean they still want to rob us?"

"Well, they'll take what we got, supposing they catch us. But it ain't just that. There's more blokes there than what we met in the forest—Uncle Sam's gone back and got his tribe. Like it says in the Bible, an eye for an eye, a tooth for a tooth."

"Burning for burning, stripe for stripe, wounding for wounding," quoted Theodore. "But it says that if you don't lie in wait for your enemy and God delivers him into your hand, then you are allowed to flee."

"Doubt if they've read that bit," said Mrs Jones drily as she took the binoculars back. "They'll be here by dinner time. We better get started. You nip down and explain to old Lung, though you'll have a job getting anything into his head this morning. He's full of his poems!"

She laughed, apparently more amused by Lung's behaviour than alarmed by the murderers on their trail. Even in the panic of the moment Theodore found this odd.

Chapter 6

Flight, but a strange exhilaration, like the flight of a wild bird freed from the hand. They breakfasted on horseback and rode all morning, stopping only to water and feed the horses at two of the strange little circular ponds that pocked the plateau almost as dramatically as the rock pillars, impenetrably deep below the mirror surface. At their midday halt by another of these ponds Mrs Jones made them fake a struggle. Lung and Theodore wrestled vigorously on a patch of softer ground, laughing between the grunts of effort. When they rose, still laughing, Theodore found he was filled with a sudden rush of affection and comradeship, something which he had never known in the God-centred community of the Settlement. It was as though the three of them were the only people in the world. They left a couple of empty cartridge-cases by the pool and one of Mrs Jones's scarves, bloodied with Lung's blood, half-hidden at its edge. They loosened two boulders and threw them in, hoping that their pursuers would see the fresh sockets and guess that the boulders had been used to weight something down. Then they rode on towards a hamlet marked on the map, the only real houses for fifty miles.

Well short of this place Theodore and Mrs Jones dismounted and walked south, choosing hard ground where they would leave no footprints, while Lung rode on into the hamlet with instructions to make a parade of guilt and haste, buy what provisions he could—feed for the horses was the most urgent—and leave the place heading north.

It was almost dusk when Lung came over the horizon. The sun, low over the mountains, threw stilted shadows from the weary horses. Mrs Jones put four fingers into her mouth and produced a screeching whistle. He waved a triumphant arm and headed towards them.

"All fine," he called, almost before he was in ear-shot. "I find Chinese trader-man. He think I rob you, kill you. I tell him going north. Find old river—no water, all rock. Ride long way. Then come round. Trader say men in village Red Lolo, men in forest Black Lolo. Black Lolo enemies with Red Lolo."

"Sounds promising," said Mrs Jones, spreading out P'iu-Chun's map on a jut of the rock pillar they had chosen for a rendezvous. "Now see here. The track we been following gets up into the mountains through this pass here, but down south here, by the river—looks like it runs through a gorge all the way—there's this other little path he marked . . ."

"Very poor road," said Lung, reading the exquisite characters at the edge of the map. "Bad bridge. Very difficult mountains."

"The worse the better, far as we're concerned, cause them brigands won't imagine us trying it. Bit of luck they'll think you done me in and shoved me in that pool, and then they'll pack it in, 'cause it was me they was after."

"This path go into Tibet," said Lung.

"Now ain't that a rum do! Just what I been wanting all along. I hope you don't mind, gentlemen both."

"You go. I go," said Lung.

"Fair enough," said Mrs Jones, smug as a well-fed cat. "Now

we'll give the horses a bite and a rest and get on as far south as we can. If there's a moon like what there was last night, it'll be good as daylight."

That night's march was the first part of a stage which lasted another five days. On the first afternoon it took them several hours to find a way across a dry ravine, but after that they rode south until on the second morning they reached the colossal gorge which they had last seen soon after they had left the forest. Here they turned west once more. All this time they saw no travellers, and only once, through the binoculars, a group of nomads herding a vast flock of browny-orange sheep.

Now, visibly, march after march, the mountains came nearer and at the same time looked ever more impassable. From a distance it had been easy to imagine clefts in the wall beneath the glittering rim, but at closer range the rock face showed no gap. It reached out of sight to north and south and at its nearest was still purple-blue with distance; to Theodore it seemed an impossible barrier, but Mrs Jones was not at all daunted. Indeed her spirits increased as the mountains neared and she sang and talked all day long, to Theodore, to Lung, to Sir Nigel if she felt like that. It was as if in her eyes the journey west was more than a haphazard line of escape, a running away. She was moving *towards*. Beyond the mountain rampart something marvellous was waiting for her, calling to her, drawing her on; and everything else that had happened—the Boxers, P'iu-Chun, even the ambush in the forest—was part of this pattern. The light persistent wind plucked at the folds of her riding-cloak as if trying to hurry her on.

On the fourth afternoon Theodore was riding alone, thinking about Father. He had deliberately let himself fall behind,

because Mrs Jones was behaving in a manner which made her
company uncomfortable. She was, to put it bluntly, flirting
with Lung. Her excuse was a song she had chosen to sing:

"The boy I love sits up in the gallery,
    The boy I love is looking down at me . . ."

She had thrown back her veil and was continually glancing
sideways at Lung from under her enormous lashes, and the
poor young man was taking her behaviour at least half-
seriously, laughing, but always with a certain embarrassment.
Theodore had come to like Lung considerably; there was an
inner dignity and pride in him, hidden at first under shyness
and uncertainty but becoming steadily more noticeable as they
rode across the grasslands. It was unfair of Mrs Jones to tease
him like this in Theodore's presence, so Theodore dropped
back out of earshot.

As he watched the pair riding ahead, he wondered how
Father would have reacted in his place. Of course Mrs Jones
wouldn't have behaved the same way with Father there—or
would she? Father would certainly have reproved her, bluntly
but without arrogance. He would have disliked her treatment
of Lung quite as much as her general impropriety and would
have said so. Ought Theodore to have done the same? No—
he wasn't Father. Father was . . .

It was strange to be thinking of Father like this, as it were
from the outside. Father had been a wonderful man, good and
clever and kind, but his personality had been so strong that it
filled the Settlement. You breathed and ate and drank Father.
Sometimes he was a cliff towering above you; at other times
you swam in the lake of his love. But all the time you were
somehow inside him, as the unhatched bird is in its shell; and

now Theodore was outside, looking back down the vista of travelled days to where Father was dwindling, just as the limestone pillars of the plateau had dwindled with the miles.

Theodore was only very vaguely aware that this sense of dwindling and distancing was a symptom of the wound in his life beginning to heal; in fact his main reaction was one of guilt at the sense of ease and freedom he had been feeling for the last few days, and for a while he actually tried to open the wound up, to bring Father nearer by working himself back into a state of shock and agony at the destruction of the Settlement and his own casting-out. But at the same time he knew in his heart that this wouldn't do. It was a lie, and Father had always taught him that unless you were truthful with yourself you couldn't be truthful with anyone else.

He was distracted from this train of thought by an absurd piece of behaviour by the pair ahead. For a moment he thought that Lung had been stung by some insect, from the way he was wriggling about; but then it became clear that the Chinese was attempting to kneel on Rollo's haunches, and having achieved that, to rise to his feet. He actually made it, and stood for two or three seconds, arms outstretched like a circus performer, while Mrs Jones applauded. Then he lost his balance and half-slid, half-jumped to the ground. Theodore would have thought that the pair of them were drunk if he hadn't heard Mrs Jones complaining the night before that Lung had forgotten to buy any wine in the village in the hollow. He smiled at their childish antics, and decided that it was not his business to judge them.

This decision, though sensible, turned out harder to stick to than he would have guessed. The nights on the plateau were very sharp. If the air was still they would wake in the morning to find the miles of grass all white with frozen dew; and any wind that swept down from the mountains was like the breath of an ice-giant that can turn all living things to stone. They would halt near dusk, pitch the two little tents, feed and water the horses, then cook a meal on the portable stove and go to bed. Despite the cold Lung had taken to sleeping in the open, saying that he slept better that way. The tethered horses were their sentries.

However hard the ground, Theodore normally slept till dawn, and if he dreamed the images were lost beneath many layers of slumber. That night, though, he chose his sleeping-place carelessly and woke at an unguessable hour with his left leg completely numb where a lump of stone had pressed into a nerve. As he turned to ease it he groaned, still half asleep, and then he was wide awake, conscious that something had responded to his groan. There had been a noise and it had stopped. There was no wind. He listened till he heard a horse fidget, and knew at once that it had not been that. Now he was tense. Wild animal? Wolf? Bear? The men from the forest? No—the horses would be making more noise. Slowly he relaxed, and as he edged towards sleep once more his mind recreated the sound he had heard. It had been a laugh, very quiet, ending in whispered words. Not one voice, but two.

He was asleep before he worked out what it meant, and in the morning had forgotten the incident until they were loading the horses and Lung said something to Mrs Jones, out of Theodore's earshot, and she laughed.

Even so, they had been travelling for some hours before he decided that he knew for certain that Lung and Mrs Jones were lovers. (Adulterers was the word he used in his mind.) After the first chill little shock—more unease than shock—at the memory of the laugh in the night, he had told himself that he must be mistaken. He was, in fact, instantly ashamed of his own nasty-mindedness. But then, as he noticed the behaviour of the other two to each other he became amazed at himself for not having noticed it earlier. It was as though they were talking, in glance and tone and gesture, a secret language to which he had hitherto been deaf; now he could hear it, though he still couldn't understand the words. He remembered a sentence of Mrs Jones's, bitten short, just after she had first seen their pursuers. He remembered their clowning the previous day, almost puppy-like in its spontaneous happiness. He remembered that first night on the plateau when he had fallen asleep in the cave and had been carried down those difficult steps to the tent . . . that was when it had started, he was vividly sure.

He came to these conclusions erratically, with many moments when he had almost persuaded himself that the opposite was true, or that he had not seen things which he knew he had seen, or that he had never heard Mrs Jones laugh to her lover in the dark—that it had all been a dream. He even wondered whether he was going mad. His own reactions to the knowledge troubled him almost as much as the knowledge itself. Here was an outright breaking of one of the Commandments, and he knew that what he ought to have felt was a mixture of pity and horror—pity for the sinners, horror for the deed. These emotions were there, but if he was honest with himself they were not his main emotions. He could summon them up if he concentrated, but as soon as he relaxed his will they disappeared in a storm of other emotions—a sense of betrayal, a curious jealousy at being left out of the secret, a slightly squeamish but inquisitive surprise that it was possible for two people so far apart in age to feel like that about each other, shame at his own cowardice in not denouncing them, in continuing to travel with them, in (to be honest) still wanting their company and their liking. What they were doing was wrong—wicked—but it did not feel like that. They were so happy, and Mrs Jones at least seemed to want Theodore to share in their happiness. In fact, when she tried to make him join in one of her songs and he rebuffed her, smiling thinly and shaking his head, he felt as if it was he who was doing wrong. It was like uprooting some cheerful little flower because it happens to be a weed.

By this time the nature of the terrain had altered. All morning the line of mountain below the snow-peaks had been losing its blue-purple vagueness and acquiring shape, ceasing to be a wall and becoming a series of steep spurs and screens, like the beginnings of roots round the bole of an enormous tree. Soon the real climbing would begin, though it was many miles still to the peaks. There was no track that Theodore could see, but the path on P'iu-Chun's map followed the line of the enormous gorge for a while, then swung away, doubled back and reached it again at a lake, right up among the mountains.

"Here's where Mr What's-is-name's poor road begins," said Mrs Jones, almost eagerly, as if welcoming the challenge.

"No way through," said Lung, shading his eyes like a hunter and scanning the whole line of mountains.

"Hark to old eagle-eye!" said Mrs Jones. "Now look here. See where that shoulder sticks out? The gorge runs in south of that, and I 'spect it is where it is 'cause it comes out through a crack in the mountains and there's no way through that side, so we got to get up behind the shoulder from the other side, and from the way he's drawn it it ain't no use heading straight up, we got to start out along that next spur there, and even that's not going to be much of a party."

She was right. After the days of easy travelling the journey slowed to an endless-seeming trudge across slant shale and scree, resting every hour and lucky to do two miles between rests, leading the horses almost all the way, seldom daring to look up from the ground for fear that a careless step would begin a hundred-foot slither, perhaps to a sheer cliff edge. The wind whipped savagely off the mountains, relaxed, and came again in buffeting gusts from unpredictable directions.

They camped that night on a slant platform of coarse grass, and almost had their tents washed away when a thunderstorm boiled up all round them in the small hours. Rollo cut a knee, wrestling with his tether in the panic, so they had to redistribute the loads, treating poor Sir Nigel as a common pack-horse. Next day they barely made ten miles, but reached at last the point where the spur they had been climbing rooted into the main mass of the rampart, and up this mass they crawled slant-wise for the next two days. Around the middle of the second day they met three men—copper-skinned, fur-booted, smiling —leading a train of loaded yaks down the barely visible path and gossiped with them for a while in shreds of Mandarin. Yes, this was the road to the lake. No, no one would stop them. So few people used this path that there was no real border. But yes, somewhere beyond lay Tibet.

Next morning they climbed the last few miles to the saddle and crossed the invisible border. It was icy cold. Patches of stale snow lay all along the level, and barely a blade of grass or other vegetation showed among the loose-lying rubble and gravel between. On either side the slopes curved up, harsh rock and loose boulders merging into the true snow-fields, never melting even in the height of summer. Mrs Jones made sure, despite the cold, that where the gentle-seeming sun beat down

on them their skin was covered all the time. "Surprising how it
can burn you at this height," she said. "All blisters I was once,
up in the Andes. And don't you go staring at them snow-fields
or you'll have a headache you'll never forget."

So, muffled against scorching as much as freezing, they
trudged across the pass, with the horses gasping all the time at
the poor, thin air. At last, after weary hours, they halted and
stood gazing down at a long gash of a valley slanting into the
tumbled mountains. The crack that had opened and let the
river through was here more than a gorge. On its far side the
cliffs rose almost perpendicular, but on this side it was as though
half the mountain had been scooped away to create this valley.
At their feet the path wriggled down a plunging bare slope
until, thousands of feet below them, it came to the trees. Even
from this height Theodore could see that it was nothing like
the clogged and rotting forest where they had met the Black
Lolo, but a pure stand of flat-topped pines with almost blue
needles and a pinkish glimmer of trunks beneath. And thousands more feet below the trees lay the lake, so dark a blue it was
almost black, reflecting the tremendous cliff beyond.

"This sacred place," said Lung in English.

"You been here before, then?" said Mrs Jones, mockingly.

"I feel excellent ghosts."

"Let's hope not. Now we'll get a move on, so we can camp
down among them trees, with a bit of luck find a clearing
where the horses can forage, poor things, or they won't be
no use to us, not after what we been through these last few
days."

She hitched up her skirt and coaxed Albert, too tired and
starved now to make trouble, down the first stretch of path.

It took them half the afternoon to reach the tree-line, but all the time the air became warmer and stronger, and sweeter too as the faint smell of the pines drifted towards them. And then, with their calves aching from the downward slope, they were among the trees, walking on pine-needles instead of rock and seeing on either side the pillars of the trees rising to the blue-green roof. There was some undergrowth—rhododendrons and trails of yellow-flowered clematis, but the whole impression was of almost ordered space, of mottled shadow and deep silence.

Still the slope plunged down, with the path twisting back and forth between the trees but heading generally west along the valley. They were beginning to look for a place to camp when Mrs Jones halted and handed her reins to Theodore before darting upwards into the wood. About twenty yards from the path she dropped to her knees in a nook between two glossy green mounds of rhododendron. She stayed quite still for more than a minute, just as if absorbed in sudden prayer, but her body hid whatever she was looking at until she rose and backed slowly away, still staring, still unmistakably worshipping. What she had found was a single lily-plant, a stem about three feet high fringed along its length with insignificant down-curled leaves, and at the top five trumpets of intense pale yellow, amid the shadowy browns and greens and blues of the wood a colour as sharp as the call of a bird.

She came back to the path shaking her head slowly from side to side. There was a shiver in her voice which Theodore hadn't heard before.

"That's new," she said. "That's me name in all the books. I'll lay my best bib and tucker no one's never seen that before. Ain't it a beauty! Where did I pack my trowel, Lung?"

"Not time for digging," said Lung, a little sourly. "Must find grass for horses, place for camp."

He was jealous. Even Theodore could hear that he resented her passion for this flower. She must have thought so too, to judge by her laugh.

"If you say so," she said. "Fair enough, I'll come along of you for a bit. We must be getting down near that there lake by now, and there ought to be somewhere along there. But I warn you, if we don't fetch up somewhere good in half an hour I'm coming back, even if it means riding half the night to catch you up again."

"Maybe we find more flower," said Lung mildly.

"That's right. There can't be just the one."

They walked on. The slope, easing now, took the path down slantwise another mile or so into an area where the pines gave way to oak and the undergrowth was much more varied and profuse. Here Mrs Jones halted again and studied the tree-tops to their left.

"Looks a bit more light down there, don't you think?" she said. "But it ain't worth taking the horses down, case it's no good. Nip off, Theo, and see, would you?"

"I go, Missy," said Lung, eagerly, and before Theodore could move he had dropped his reins and was darting down between the bushes, leaping like a deer to clear the lower ones. He vanished from sight, but still they could hear the crack and rattle of his progress, loud in the forest quiet.

"Changed, hasn't he?" said Mrs Jones. "He wouldn't of been dashing about like that a fortnight ago, would he? You've spotted there's something on between us, young man?"

Theodore wasn't ready for the question.

"I guess so," he muttered.

She lifted her veil and looked at him, smiling gently. Beneath her make-up he could see the lines of exhaustion creasing her face.

"And what do you say to that?" she whispered. "No, it ain't fair to ask. You can't go telling me to my face what sort of woman I am, can you? But let me tell you this—I ain't ashamed of myself. He's a duck, ain't he? You ever seen a young fellow so happy? You'll be lucky if you feel like that yourself one day. I tell you, it was seeing I could still do that to a bloke as begun it in me, and now I don't know as I'm not a bit head-over-heels myself . . . disgusting, ain't it, in an old baggage like me?"

Theodore shook his head. It was sinful, but it was not disgusting.

"Glad you think so, 'cause I see it's rough luck on you. It ain't easy living along of a pair of love-birds, and never mind your principles. But you ain't going to go all haughty on us, are you? You'll put up with our doings? Not that you got much choice."

He nodded, dumbly. Certainly he had no choice, not just because he was forced into their company, but because it was impossible to resist her pleading.

"Tell you what," she said. "I'll teach you drawing. That'll be something, to make up like. Here comes young Galahad— he better not see me holding your hand, or he might hit you."

As Lung came crunching up through the wood Theodore discovered that her small fingers had been gripping his wrist like a steel bracelet. He rubbed the place, feeling dazed and uncertain.

"Number one fine place," panted Lung. "Plenty grass, plenty water."

"Fair enough," said Mrs Jones. "You two take the horses down, set up camp, while I nip back for my *Lilium Jonesii*. How's that strike you, Theo? *Lilium . . .*"

"Missy come along this way," interrupted Lung. "All day walk too far. I fetch this flower."

"So who's being masterful?" said Mrs Jones, only half-mockingly. "All right if you say so—I'm fair tucked-up, to be honest, and I'm surprised you ain't too. You got to promise to do the job proper, like you seen me doing it. I want every hair off every root. First off you got to dig . . ."

"I know. I dig very well," said Lung, seizing Mrs Jones's wrist in his impatience and trying to drag her from the path. She shook him off, laughing.

"All right, all right," she said. "Here's the trowel. You cut along up the path or it'll be too dark to see where you're digging. Come on, Theo."

For a moment Lung seemed reluctant to obey, but then he made up his mind and started back along the path.

"See any hoof-prints, try and wipe them out," called Mrs Jones as she led Albert down between the bushes. "We'll have to make a proper job of that tomorrow, if we're going to have a bit of a rest here."

Theodore saw that she was already picking her way with extra care, choosing patches of fallen leafage that left no trace of their passage, and making wide circuits to avoid breaking through undergrowth.

"Do you really think they've followed us this far?" said Theodore, after a while.

"You can't never tell with blood feuds. Besides, they ain't the only ones we got to look out for—there's other people use that path, and some of them might think as we was easy pickings like that first lot did. Nearly there. Hi! What's this? Ooh, the yellow monkey! I thought as he was up to something!"

The spate of exclamations had begun with a squeak and ended in a whisper. Theodore, his eyes on the ground to choose the least betraying path, looked up to see what had caused that note of hushed excitement, almost of awe. At first all he noticed was that she was standing beside Albert on the edge of open ground; a mile beyond her a wall of dark cliff reared up, but in the middle distance was only the pale and mist-tinged luminosity of evening. He led Rollo up to her side and found that he was looking down a green coomb that reached right to the lake shore. The green was grass and looked good for grazing. A thin stream threaded through it.

Slowly his eyes were drawn away from these practicalities by the mountain opposite, the enormous wall of granite rising from the water, and above it the glittering ice-peak, pink and gold with sunset. The lake surface mingled the colours of the dark cliff and the pearly sky into a silky shimmer. The mountain was a huge presence, imposing awe and quiet.

"It's beautiful," he whispered to himself.

"Don't tell me you haven't noticed 'em!" said Mrs Jones, flinging out an arm. Theodore followed the direction of her gesture.

The flanks of the coomb were not as steep as its head, where they were standing. The trees reached the rim and stopped, leaving caves of shadow beneath their lower branches. In this shadow the lilies glowed.

"Did you ever see anything like it?" said Mrs Jones. "In your wildest dreams, even? Ooh, where's that fancy-dan of a poet? I could of told he was being artful!"

"Here, Missy," said Lung with a chuckle in his voice, coming quietly up behind the horses. "You find plenty flowers?"

"Oh! You!" cried Mrs Jones, spinning round to sieze and hug him. "I'd kiss you, too, young man, only I'm scared what he might do to us."

"Missy go see flowers," said Lung, disengaging himself. "I make tent."

There was a note in his voice as though he had created the coomb for her sake and was now presenting it to her, like an emperor giving his beloved a kingdom. But Mrs Jones stayed where she was.

"Funny thing," she whispered. "Ever since we crossed the Yangtze I've had a feeling something was sending for me, calling me westward. Perhaps this might of been it."

Chapter 7

From the very first day in the valley a routine seemed to spring into being, ready made. Mrs Jones's mornings were for Theodore, her afternoons for Lung, and the evenings for the three of them to eat a slow supper and then sit round and talk a little, and listen to Mrs Jones's songs, and watch the stars moving behind the mountain-tops or the big pale moths that came from nowhere and floated among the lily-banks, settling to drink their nectar or floating soundlessly from flower to flower. As the dusk came on the lilies began to produce a pungent, peppery scent and it was that, Mrs Jones said, which attracted the moths.

On the first morning, after they had groomed and tethered the horses and had breakfast, Mrs Jones sent Lung down to the lake and told him to see if he could catch some fish.

"You're always on about old fishermen in them poems of yours," she said. "Let's see if you can do anything more than talk about it. Now come along here, young man. I got to start painting my lilies before they goes over, but you'll find that a bit dull. What'd you like to have a go at?"

"The mountain," said Theodore immediately.

She shook her head.

"Bit of a mouthful," she said. "Surprising how tricky that sort of subject is. No, supposing you settle up there and have a go at that bit of the hollow. You got the tents there, give it a bit of shape, and Albert. Not that horses is easy, but they're easier than mountains ... Don't waste more paper than you can help ..."

She gave him two pencils, a piece of charcoal and a brand-new notebook, and he settled down to do as he was told. He drew a tent and decided it looked quite like, so he put the other one into the same picture. He started to draw the bottoms of the tree-trunks beyond but found that they seemed to be floating in mid-air, so he experimented with grass-tussocks to try and suggest the bank of the coomb, but they floated too. He was beginning on Albert when Mrs Jones came over and sat beside him.

"Why, that's not so dusty," she said. "Who's been teaching you?"

"Nobody. Mother was an artist, but she died when I was four."

"Then you got it in you. I see we're going to have to take this serious. Look, I'll show you a trick for doing shadows. Lend me that pencil. Ta ... like this, see. It ain't the only way, course, but it's the easiest. And this bit here ... you don't want to draw quite so careful as I do, mind you. Its the only way I know how, but except for flowers it's a bit ... oh, I don't know. Remember how Mr What's-is-name drew? That's the thing to aim for."

Theodore could see what she meant. She had added several touches to his picture which had anchored the trees to the top of a definite slope, but there was something vaguely niggling about them. It was as though the richness of her personality stopped at her finger-tips and could find no way out through her pencil. When she left him he practised shadows for a while and then went back to Albert, achieving a shoulder and a haunch that were quite horse-like but a head that was far too small and looked more like a dragon's or even a sheep's. Not that Albert's head was really a model for all horses . . .

He was surprised to find how high the sun was above the mountain by the time of the next interruption. At a low whistle from the bottom of the coomb he glanced up and there was Lung, looking both shy and triumphant and carrying something hidden behind his back. He marched up to Mrs Jones, still hiding his booty.

"I catch fish," he said, grinning.

"I'll believe it when I see it," said Mrs Jones.

"Flying fish?"

"Garn!"

She grabbed at him and he dodged away, slipping on the slope and almost falling. He flung out his hidden hand to steady himself, revealing the body of a dark brown duck.

"Ho! Mighty hunter!" said Mrs Jones. "How did you manage that? Make yourself a bow and arrow?"

"I make trap," said Lung, producing a length of cord with a noose on the end. "Tomorrow I make better trap, with basket. Plenty reed for basket."

"Good for you. Let me have it. H'm, bit of meat there. I better pluck it while it's still warm. Now, you two, you can go up to the path, back along the way we come, try and wipe out any marks we might of made . . ."

Theodore and Lung spent the rest of the morning doing that, smoothing out hoof-prints and foot-prints and sprinkling pine-needles over them. After lunch Lung showed no inclination to leave the coomb, so Theodore climbed up through the wood and continued to work alone, doggedly smoothing and scattering till he reached the beginning of the trees and found that the sun was almost down behind the mountain ranges to the west. He had to pick his way down in near dark, trying not to spoil his work by leaving yet more foot-prints, and met Lung coming up the path to look for him. They smelt the roasting meat before they reached the clearing.

The duck was oily and incredibly tough, but they chewed up every scrap and threw the bones on the fire. After the chill nights on the plateau it was strange to be sitting out under the stars without having to creep at once into a blanket-roll; they talked, and tried to prevent the big moths from flying into the fire, and listened to the steady tearing rasp of the grazing horses. Mrs Jones began to tease Lung into translating his poem about her and he made up uncomplimentary lines and pretended they were parts of it, but when he quoted in Mandarin it was clearly the real thing. Mrs Jones answered him with flowery speeches from old pantomimes, and even once a bit of Shakespeare. Then she started to sing.

"The boy I love sits up in the gallery,
    The boy I love is looking down at me . . .

"Not that I'm the right type to sing that one," she broke off. "What you want is a neat little ingenue, all pink and white and countrified, rolling her big blue eyes up at the clerks and 'prentices in the top of the house. Never mind. You'll have to make do with what you got . . .

"There he is, can't you see, waving of his handkerchief . . ."

It was a sign which Theodore understood perfectly well. She wanted to be alone with her lover. He rose, muttered a good-night and walked up the dell to his tent, where he slid between his blankets and started to say his prayers. The singing stopped, replaced by whispers. A low laugh reminded him that he ought to pray for the other two, that they should recognise their sinfulness and be forgiven, but he had hardly begun when he stopped, feeling that it wasn't right. The peppery wild scent of the lilies drifted through the night. He felt the stillness and the isolation of the valley all around with the three humans at the centre of it, as though they were cradled in the palm of the mountains. Things that happened here seemed to him to have no weight, no effect on the rest of the world. Any act was simply itself, neither good nor evil. It existed, and that was all, like one of the lilies.

So day followed day, restful and quiet. The only serious effort anyone made came on the third day when Lung, irritated perhaps by Mrs Jones's obsession with her lilies, announced that he was going to explore the path to the bridge marked on P'iu-Chun's map. Theodore went with him.

They followed the track through the wood and came quite soon to a place by the water's edge which was clearly used as a camp-site by other travellers. There were remains of cooking-fires, and scatterings of yak-dung. After that the path climbed for a couple of miles through the wood and came out on a vast slope of sour-looking earth, above which the rock face rose precipitously to the snow-fields. The path continued to climb, but far less steeply than it would have needed to if it had been aiming to leave the valley at the skyline. Instead it led towards a point where the mountain cliffs seemed to come down and close the valley off. Steadily, as Lung and Theodore climbed, the tilt of the slope became steeper, until it was a slope no more, and the path was a mountain ledge running with vertical cliffs above and below, and the cliffs of the opposite mountain now incredibly near. They were, in fact, now walking along the wall of a vast ravine, with a river growling towards the lake a thousand feet below. An unsteady wind whipped through these narrows, with sudden little lulls, as though it was trying to trick the traveller into unwariness and then hurl him over the edge with its next gust.

After a couple of hundred yards the ravine began to open out as the opposite cliff tilted away, but before that happened, at the narrowest place of all, the path ended and there hung the bridge.

It was a single strand of rope, sagging hideously over the drop, and that was all. At either end was a fair-sized platform, with the rope running a few feet above it; on the further side the rope seemed to start from a timber structure, but here it was anchored into a big iron ring set into the cliff. Theodore stared at the curving rope, which swung slowly from left to right as the wind gusted down the gorge. His palms began to prickle with the idea of height. Yes, he could imagine hooking his legs over the rope and hauling himself across, hand over hand, though when he reached the far side his weight would drag it down to such a steepness that perhaps he wouldn't be strong enough to pull himself up those last few feet. He could see on the far side where the path led across another barren slope and vanished into a steep wood of larches. Perhaps he could reach there, and Lung, and even Mrs Jones—she could do anything—but the horses? The baggage?

"This is a place of devils," said Lung. He usually spoke Mandarin to Theodore, though his English was steadily improving.

"People get yaks across here, I think," said Theodore.

"Perhaps. Perhaps there is another path, though none is marked on the map. I think we will return and tell the Princess that we can go no further."

He turned decisively away and began to walk back along the ledge. Theodore understood very well—if it was impossible to go on and dangerous to go back, then they must stay where they were, and the idyll could be prolonged. He smiled and shook his head in sympathy, but from that moment there started to grow inside him a conviction that the idyll was not free. It would have to be paid for in the end.

Mrs Jones took the news very calmly, saying that the valley was as good a place to be as any while the weather lasted, and there were enough plants around to last her another couple of weeks, at least, and after that they'd start thinking what was the best thing to do next.

In fact it was an extraordinary relief to settle back into the coomb of the lilies, and to know that they would be staying here for another day, and another after that. Theodore hadn't realised how weary he was with travel, not simply weary in nerves and muscles, but soul-weary with ceaseless change. Time on the journey had been like a muddy spate, full of whirling and uprooted objects, but here it settled to a clear, still stream, with even the eddies in it returning again and again to the same pattern.

Mrs Jones botanised and sketched her finds, including a small dark-red clematis which she thought was new. There were delicate little plants too in the barren-looking slopes above the tree-line, which Theodore helped her press. But the lily remained her chief delight. It grew in drifts in several places along the lake shore, often mixed with a shorter, dark-orange

lily which Mrs Jones said was quite common. The yellow one
stood up to four feet high and carried as many as a dozen
trumpets at the top of its scrawny and metallic-looking stem;
the flowers were about five inches long and less than three
across at the tips of the outcurved petals; from a distance they
seemed to be all of a uniform intense yellow, but in fact each
petal had a streak of green along its outside, and inside the bell
the colour slowly darkened from the rim and was flecked with
a pattern of small orange spots; at the mouth of the trumpet
poised the six large anthers on their curving stalks, the colour
of plain chocolate.

"I seen bigger lilies, of course," said Mrs Jones. "I mean,
there's *Lilium auratum*—I seen that a foot across, and with
twenty flowers on a stalk—dead vulgar if you ask me—not a
patch on this little beauty. How are you getting on, young
man?"

Theodore had become obsessed with a desire to produce a
drawing of Sir Nigel that would do justice to that animal's
look of utter nobility, a problem, he found, far subtler and
more difficult than rendering Albert's coarse-grained ill-will.
He was developing his own style of drawing, neither like Mrs
Jones's nor P'iu-Chun's, but chunky and stolid, as though he was
as much interested in the weight of things as their shape and
texture. He was unaware of this—or rather he was only aware
that he liked certain effects when he got them right—until Mrs
Jones pointed it out.

"That's not at all dusty," she said, looking at a picture he had
made of a tree overhanging the lake shore. "You got it in you,
more than what I have. You draw like you are."

"What do you mean?"

"Oh, I dunno. Someone as didn't know you, suppose I

showed him this, he might make a guess what kind of person you are, and that's good. It ain't true of my pictures."

"If it was you'd keep running off at the edge of the paper," said Theodore.

She laughed and went back to her fiftieth attempt to render the spirit of her lily.

In the afternoon Theodore explored. They did not have the valley to themselves. The wood was full of birds, which sometimes called until the cliffs echoed and at other times for an hour on end failed to break the intense silence of the place. There were porcupines, and a lot of other small animals too briefly glimpsed to be sure of. There was something larger, perhaps a bear, which raided the camp one night, frightened the horses and upset one of the baggage baskets—Theodore slept through this episode, but Mrs Jones and Lung woke and drove it off. Next day they moved camp to another lake-side clearing Theodore had found, an even more secret place, further from the path because of a curve of the shore and screened by thicker undergrowth. It too had its drift of lilies, but no stream.

They would have had to make a move in any case, because the horses by now had eaten almost all the thin grass of the clearing, but the episode with the bear decided them. In the new camp Lung devised an ingenious arrangement of ropes that allowed him to haul all the baggage out of reach of bears, up among the branches. He astonished Theodore by his knack of doing this sort of thing, and the neatness of the fish-traps he wove, and his general practicality, though he pretended to despise the work.

"A scholar does not do these things," he said, weaving a length of split reed between the ribs of his latest trap.

"My father said we must worship God with our hands as well as our minds," said Theodore. "You ought to have seen the bridge he made."

"Good," said Lung. "Then I am worshipping the Princess with my hands."

He tied the reed's end in with mocking precision, as though he were making a true-love knot.

Theodore laughed aloud, though a month ago the joke would have appalled him. But now all that part of him seemed dead. Of course he said his prayers morning and evening and read a little from his Bible each day, as he had always done; but this was mere habit and he knew it needed only one more violent event to break it. It was as though deep inside him was a chapel which had once been lit and gleaming, loud with hymns or full of silent prayer; now it was shut, its air never changed, its ornaments gathered dust and mildew.

A few mornings later Theodore was lying on his stomach, drawing Sir Nigel once more. It had started as a practice study on the blank part of one of Mrs Jones's rejected lily-drawings; but of course, being only practice, it was going particularly well, with eye and mind and hand and pencil forming a smooth-linked system so that what appeared on the paper was not only a real horse, living and solid, but was this particular horse, with its own striking combination of dash and dignity.

"Hullo," said Mrs Jones, "here comes my admirer. What's brought him back so soon?"

Theodore looked up and saw Lung walking towards them, carrying something slung on a stick over his shoulder. He smiled, lifted down his burden and laid it at her feet like an offering. It was a fish, more than twice the size of any he had so far trapped, blue-black above and brown below.

"My, that's a beauty!" said Mrs Jones. "Three good meals on there—at this rate we could stay here all summer, and I wouldn't mind hanging around till my lilies have seeded."

Lung settled onto the grass and watched her manipulating her flower-press. For a while Theodore went on drawing, but gradually became aware of a change in the atmosphere, a sense of stifled energies beginning to fill the glade. He looked carefully up and saw that Lung was watching Mrs Jones out of the corner of his eyes while his hand stroked the sleek side of his fish, and she was merely twiddling and then untwiddling the brass butterfly-nut at the corner of her press. It had happened sometimes before, but they had always been extremely strict with themselves; perhaps, without telling him, they had agreed rules, but if so it had been for his sake. He had seldom seen them even touch, and when talking to each other in his presence they maintained a slightly teasing relationship, as though their love was not really serious and he needn't worry about it. But he was often aware of it, a deep, intense, unspoken shared emotion, more like hunger than anything he could understand as love. Being with them in this mood was like living too near some source of power—a furnace, perhaps, the by-product of whose energies is enough to make one want to move to somewhere cooler.

"Shall I go and look at the old traps," he said. "If that one's going to last three meals we don't want to catch anything we can't eat."

"I think that would be a very good idea," said Mrs Jones in her drawing-room voice.

Theodore folded his picture and tucked it into the breast-pocket of his jacket. He rose and walked away without looking back.

Normally it took about ten minutes to walk to the coomb where they had first camped, but Mrs Jones had made a rule that for regular journeys like this they must always try to use a different path, so Theodore decided this time he would stay right down by the lake shore, which would delay him because the undergrowth was thicker here. He slowed himself still further by walking with a hunter's silence. There was no real difference between deliberately going a slow way and going a quick way and then hanging around for a while, but there seemed to be. He was angry about the interruption of his drawing when it was going well, and the stealing of his share of the day, and he was ashamed of himself for being angry.

About a hundred yards short of the coomb he ducked below a branch that hung right out over the lake and saw that something was disturbing the water near where the little stream ran out—close by Lung's fish-traps, he thought. He couldn't actually see the shore at that point, but after watching for a moment he became almost certain that something was actually meddling with one of the traps. The bear, perhaps. He wasn't at all anxious to meet the creature at close quarters, but he would be glad to see it at a distance, so now he struck up away from the shore, aiming for a point about half way up the coomb; the lakeside undergrowth thinned, and he was able to move quite quickly between the trees until he came out behind one of the ranked drifts of lilies and could gaze down from tree-shadow into the bright-lit arena beyond.

Down by the stream, a few yards up from the shore, a man was making urgent gestures. Near the head of the coomb

another man was kneeling by a rectangle of paler grass where
Mrs Jones's tent had been pitched. This second man looked up,
saw the gestures and came hurrying down to meet his comrade.
Together they went to the lakeside and pulled out one of the
fish-traps. Even from where he watched Theodore could see
the sudden agonised writhings of a fish brought into the air.
The men looked at it for a moment, then slid the trap back into
the water and backed away, stooping as they did so to erase
their foot-prints in the water-logged earth.

They came slowly up the coomb, pointing at things that
caught their attention—the interlocking rings of shorter grass
where the tethered horses had grazed, a pile of old horse-
droppings, the patch by the stream where Lung had usually
washed the dishes. They darted eagerly up the far slope and
stared at a point among the lilies, inexplicably as far as Theodore could see, until one of them fell to his knees and began to
dig with his bare hands; then he remembered that Mrs Jones
had dug one of her precious lily-bulbs from there. What were
they after? Treasure?

The standing man began to argue. He snatched at his companion's shoulder, dragging him to his feet. They came back
down to the stream, still arguing in low voices. They were
small men, wearing what looked like rags which were held in
place by a tracery of criss-crossing thongs; plaits of coarse black
hair stuck out all round their heads under small grey fur caps
with tight-rolled brims. They were Lolo, that was certain.
Then one of the men in the frenzy of argument pushed his face
to within an inch of the other man's nose. He held his head
poking forward on his neck and cocked a little to one side—an
extraordinary posture which made it look as though his spine
were double jointed. Theodore had seen a man do that only

once before, in an argument over who should carry which burden when the porters were loading up in the Lolo village before the ambush. This was that man.

Theodore stayed perfectly still, his muscles locked by the ancient instinct of the hunted, while the men finished their argument and peered hither and thither, eager but scared, into the lily-glowing darkness beneath the trees. He began to feel that at any moment the wide, snub noses would pick up his scent, but at last the men started back up the coomb and disappeared under the trees. He felt certain that they were going to find their comrades and report what they had seen.

It seemed important to him to know whether the enemy were behind or in front, so, using known tracks, he followed the men up through the wood, keeping them right at the limit of his vision. They never looked round but the moment they reached the track they started eastwards up it at a quick, effortless jog. He held his breath until they disappeared and then, still careful to leave no traces, made his way down to the camp.

Normally when he came unexpectedly into the glade he would have coughed, or hummed a few lines of one of Mrs Jones's songs. It was like knocking at a door. But this time he didn't dare make even that amount of human noise, so he caught the lovers unprepared. Lung was lying on his back with his head in Mrs Jones's lap. She had let her hair down and was bending over him, gently stroking his head with one hand. He held the other clasped against his chest.

Theodore paused in his approach. Despite the urgency and fear he found it hard to break the weightless bubble of their happiness. He saw for the first time how streaked with grey was Mrs Jones's hair.

"Pardon me," he whispered.

They looked up. Mrs Jones stared for a moment through the curtain of her hair, then tossed it back.

"What's up, Theo?" she said in a low voice.

He crouched in front of her and in a straining whisper told what he had seen. She nodded, accepting without question that he was sure that he recognised one of the men.

"That's rough," she said. "The others can't be far off, neither, or they'd have spent more time scouting. First thing, we got to get out into the open—up by this bridge of yours might be favourite, then if things go sour we can try and cross it and cut the rope behind us. Before it comes to that we'll try and parlay with them, buy them off for a blood-price. But we haven't a hope if they catch us down among the trees . . . oh, it's all my fault for saying we could hang on here for ever! Lung, my love, you better get up. I'm afraid our prettytimes are over."

Chapter 8

It took an agonising time to strike camp, far longer than when they had been on the march. During the days in the valley they had unpacked more, settled in, grown used to the notion of staying. The horses, too, were out of the habit, troublesome with idleness and perhaps infected with the sudden renewal of tension. Mrs Jones decided to give them an extra feed while they were being loaded.

"Help keep 'em still," she said. "And there's no telling when we'll next get a chance for a halt. We'll ride, soon as we're on the path."

"The hoof-prints will show," said Theodore.

"Yes, but if these blokes got any sense they'll split up, send one lot on ahead and leave the other to hunt through the wood. Last thing we want is get ourselves cut off while we're making our way up by rabbit-tracks. Cut a couple of switches, Theo, case you want to make the ponies hurry. You better have the shot-gun, Lung. This is the safety catch, see . . ."

They were ready at last, and led the ponies sidelong up through the wood, striking the path a few hundred yards above the camp-site which the yak-drivers used. Theodore scrambled up onto Bessie's rump, and she accepted him placidly, just as if he were another piece of baggage. He led the way. Next came Lung, sitting sideways behind Rollo's pair of baskets, with the shot-gun slung across his back and looking

every inch the soldier-poet; last of all Mrs Jones, riding Sir
Nigel and leading Albert. They rode steadily down to the lake
shore and started up the further slope. The sense of panic flight
dwindled, though the urgency remained. Theodore began to
make calculations. Say two hours to the bridge—that would be
early afternoon. One person with a gun could hold the cliff
path, at least while it was daylight, so there would be four
hours to cross the bridge. They must start preparing to cross at
once, because the path couldn't be held in the dark, and Mrs
Jones would have to be able to see across the gorge to protect
Lung with the rifle while he crossed. He would have been
holding the path with the shot-gun while *she* crossed ... Crossing—you'd have to have a rope round your waist with a loop
over the bridge rope ...

A whooping cry rang through the trees. Theodore looked
over his shoulder and saw Albert, loose, walking uncertainly
up the path. Beyond him Sir Nigel stood still, with Mrs Jones
twisted in the saddle, her gun raised and aiming. And beyond
her was movement, barely fifty yards away, men, running.
Her gun cracked twice. Albert gave a scream of terror and
came bolting up the track, almost knocking Lung off Rollo's
back where the wide-hung baskets crashed against each other.
Theodore tried to nudge Bessie across the path but only
succeeded in making her pull to one side and open the way for
Albert to come tearing through. The gun cracked again just as
Theodore brought his switch down hard across Bessie's
haunches. She squealed, more with fright and the infection of
Albert's bolting than with pain. Another shot, louder and
deeper, rang out, and something tore through the leafage
overhead.

Theodore gave a gulp of fright—he had never thought that

the attackers might have a gun—and lashed violently at Bessie's haunches. There was no need, for by now she was bolting too, wallowing up the path in a bucketing canter, and his saddle— nothing more than a pad of blanket—was slithering away. He clutched at the basket-harness and dragged himself forward till he lay spread-eagled along the hollow of her back with his legs dangling behind the baskets and his arms in front, while Bessie steamed uncontrollably up through the wood. The breath was jolted from his lungs. Tree trunks flickered past. All ideas left his mind.

Slowly the slope took its toll. Bessie's pace eased as her breath came in slower and louder snorts and he was able to raise his head and peer forward. There was no sign of Albert, but his hoof-prints showed that he had stuck to the path this far at least. Theodore stayed where he was until Bessie slowed to a gasping walk, then he slid to the ground and led her for a while. Another shot echoed through the wood, but far off now, at least half a mile, he thought. No point in waiting. The first thing was for him to get to the bridge and set about making arrangements to cross.

He found Albert about ten minutes later. He had evidently tried to leave the path at a point where its slope became much sharper but had almost at once caught his reins on a broken branch and been too stupid to back off and release them. He was half-exhausted with his fresh bout of panic at being thus trapped, and by the time Theodore had him back on the track he was apparently ready to do what he was told. Theodore tied Bessie's reins to Albert's basket-harness and led the pair of them on up the track.

His instinct was to run, but he schooled himself to a steady walk. The bridge filled his mind, so that he could feel in his imagination the weight of his own body trying to tear the rope from his tiring grip. It was no use getting to the bridge exhausted . . . he began to think about hauling the baggage over . . . a length of cord the full width of the gorge . . . no, twice that, so that it could be hauled back again to take the next load, otherwise he'd have to cross and re-cross every time . . . there wasn't nearly enough. Not enough even for one width, perhaps. Reins, and tent ropes . . . And the tents could be cut into strips and tied . . . it would take hours!

Where the trees ended with the typical abruptness of mountain scenery, the path zig-zagged up a couple of hundred feet and then eased to a far gentler angle as it slanted up towards the narrows of the gorge. Here he rode Bessie again, letting her pick her way along but keeping her moving at a fast walk. All three ponies had turned out to be sure-footed, and Albert's temper even improved a little when he had a plummeting drop below him, so they crept with agonising slowness across the great bare sweep. For a long while there was no sign or sound from the wood, and Theodore was almost two thirds of the way across when a figure emerged from the trees—Lung, still on horseback.

Theodore waved, waited for Lung's answering gesture and decided that it was encouraging, so rode on. The last he saw as he dismounted for the final slope up to the cliff ledge was Lung halted about a hundred yards from the trees and Mrs Jones coming trotting out into the open. He sighed with relief and led the horses into the gorge.

Albert was fidgety again, troubled by the erratic gusts of wind and the ceaseless rumble of the river. His reaction to height was to walk on the extreme outer edge of the ledge, as though he were more frightened of the cliff above falling on him than of himself tumbling into the gorge. Theodore's palms were sweaty once more with the prospect of the coming climb. He would tie the horses, then make himself a waist-loop, and then set about manufacturing the travelling rope. He kept his eyes on the path, gathering his moral energies for the next effort. Not far now. There was the clump of pink daisies which Lung had picked from to show Mrs Jones. Round this next buttress of rock he would see the bridge . . .

It was still there, but the curve of it was clean no more. It was swaying, and a loop of cord dangled below. There were men on the far platform, watching . . . A few more paces and he saw that the rope dipped to a heavy bundle which hung from a yoke-shaped wooden runner, made to slide along the top of the rope. And there were four men on the near platform, too, hauling at another rope to drag the bundle over. These were Tibetans, like the yak-drivers, wearing fur caps and knee-length loose coats tied at the waist with a great sash. None of them paid any attention as Theodore led his horses onto the platform.

He hesitated a moment, then crossed and spoke to the hind-most man, slowly and clearly in Mandarin.

"Can you help us please? We are being attacked by bandits and must cross the river."

The man looked at him, one quick stare, and returned to the rhythm of hauling. Theodore tried Miao, and then assembled his smattering of Cantonese into a sort of sentence. The man didn't even glance at him now. In desperation he tried English, but the man only grunted, and that might have been because of the extra effort of dragging the load up the last steep section of curve. He and his neighbour took the strain as soon as the bundle was over the platform, while the other two unlashed it and lowered it to the ground.

The moment the weight was off Theodore stepped forward
and put his hand on the rope, as if laying claim to it. The men
stared furiously at him. One of them spoke in Tibetan, and the
nearest man snatched Theodore's arm off the rope, gripped him
by the shoulder and flung him back against the rock wall.
Somebody hallooed to the party on the far platform, and by
the time Theodore got to his feet the wooden traveller was
already sliding back along the rope. A man led the horses up to
him and made signs that he was to hold them and stand clear;
this man's face was a dark scowl of anger and disapproval, and
he finished his gestures by patting the large dagger in his sash
several times.

The men were strangely silent, not at all like workmen chat-
ting over a routine task, but almost more like worshippers
engaged in a ritual. The rhythmic movement of paying out the
cord ceased, and there was a long pause, but their bodies
blocked his view of the far platform, preventing him from
watching whether there was any special trick of attaching
bundles to the traveller. At last a yodelled shout floated across
the gap and the men went to their positions and began to pull
the cord in, using no force yet because the load was still sliding
down the further curve. Before it dipped from sight below the
rim of the platform Theodore saw that this was not a bundle
but a man sitting bolt upright in a chair.

Now the men began to heave, working against steadily
increasing gravity and friction. Where was Lung—he should
be here by now, surely?—he might know a few words of
Tibetan. Or Mrs Jones might use her strength of character, to
make the men understand the urgency . . . there was no sound
along the path, no sign of either. Now the chair came into sight
and Theodore could see that the man sitting in it was different

from the others, elderly, with a many-wrinkled face of a yellower tinge than the bronze of the men working the ropes. He wore a pointed dark red cap with flaps to cover his ears, and a heavy robe of reddish brown, which flapped around his feet in the gusting wind. His eyes were closed, but obviously not from fear of the drop. In fact he looked as if he were asleep, sitting still as an idol in the swaying chair.

Again two men took the strain while the other two unfastened the chair and lowered it onto the platform. The newcomer rose, opened his eyes and intoned a few words. The men looked pleased. He was nearly a head taller than they were.

"Honoured sir," called Theodore in Mandarin. "Can you help us? We are being attacked by bandits and must cross the river."

The men who had pulled the rope glanced angrily at him and made shushing gestures, but the newcomer turned and gazed at Theodore with strange, vague eyes, as though he were seeing him through layers of mist.

"I am on a holy search," he said. "Let none distract me from my path."

His voice was clear and deep and he spoke good Mandarin, apart from a metallic twang at the end of many syllables.

"But, honoured sir," pleaded Theodore, "could your men show us how to cross the river? Many men are attacking us, and we are only three."

"Three?"

The newcomer spoke as though the number were much more interesting than the idea of bandits. His gaze sharpened, and he moved towards Theodore with gliding paces that made it seem as though he were floating above the rock surface. A hand drifted from his robes and plucked at something in Theodore's breast pocket, then drifted away again, holding the folded piece of paper on which Theodore had been drawing that morning. Another hand—they seemed to be moving of their own will, almost unconnected with the mind behind the quiet, distant gaze—helped unfold the paper. The eyes studied it. The hands refolded it and put it back in Theodore's pocket.

"What is your age?"

"Thirteen, honoured sir."

"And your companions?"

"Mrs Jones is about forty. Lung is over twenty."

"A Chinese?"

"Yes."

"You wear Chinese dress and hair, but you are not Chinese."

"I am American, sir."

"Your name?"

"Theodore. It means Gift of God."

Theodore had no idea why, at this moment of desperation, he should feel compelled to utter these unnecessary syllables, but the old man's gaze which for a while seemed to have been dying back into distance now steadied and returned. He muttered to himself in Tibetan and then, suddenly as sunburst through clouds, smiled and became an ordinary person. It was as though his soul had swooped down from heights where it had been hovering and now stood in his body beside Theodore on the rock platform.

"I am confused," he said. "My name is the Lama Amchi. I follow certain signs, some of which you bear but not others. I must enquire further."

"Honoured sir, there is no time. We are being attacked by bandits. If you help us across the gorge . . ."

"I must not go back till I am sure. But I travel well protected, so that I may have a suitable retinue for the one I seek."

He turned and spoke in Tibetan to his followers, one of whom shouted across the gorge and made urgent signs; the others opened one of the bundles on the platform and brought out a number of savage-looking daggers and a couple of elderly rifles. The men on the far side began to cross the bridge, but Theodore was only aware that they were doing so when the first dropped grinning onto the platform. He moved to where he could see the traveller being rapidly twitched back over the gap. As soon as it was within reach another man leaped for it, twisted and swung his legs up over the rope. With nothing else to hold him but his hands gripping the traveller on either side he walked himself across, monkey-fashion. Theodore felt cold in the pit of his stomach.

"Tie your horses," said the Lama Amchi. "We will go and investigate your predicament a little further. The thought comes to me that in itself it is perhaps a sign."

He spoke softly and kindly, as though a confrontation with the savage tribesmen from the forest were a problem such as a scholar might meet in his books.

They found Lung waiting with his back towards them at the point where the cliff began to tilt from the vertical and became an immensely steep slope. Rollo had lost his baskets, and was standing on the path with his head bowed, snorting at the thin air for breath. Lung seemed to hear or sense the newcomers and swung round with the shot-gun rising to his shoulder. Theodore, half-hidden from Lung by the Lama Amchi, scrambled a little up the slope.

"These are friends," he called in Mandarin. "They have come to help us."

Lung lowered his gun, stared in astonishment at the Lama Amchi, and bowed deeply.

"Revered and honoured Sir," he said in Mandarin. "We are peaceful travellers but we are attacked by violent men. Pray condescend to make room for us under the umbrella of your benign protection."

The Lama Amchi didn't answer, but strode past him and Rollo and on down the path. A shot snapped through the whistling air.

"Who is this? What does he want?" whispered Lung as Theodore reached him.

"I don't know. Something about a search, and signs, but I think he'll help us cross the bridge."

With the jostling escort they followed the Lama Amchi down until he halted where a small ridge made a level and they could all crowd round to watch the scene below. About two hundred yards down the slope Mrs Jones was sitting on Sir Nigel's back, facing the woods with her gun half raised. For a moment the rest of the drear expanse seemed empty, and then, a hundred yards beyond her, Theodore noticed a movement, and another further to the left, and another beyond that. The attackers had spread themselves into a wide curve and were creeping up the hill towards her, using what cover they could from tussock and outcrop.

Lung put his hand to his mouth and gave a shrill yell. Mrs Jones twisted in the saddle, stared for a moment, then waved an arm, nudged Sir Nigel round and came cantering up the path. The horse's huge lungs laboured and his ears were flat on his head. Twice he almost fell, but Mrs Jones somehow hauled him up and kept him going. Behind her the attackers rose to their feet and came trotting up the hill, some of them waving weapons. Theodore hadn't realised there were so many of them—more than twenty, he thought.

"These are not here for vengeance," muttered Lung. "Some are from other tribes. Look at their dress. They are here for loot, mere bandits, brought by chatter of gold."

Mrs Jones at last let Sir Nigel slow to an exhausted walk.

"What's up?" she called.

"Holy Lama on search," called Lung in English. "Maybe help. Missy cover face, please."

She had been riding with her veil thrown back, no doubt for better shooting. Obediently she twitched it into place as she brought Sir Nigel round once more so that she could face down the slope. The attackers came on steadily, but as the slope tilted they bunched towards the path, so that by the time they were fifty yards away they were trotting up in a ragged file, silent, panting, but still tireless.

"That's close enough," said Mrs Jones. "I'll stop 'em there."

She was raising her rifle as she spoke. The men on the path jostled to a halt.

"Do no violence," said the Lama Amchi. "I will speak with these foolish people."

"Missy, holy Lama say no shoot," called Lung.

"I might have to," she said. "I been aiming to miss so far, but . . . Hey! Stop him, somebody. Oh, why didn't one of you stop the old goat?"

It was too late. The Lama Amchi was striding down the path with the confident long pace of a man used to steep places. His followers whispered uneasily but stayed where they were. A bolt clicked.

The attackers closed to a tight cluster and waited to meet the old man. He halted a few feet away from them and spoke, too far off now for Theodore to hear words, or even language.

"I can't pick the beggar out," cried Mrs Jones. "Shout to him to watch out, Lung."

Even as she was speaking Theodore saw metal glimmer, shoulder high, somewhere near the middle of the bunch, a pistol barrel. He couldn't tell whose hand was holding it, but in the thin air and slowed time of helpless watching he saw the clumsy flintlock hover over the pan. The Lama's robe flapped violently in a sudden gust, so that for a moment the old man seemed to waver, to separate into two images at the instant when the shot cracked and the dark smoke puffed among the faces. On the ridge there was one quick gasp of horror, followed by a wild yell as the Lama's escort broke into a charging rush down the hill, waving their weapons and leaping from tussock to tussock, screaming like animals. The Lama stood still, apparently unharmed, but in front of him the bunch of bandits broke and ran streaming down the path, jostling and stumbling, though they must have outnumbered the attackers two to one.

"Missed at that range!" said Mrs Jones. "Thank Heavens!"

"Lama make himself two men," whispered Lung. "Missy no see?"

"I saw a bit of rotten awful shooting," snapped Mrs Jones. "Now I suppose we better try and make a good impression on His Reverence."

The Lama Amchi had stood unmoving while his escort charged past him, then turned and come striding up the hill. He looked neither sad nor exhilarated as he approached. Beyond him the escort had caught up with the hindmost bandits and were hewing at them as they ran. The bandits made no attempt to turn and protect themselves. Already two bodies lay on the hillside.

Mrs Jones slid gracefully from the saddle and gave a little curtsey, but the Lama turned to Theodore.

"These are your companions, child?" he said in his twanging Mandarin.

Theodore made formal introductions.

The priest gazed for a while at Lung, who faced him uneasily and seemed relieved when the old man turned away. Mrs Jones stood her ground until the creased, blue-veined hand rose as if to pluck her veil; then she backed politely away, raising the veil as she did so, and stood answering his gaze with her own. The sounds of the valley—the hiss of the wind, the growl of the river in its gorge, the cries of fighting men down across the slope—all dimmed, became almost part of some other scene as the world closed in to make a sphere of calm around the group by the path. Intangible energies flowed, as if round the twin poles of a magnet, creating and maintaining this sphere until, like duellists or dancers at the end of an encounter, Mrs Jones and the Lama bowed their heads to each other and turned away.

"Now we will return to the bridge and prepare to cross," said the Lama.

Chapter 9

Tibet. The Yak-drivers they had met on their way to the valley had said that there was no real border. The Lama waved a vague hand eastward and explained that two whole provinces had been stolen by China a hundred years before, so Theodore's party had really been travelling through Tibet for many days. But for Theodore the border lay, sharp as a shore-line, at the bridge. From then on the grammar of all things, large and small, changed. There was the change from stillness to travel, from the simple triangular relationship with Mrs Jones and Lung to the far more complex pressures of the Lama and his half-hostile escort. There were the yaks, brooding, slow-paced, utterly alien; even their drivers, who drank their milk, ate their butter, wove their hair and wore their hides, seemed to have no feeling for them.

There was Tibetan tea. The only time Theodore attempted to drink this on the journey his mouth spat it back into the cup before he could will himself to swallow. The first taste was of half-rancid grease, disgusting but manageable; then, inside that—wrapped in it, so to speak—his tongue met scouring soap and sharp salt and a thick woody flavour like the bark of a tree. He looked up, flushing with shame, and saw the Lama watching him with an intense but unreadable stare.

"I'm sorry," he stammered. "I couldn't help it."

"It is a strong taste," said the old man. "You do not remember it, child?"

"Tibetan tea notorious," said Lung in English. "Boil leaf long time. Put in salt, soda, sour butter."

"It is as well to acquire the taste," said the Lama mildly. "The drink is full of strength for those who travel in the mountains."

He didn't seem at all put out by Theodore's ill manners, but oddly interested. Then he and Mrs Jones and Lung fell into bilingual small-talk about the tea ceremonies of different countries.

Yaks and tea were trivialities. There was a more important change, which Theodore sensed at once—had in fact sensed in the escort's behaviour as they had prepared to haul the Lama across the ravine, the very first time he had seen the old man. Tibet was a priest-ruled country. Father had in a sense ruled the Settlement, but had done so as its first citizen, with the consent of his converts. He had been respected, and loved. But in Theodore's eyes the escort, as well as the inhabitants of the flea-swarming farms where they billeted themselves each night, treated the old man as if he were in some way God. And this strong uncomfortable awe applied not only to the Lama but to everything. Wherever a stream ran near a village it drove at least one prayer-wheel, a tinkling device which at each turn was supposed to repeat the same meaningless syllables of devotion, inscribed on its rim. Prayer-flags—mere rags on sticks, like wash-day in the slums, Mrs Jones said—fluttered from the roofs of houses or in groves along hillsides, to perform the same function. Shrines—little box-like stone buildings, each with a fantastic bobbly spire ending in a crescent moon—dotted every slope. Monks stalked the roads.

Father had always pitied heathens, never hated them, even at their most superstitious. His anger and his hatred had been reserved for those Christians who had, in his eyes, been shown the truth and refused it. But despite himself Theodore couldn't help a distrust and dislike which was almost hatred. The wheels and flags offended him most. Prayer was not like that. It was a thing which needed to be done each time afresh, with intense personal effort. And yet . . . and yet how different, really, were these meaningless devices, repeating their formulae without a mind behind them, from Theodore's own useless attempts to pray?

Strangely, this very revulsion made him pray with greater earnestness, as well as with a new sense of frustration. In the valley of the lilies he had felt it would need only one more violent event to break the habit of prayer, but now that event had come and the habit was strengthened.

Perhaps it was the mountains which caused this change. They were, in themselves, the biggest change of all. The peak that had faced across the valley of the lilies had seemed colossal, but soon the party was moving through country where the out-crops and buttresses of the main mountains were larger than that; and the saddle they had crossed into the valley seemed low and easy now, compared with some of the passes they trav-ersed. The ranges were split by immensely steep, thick-forested valleys, each with its rushing river at the bottom, and here and there a huddle of flat-roofed stone houses in a patch of tiny fields. In the valleys the tracks were often tolerable, sometimes even surfaced with logs laid side by side. But then the route would zig-zag up to the bare slopes above the tree-line, higher and higher, until they were trailing among wastes where snow lay in crackling drifts between the wind-eroded boulders. Here the paths were usually invisible, except to their guides.

Even Mrs Jones would look at some barrier—a cliff carved by
frost and blizzard into vertical pleats and pillars, and lined with
horizontal layers by the rock-strata—and shake her head, but
the Tibetans would find a series of cracks and gullies and yard-
wide ledges where only a few worn foot-holds showed that
anyone had ever passed this way before. Theodore learnt to
walk at these heights with a short-paced shuffle, drearily slow
but not using one breath more than was needed of the sparse
oxygen, one extra pump of his straining heart. He learnt that it
was possible to sit at the midday rest with one's head in the sun
and one's feet in shadow and suffer sunburn and frostbite at the
same time. He learnt to trudge for hours with his eyes half-
closed against the brilliant light, though the temptation was to
gaze and gaze at the enormous, sharp-seen distances and the
piercing colours.

But all these discomforts were overwhelmed by the sense of
awe which the mountains imposed. It was no wonder that such
a country had come to be ruled by priests who were almost
gods. Even Mrs Jones, despite her restlessness at the slow pace
of travel, and the feeling that the Lama, by pressing steadily on
at that pace, was preventing her from exploring the valleys
properly for plants—even she seemed to feel the solemnity of
the mountains. They changed her, as they changed everything.
Her personality, which in earlier days had been so elusive and
at the same so enveloping, withdrew into itself a little. There
was no less of it—supposing you could measure such things—
but it seemed somehow more concentrated, and more coherent.

This was the change poor Lung took hardest. For some
reason the hostility of the escort, never voiced, but expressed in
glances, in an angle of the head or a gesture of the fingers,
concentrated on him. The Lama, though carefully polite, never

allowed him the curious and penetrating interest he often showed in Mrs Jones and Theodore. No doubt Lung could have borne this, and worse, if it had been possible for the idyll of the valley of the lilies to continue, however changed by the changed circumstances. But Theodore could see that the idyll was ended. Mrs Jones might spend whole stretches of the journey, or long hours in the evening, talking quietly with Lung, but they were lovers no more.

To his own astonishment this change filled Theodore with sadness. He should have been rejoicing at the end of the sinful affair, but now he knew what he ought to have known all along, that his own content in the valley was not simply a product of the peace and beauty of the place; it had been caused just as much by his companions' happiness; he had been infected, so to speak, by their joy in each other; so now Lung's loss was his.

He saw this with sudden sharpness on the second day of their journey, when during the midday halt he found Lung brooding beside a bleak upland lake, whose slaty waters and treeless shores seemed a world away from the brilliance and richness of the valley.

"Changed, changed, all changed," muttered Lung.

"Are you going to write a poem about it?"

"No poems. Not any more."

"I'm sorry."

Lung turned away with a noise that began as a laugh and ended as something like the cry of a fox.

On the fifth night they stayed not at a farm but at a monastery called Daparang, an erratic line of almost windowless slabs of building, punctuated by spired shrines and spread along a hill-side. Here they were shown to a guest-room near the gate, and for once had some privacy and comfort. (The people in the farms were friendly, but almost as pestilential in their inquisi-tiveness as the fleas.) The Lama Amchi disappeared into the monastery, but later that evening brought another Lama, a very old man who was Abbot of Daparang, to drink tea in the guest-house. The Abbot spoke about three words, all Tibetan, in the hour he was there, and never took his eyes off Theodore.

When they travelled on next morning they found the escort was increased by two men who wore monks' robes but were built like wrestlers, and indeed turned out to be just that. At their next halt they engaged in a highly formalised fight, accompanied by sharp barks and grunts. Mrs Jones watched the bout with a keen and knowing eye. Apparently they were soldier-monks, employed to escort important men, and even to fight with monks from other monasteries in disputes over territory. They wore their hair combed over one ear in a great curling swag. Mrs Jones was delighted by them, but to Theo-dore it was just another example of the absurdity of these heathen beliefs, that a religion which claimed to be founded in peace and the rejection of earthly vanities, should train such men.

That night the three of them were sitting on a pile of rugs in the corner of a single upstairs room in a large farm. The Lama had vanished, as he sometimes did. The escort and the farm family were clustered round the stove in the middle of the room. Mrs Jones was trying to tease Lung and Theodore into asking impertinent questions about the family, which seemed to consist—as in the other farms they had stayed at—of one wife, three or four husbands and a few children.

The door on the far side of the room opened, producing a

come-and-go of the chill night air as the two soldier-monks entered. They crossed the room and bowed formally to Theodore.

"Lama say come. Bring woman," said one in grunted Mandarin.

"'Bout time too," said Mrs Jones, when Theodore had translated. "We got to sort out how far we're going along of him, and find a proper magistrate or someone what can give us some travel papers, so as we can go off on our own. I wouldn't mind staying round these parts for a month—there's hundreds of things to find in some of these valleys."

She rose, drawing her cloak round her. Theodore reached for his coat. But as Lung got to his feet the soldier-monk who had not spoken made a vehement gesture with his arm, palm forward, as if to push him back onto the rugs.

"Lama see boy. Lama see woman. Lama not see man," said the first monk.

"I go where the Princess goes," snapped Lung.

The monks frowned at him. He gazed hotly back until Mrs Jones laid her hand on his arm.

"Best do like he says, love," she said. "Theo and me'll look after each other, and somebody'd best stay here, stop the beggars going through our baggage."

Lung shrugged, sighed and returned to the rugs. The silent monk joined the group round the stove. The other one held the door and let Theodore and Mrs Jones climb down the ladder to the farmyard. After the fug and reek of the upper room the night air, crisp with its passing over frosted snows, brought Theodore's weary nerves to wakefulness; but as they followed the monk up the hill by the light of a half moon, this sense of energies renewed ebbed away. The monk led them not to one of the other houses in the hamlet but straight up a steep meadow into whispering woods. Calves and thighs ached with each step, and the fresh-seeming night air was only a rasp in the throat, with no substance for the lungs. It was very dark under the trees, but Theodore sensed a beetling mass close ahead. The path twisted as if to avoid it and climbed again, more steeply than ever. At last, when Theodore felt he could go no further without a rest, the monk grunted "Wait," and moved away to the right. For a while Theodore could hear nothing through the sound of his own gasping breath, but then he was aware of voices that seemed to be coming from the middle of the night sky, somewhere out over the valley.

"Bit of rock buttress there," whispered Mrs Jones. "They're out near the end of it."

The voices ceased and the monk returned. They followed him up to the right and then, as Mrs Jones had guessed, out along a level platform of rock that led them through the tree-tops and into the open air. At the end of the platform was a small shrine, just like the hundreds of others they had seen in the last six days, a square stone box surmounted by a pointed dome, and at the very top the symbol of a crescent moon, a black shape that echoed the silver crescent now riding above the snow-fields. Round the far side of the shrine, sitting cross-legged on the ground, they found the Lama Amchi. Despite the bitter night air he was naked to the waist.

He spoke briefly to their guide who bowed and left without a word.

"Sit," said the Lama.

They settled, fidgeting a little for comfort on the smooth but icy rock. Below them the few lights of the hamlet glimmered in the mass of dark which lay impenetrable, almost as if it were a liquid, all up the valley's side to where the tree-line ended; above that in lesser blackness rose the rock screes and the cliffs; and above these, brighter-seeming than the moon itself, the glaciers and the glittering wastes of snow. As the body-warmth engendered by the climb faded, the chill of those snows seemed to fill the slow breeze and seep like water through Theodore's clothes.

"I am troubled," said the Lama at last. "I think you are not after all the one I seek."

"I don't know what you mean."

"You tell me you are thirteen years of age."

"That's right."

"There is no mistake about this? You count the years in the same manner as we do? A child who has lived for one whole year and is now in his second year, you call him two years of age?"

"No. We call him one. We only count whole years. I am thirteen years and five months old."

"Ah. And this woman is not your mother? It is necessary for me to know, even if you have reason to pretend other than the truth."

"No. Honest. My father was a Christian missionary in Kweichow. My mother died when I was four."

"Six days you have been in Tibet. You have eaten our food and drunk our drink, travelled our paths. You have slept in a certain house, met a certain man. All this was wholly new to you?"

"I don't know what you mean."

"In these six days you have not seen or smelt or heard anything which woke in you a feeling that you already were acquainted with that thing?"

"No. I don't think so."

The Lama sighed and fell into silence.

"What's he on about?" whispered Mrs Jones.

"I don't know. He's asking questions about me, and whether I remember seeing things before."

"Not much help," she muttered. "Ask him why he wants to know. Go on, he won't bite you. That way we might be able to tell him something he didn't know he was after."

Before Theodore could frame the question the Lama sighed again.

"And yet the signs seemed so sure," he said. "Tell me, child, how you came to the valley, you and this strange woman and the Chinese, pursued by murderers."

"It will take a long time," said Theodore, reluctantly.

"You are cold? Take my robe. I do not need it. I am warm. Feel my flesh."

It was a command. A little embarrassed, Theodore wrapped himself in the harsh cloth and then reached out and touched the naked shoulder. It was warm, not simply with the warmth of health but as if with a fever.

"He's hot!" he exclaimed in English. Almost languidly Mrs Jones peeled off her glove, touched the Lama's arm and withdrew her hand.

"Fancy that!" she said. "Mind you, it's not at all that surprising. I can think myself warm sometimes—not that warm, mind you."

"What does she say?" said the Lama, his voice suddenly sharp with interest. He grunted with approval as Theodore explained.

"Now tell me your tale," he said. "For six days I have not enquired, nor told you the nature of my search, because I did not wish to plant seeds of thought in your mind until I found whether the thoughts were already there. They are not. Moreover, the Abbot of Daparang, who knew the one I seek in his previous childhood, could find no echo in your soul. And furthermore your age, which I misunderstood at our first meeting, makes it impossible. So we may speak more clearly now, I think."

Theodore started into his story. He tried to begin with the destruction of the Settlement, but the Lama made him start with his own birth, and was both surprised and disappointed that he had no idea what astrological signs he had been born under. Then the details and timing of Mother's death were apparently important, but Father's work and the success of the Settlement quite uninteresting. When it came to the meeting with Mrs Jones, Theodore expected to have to go back and explain all about her, but the Lama cut him short.

"We can consider that later, perhaps," he said. "But ask the woman now why does she roam through wild places, seeking flowers. Whence is this need?"

"Tell him . . . oh, don't tell him about Monty—that'd take all night. Tell him I don't know—I just like the seeking and finding, that's all. It's true, too."

"A search," muttered the Lama. "I have read that all searches are the one search. And has the woman found satisfaction?"

"Funny he should ask that," said Mrs Jones. "You remember me saying, first time we saw them lilies in the coomb, as how I felt they might of been sending for me, somehow. I really did feel it, all while we was there. But since then, I dunno, I've been thinking that wasn't really it. There's something else, and them lilies was only a sign-post on the way. Go on. I know it sounds nonsense, but you might as well tell him, since he asked."

Theodore translated as best he could. The Lama listened with close attention and then began to make a curious humming noise in his throat, a purring vibration that seemed to involve no movement of air in his lungs.

"A sign," he whispered at last. "The lilies. And the horse. Child, who drew those pictures which you carry?"

"Mrs Jones drew the lily. I was trying to draw the horse. Why do you want to know all these things? Where are you taking us?"

The old man ignored the questions.

"The Chinese with whom you travel," he said, "is he a servant of his Government? He is no ordinary servant, I think."

"Course not," said Mrs Jones, when Theodore had translated. "What the old geezer means is he thinks Lung is a spy. Tell him I picked poor Lung up in Canton, 'cause his uncle swore he could talk a lot of Chinese lingos, besides Miao and Lolo what he only knew three words of. He's a poor scrap of a poet what can't get a government job, 'cause he failed all his examinations from thinking beautiful thoughts—and if he's got the gumption to go spying, why I'm Queen of England. Besides, I never let on as I was hoping to get to Tibet, or he wouldn't of come in the first place. Tell him that. And ask him what it's all about, while you're at it."

It was hard to fit her rush of speech into staid Mandarin, but Theodore did as well as he could and added the question at the end, expecting to be put off again. But this time the Lama answered quite straightforwardly.

"Yes, I will explain," he said. "Then perhaps you, who carried the signs of which the oracle spoke, will be able to tell me the next step of my search. I seek a child. It is our belief that the soul does not die with the body, but begins a new life, forgetting all that went before. Only when a soul has attained enlightenment is it freed from this endless wheel of death and re-birth and can go to join the great soul. I know that you, being Christians, do not share this belief.

"Now, there are certain great souls who, though they have reached enlightenment, choose to continue in the world of death and birth in order that they may show their fellow creatures the path to freedom which they themselves have chosen. And these men have reached such spiritual mastery that they can overcome the forgetfulness which ordinary souls experience at death and birth. They can will their own consciousness to continue from one life into the next. Their memory does not remain whole, however. At first it is all unrelated fragments, but as they grow they can be helped to piece these fragments back into the whole it once was, so that all their lives and all their old learning become present once more to their consciousness."

"Yes, I've heard of that," said Mrs Jones when Theodore had finished translating. "They've got this head priest called the Dalai Lama, and when he dies they go and look for a boy born at the same time to be the new Dalai Lama, and they say it's really the same person."

The old man must have picked the known syllables out.

"He whom you call the Dalai Lama," he said, "we know to be the Tulku, or reincarnation of Avalokitesvara, the Great Compassionate One. But he is not the only Tulku, and the Abbot of my own monastery of Dong Pe was also such a one, Tulku of the Siddha Asara. In his latest body he was known as the Lama Tojing Rimpoche, and though he was not yet thirty

years of age, all who knew him bore witness to his spiritual
mastery and holiness and wisdom and learning. But for twelve
years we have not seen him. He set out on a journey to Daparang, where we rested last night, and never arrived. It was his
custom to travel alone, and often to wander into waste places
to perform his spiritual exercises, so we did not find his disappearance surprising. But winter came on and he had not
returned, and then a rumour grew that he had been waylaid
by traitor monks and sold to the Chinese.

"I must explain that the Chinese have long claimed lordship
of Tibet, and there is in Pekin the Tashi Lama, who they say is
the true spiritual head of our people. Dong Pe is the nearest
great monastery to the Chinese border, and if its Abbot were to
acknowledge the claims of the Tashi Lama that would be a
victory for the Chinese. Tojing Rimpoche, however, was
always loyal to the Dalai Lama at Lhasa."

"That explains why he's been looking so beady-eyed at
poor Lung," commented Mrs Jones.

"Now we have a famous oracle at Dong Pe," said the Lama,
still talking as though he were discussing the most ordinary
things in the world, such as weather or crops. "But when we
consulted it, it told us nothing, not even whether Tojing
Rimpoche lived or died. We sent to the State oracle at Lhasa
and received only riddling answers. And so matters rested until
this year, when two things happened. First a story reached us
that the Chinese were preparing to announce the discovery of
the Tulku of the Siddha Asara; and second our own oracle at
Dong Pe spoke plainly for the first time, saying that Tojing
Rimpoche was dead, and it was now time to search for the
Tulku. It gave us certain signs, but did not tell us when Tojing
Rimpoche had died, so that we could not know the age of the

child we sought, except that he must be less than thirteen years of age—which you call twelve years of age.

"I will tell you the signs. Towards the south-east we must search. There would be a river. There would be a guide, and symbols of lower creations. There would be three people, one of them the mother of the Tulku. And there would be danger to the Tulku. Furthermore, it is usual in such cases for the oracle to describe some point by which the house in which the Tulku is born may be recognised, but this time there was no hint of any house at all. Lastly, though in this the oracles spoke even more obscurely than in the other matters—and oracles are seldom wholly clear—it seemed that the child we sought was begotten in a foreign land. This last sign we greatly feared for it seemed to us that it might be taken to show that the child from Pekin, of whom the rumours spoke, is the true Tulku of the Siddha Asara.

"Therefore we decided to search for our Tulku. It is normal to form a commission of several experienced Lamas to conduct this search, but in this case we decided to send only one man and to conduct the search in secret. And since it was I who had first recognised the child who became Tojing Rimpoche as the Tulku of Asara, it was thought best that I should conduct the search alone.

"So I set out, journeying south-east, enquiring in the villages I passed for children of unusual learning. But more and more as I considered the matter, and the signs I had been given, I dwelt on the absence of any sign concerning a dwelling place. Therefore, though I had come to the last village for very many miles, I did not turn back, reasoning that I might meet the one I sought far from houses, and that a child begotten in a foreign land might dwell still in that land. And behold, at the very edge of what is now Tibet I met with a child who said he was in danger and who bore in his pocket pictures which were symbols of lower creations, a lily and a horse. Next he spoke of a foreign woman, who might well be his mother—for how else should he be travelling with her in these wild places? And it was to be surmised that the Chinese of whom he spoke was their guide. When the child told me that his name meant Gift of God I felt assured that I was near the end of my search, though the child gave me no new sign.

"This might have troubled me earlier, but when I encountered the woman I recognised her as being a soul of great spiritual power, untamed and undirected, and I told myself that such a one might well be the mother of a Tulku and took this for a sign. It was then I decided that we must return to Dong Pe and ask the oracle whether I had read the signs correctly.

"But during our journey I have become increasingly aware, both from outward observation and from inward searching, that the child is not the one I seek. There were many small signs of this. He felt all around him to be strange. I watched him reading from his Christian book and sensed his active dislike of all our ways and thought. I felt no echo of the Tojing Rimpoche I had known for more than thirty years, and last night the Abbot of Daparang confirmed my thought.

"And yet the signs were so sure. Even now, though I know my reading of them to have been mistaken, I feel assured that these were the signs I was sent to seek. It is as though I had pieced together a torn sheet of paper, but done so in the wrong order, so that the message I read is not that which the scribe wrote; so I must study the scraps again to discern the true order. Reason tells me that the search is not at an end, and that with your help I may yet find the one I seek. It is possible that the woman is the guide of whom the oracle spoke, and that she will recognise the Tulku when she sees him. I do not know. I have sat here in meditation, cleansing my soul of all old thoughts, so that I may look afresh at the signs and question you further."

"So that's it!" said Mrs Jones with a teasing chuckle. "What do you make of that, Theo? I 'spect you're glad you're not some kind of incarnation, ain't you?"

"Of course I'm not!" said Theodore in a spitting whisper. "It's . . . it's rubbish!"

He surprised himself with his own fury. The calm of the Lama's voice, and Theodore's tiredness, and the complexity of turning one language into another, had softened and somehow made remote the actual meaning of what was being said. Fear and repugnance shook him now in the silence. And it wasn't any use saying it was superstition, to be pitied and disregarded, because the Lama Amchi was what he was, neither pitiful nor stupid, but a man of intelligence and authority. You would need an inner power equal to his own to argue with him, and Theodore felt now that you might never reach the limits of that power. How had he known at once that Theodore wasn't Chinese when in the past many Chinese had been mistaken about that? How had he caused the bandit with the pistol to miss him at point blank range? How did he keep his body so unnaturally warm in the Himalayan night?

Mrs Jones chuckled again.

"Wonder what he'll think of now?" she said. "He can't go back like this, can he? Must of been a disappointment for him when he seen how set you were on your Bible-reading."

She was interrupted by a movement. In the moonlight

Theodore saw the Lama lean forward from the waist and reach out a thin arm to touch her wrist.

"I sense more lives than our three," he said, in that remote and dreamy-seeming voice with which Theodore had first heard him speak. "The woman carries a child in her womb. He must be the one I seek."

Theodore hesitated. Flushing with embarrassment in the dark he stammered the translation. Mrs Jones drew in her breath sharply and let it slowly out.

"Lord, I hope not," she whispered. "I been beginning to wonder. How on earth did the old geezer know?"

"We will go to Dong Pe and ask the oracle," said the Lama.

Chapter 10

At noon next day they halted among the snows on the highest pass they had yet tried to cross. Theodore had lost all sense of direction among the intertwining mountains, though the position of the sun seemed to say that three days ago they had been heading south and now they were going north again.

"We done a detour," explained Mrs Jones. "He went out of his way south, so as the old holy man at Daparang could have a dekko at you, and now he's taking a short cut north, save time, instead of going the whole way back and round."

They had halted not for the noon rest—the thin icy air made stillness seem half way to death—but because a wall of snow had slid down from the peak on the right and was lying, twenty feet high in some places, across the narrows of the pass. Two of the escort were stamping and digging a narrow passage at the lowest part, but they hadn't gone more than a few feet in when the wall of the passage collapsed on them and they had to be dug out; the hindmost man emerged laughing, as though being buried alive was a splendid joke, but the leader took longer to rescue and therefore longer to see the humour of it.

Meanwhile three of the escort had been expostulating with the Lama, clearly from their gestures saying it would be better to go back. He listened to them without a word, then turned away and moved along the obstacle, wading knee-deep through loose drift. He stopped and stood with slowly nodding head by a place in the wall that looked no better than the first they had tried. The escort, grumbling and unwilling, started to hack and dig and stamp again until they were out of sight. This time they wore ropes round their waists in case of another collapse. Lung was holding Albert's head while Mrs Jones cleared a ball of snow from his hoof. Sir Nigel, unloaded and swathed in blankets, hung his head and gasped at the useless air.

Suddenly there was an excited cry and the escort started to lead the yaks into the gap. Theodore followed in his turn, leading Bessie, and found that at the point which the Lama had chosen the ground on the far side fell sharply away and most of the thickness of the snow wall had spilt down it. Now the escort were stamping a ledge back along to the path, which dropped precipitously down through snowfields to another of the lushly forested valleys that threaded among the peaks.

They had not reached the trees when they heard from above and behind them a long, slow grumbling roar; the air quivered with shock-waves below the threshold of hearing, and lesser roars followed as snows loosened by the first vibrations slid and settled. The escort broke into mutters, which seemed centred as much on the Lama as on the noise in the mountains.

"Avalanche," said Mrs Jones. "I bet his Reverence has managed to make 'em think it come just where we was standing. He's a sly old geezer, ain't he?"

"He was right about where to make the path," said Theodore over his shoulder.

"Fair enough," said Mrs Jones. "But you mustn't go thinking that proves he's right about everything else."

There was a note in her voice which made him look round to where she was leading Albert down the path. Even through the dimness of the veil he saw one large eye wink.

"Are you sure?" he cried.

"Course I ain't," she snapped, suddenly angry. "And watch where you're walking. *And* keep your voice down."

Theodore turned his head and trudged on, confused. The night before, on their way down from their interview with the Lama, she had suddenly said, "I'm not telling old Lung till I know for certain, one way or the other. I don't want him puppying round, all anxious, right? And that means you'll have to ask His Reverence not to mention it in front of him—don't tell him why—perhaps he won't fancy the kid having a Chinese Daddy. Just let him think I don't want Lung to know 'cause I'm a bit ashamed, like." No doubt that accounted for her asking Theodore to keep his voice down now, but not for the violent shift of tone. She had sung most of the time on their way up to the pass, until the air became too thin for wasted breath, but between whiles Theodore had noticed her riding or walking with an unaccustomed slouch, as if deep in thought.

He was confused at a deeper level too. Obviously it would be best if there were no child—an infant conceived in sin, born out of wedlock and doomed to be reared in an idolatrous creed . . . but Theodore had slept uneasily, and in the timeless slithering intervals when he was neither awake nor asleep he had been conscious that somebody or something was standing at the top of the ladder outside the upper room in the farm, waiting to be let in. Sometimes he thought it was the Lama Amchi, come down from the hillside; once he had been certain that it was Father, alive and safe; but several times it had been a vaguer being, a bodiless cloud, the soul of the unborn Tulku. Theodore had even dreamed that he had slid out of his cot and opened the door and found nothing there but the starlit mountains—and then he would be awake in his blankets, raging with fleas and knowing he had never opened the door at all. Of course it was only dreams, but the memory was still strong as he picked his way down the tilt of the track towards the cedar-scented woods.

They slept that night in a village in the valley, where the villagers held an impromptu festival to celebrate the Lama's presence. It seemed that the expedition was now returning to territory where he was well known and revered. Next day they climbed a good broad track up the far side of the valley and came to a wide plateau, ringed with ridged peaks, quite barren and without even snow to vary the deadness. For two hours the track wound north across this desert and all the time the peaks funnelled in until, about the middle of the afternoon, they crossed a slight ridge and looked down on an extraordinary bowl or plain. It was four or five miles across, almost circular, reaching on this side to the foot of the ridge where they stood, rimmed to left and right with cliffs which were really the beginnings of the peaks, and on the far side apparently ending with a steepish slope of bare ground which rose to a horizon between the flanking mountains. The floor of the plain was made entirely of close-packed rounded boulders, some as small as a clenched fist and others large as a hay-bale, but all lying so level that from the distance they looked like dark grey water, made opaque by the ruffling of a breeze.

Here, to Theodore's surprise, the escort started to make camp by unloading the yaks and building a larger-than-usual fire of dried dung. Anywhere would have been a more appealing place than this, he thought. Surely they could have crossed the plain—it was still three hours till nightfall—and found somewhere better beyond it. The wind, which was full of fine, abrasive grit, slashed at them from erratic directions and set up vague hootings among the stones. They ate their meal early and then simply sat and waited for nightfall, but when Mrs Jones set out for a stroll towards the nearer cliffs the Lama immediately sent two of the escort to fetch her back.

"There are fourteen devils in this place," he explained solemnly. "Within my protection you are safe, but beyond it they will cast you down and break your limbs, howling."

Indeed at dusk he performed a ritual, circling round the camp with a weird, gliding step and stopping at four points to make an invocation which sounded like no language at all, but a mixture of whooping cries and sharp barks and a booming hum with bits of gabble threaded through. The escorts turned inwards towards the fire, shutting their eyes and stopping their ears while he performed, and as soon as he had finished rolled themselves in their blankets and lay still. Lung and Theodore copied them and Mrs Jones went to her tent, but Theodore spent longer than usual saying his prayers. Though he was praying to the emptiness which was all he had found for many days, it crossed his mind to ask that Mrs Jones should turn out not to be pregnant after all; but before the thought had formed itself into words he tried to erase it—there was something appalling about the idea of praying that a life should not exist.

Again he slept badly, and whenever he woke he saw the Lama sitting a little further up the hill, bolt upright, staring out across the mysterious plain, cross-legged and motionless, sentinel against the princes of the powers of the air and spiritual wickedness in high places. St Paul's strange phrase repeated and repeated itself in Theodore's muddled brain. He kept

telling himself that these fourteen silly devils didn't exist, and
suppose they did, there was nothing a heathen priest could do
to control them; but at the same time he knew quite well that
he was scared, and that if the Lama hadn't been there he would
have been more scared still.

Early next morning they set about crossing the plain, and
Theodore at once discovered why they hadn't tried the
previous afternoon. Night would certainly have caught them
somewhere out in the middle. Each stone, though apparently
just like all the others except in size—a flattish dark blue-grey
oval, very smooth and veined with paler lines—seemed to
have a life of its own. In places they lay loosely on beds of the
sharp grit and it was possible to pick a way between them,
but mostly they were many layers deep and one had to pace
across them as if they were stepping-stones, never knowing
whether they would stay firm or shift with one's weight. All
the while the stinging, buffeting wind came and went, seeming
to strike at the exact moment when one was balancing for
the next pace.

"Don't need no devils to cast us down round here,"
grumbled Mrs Jones. "This wind! We'll be lucky if we get
the horses across in one piece."

Certainly, though the stones were trying enough for the
humans, for the animals they were almost impossible. The
yaks managed a little better than the horses, being more sure-
footed, lower-slung, and readier to take a stumble, but even
they had to be coaxed or prodded almost every yard. In the
worst places the escort gathered all the bedding and laid it
out, several layers thick, to make a pair of rafts. An animal
could be led onto one of these, then the other one laid in
front and when it was standing on that the first one could be

taken round to make another short stretch of tolerable footing.
Elsewhere the escort piled the larger stones together to make
a rough causeway. There were stretches where the remains of
previous causeways showed clearly, the results of earlier
crossings by other travellers, and they used these where they
could. But frequent repairs were necessary, as though something had come since they were made and started to tumble
the stones into their normal loose ruin.

Lung was leading Rollo along one of these stretches of old
causeway when a stone, apparently as stable as any other,
tilted sideways under Rollo's hoof. The movement was so
sudden that to Theodore, following next behind, it looked as
though the other end of the stone had been violently flipped
up from below. The pony's leg shot down as if into soft bog
and through the beginnings of its squeal Theodore heard the
bone snap. The Tibetans left their yaks and came crowding
round, gabbling at each other as they tried to drag the
struggling animal free. It squealed with fresh pain. Mrs Jones
strode past Theodore with her gun under her arm, her face
invisible beneath the veil. The click of the bolt stood out
sharply through the clatter and scrape of hooves on stone.
Theodore looked away. The shot rang out, clapped against
the nearing cliffs and came back in echoes that sounded like
laughter from stone lungs.

The Tibetans dragged the pony's body a few yards to one
side and began to pile a heap of stones over it. The Lama turned
to the cliffs and intoned a few short sentences in Tibetan.

"The old ones have taken their sacrifice," he said in
Mandarin. "We will have no more trouble."

Indeed from that moment the causeway became wider and
better-built, leading them in twenty minutes out onto a sound

track which climbed across a long slope of thin-grassed soil and bare rock and disappeared round a buttress of brown cliff. By now it was well into the afternoon, so they fed the weary horses and yaks and improvised a hurried meal for themselves.

"We're getting somewhere near," said Mrs Jones in a low voice to Theodore while Lung was still with the horses. "Soon as the old boy's finished his hobson-jobson, ask him how much further, and while you're doing that see if you can ask him, natural like, if there isn't an easier way than this. If I find he's right, what he said about me, I'm getting back to civilisation double quick, where there's proper doctors. But don't let him see that's what you're on about."

The Lama was standing at the end of the causeway, arms raised, crying aloud in a series of wailing repetitive phrases as though he were preaching or singing to the stones; sometimes in a pause between the phrases the distorted echo of his voice came whining back, as though the stones were answering. When he had finished he turned to Theodore and answered both his questions without being asked.

"We are in the territory of Dong Pe," he said, smiling like a host welcoming expected guests. "This night I shall sleep in my own house. I am sorry that the journey has seemed so difficult, but the old ones who dwell round the stone lake are our guardians as much as our tormentors. This is the only path to Dong Pe, and close though we are to the border I do not think that even the Chinese could drag cannons across here."

"Cannon?" asked Theodore.

"When I was a young man I walked all across the mountains and plains, both to seek wild and waste places in which to perform my spiritual exercises and also to visit monasteries and learn from their teachers. I went to the great monastery at Nachuga, in the far west, a place famous for learning and for its many shrines, but I did not stay there long because I found that the monks had begun to quarrel among themselves, and all learning was forgotten in the arguments. The summer after I left, this argument broke into fighting and the Abbot drove his opponents out of Nachuga. They, however, journeyed to Lhasa and complained to the Dalai Lama. Now in those days the Chinese had much influence in Lhasa, and they persuaded the Dalai Lama that the time had come to break the power and independence of Nachuga, so he sent a message to the Abbot ordering him to restore the rebel monks and reform the monastery according to their wishes. Naturally the Abbot refused. Then, with Chinese help, soldiers came from Lhasa, bringing cannons, and they bombarded Nachuga until most of its rooms and shrines were rubble. It was a poor inheritance those rebel monks came into . . . But with the help of the old ones I will see that this does not happen at Dong Pe. Come now. We will ride these last few miles, so that the Mother of the Tulku shall see Dong Pe in daylight."

"We've only got three horses now."

"The Chinese can follow with the yaks."

Lung did not like this arrangement at all, but in the end he accepted it, scowling. Theodore perceived suddenly that Lung was aware that something was being hidden from him, something which Mrs Jones and the Lama and Theodore knew. This would have been wounding enough if they had merely been companions, but for poor Lung, already half-sick with the ending of his idyll, it must have seemed a sign like the ending of love itself.

While they were redistributing the horse-loads among the yaks, Theodore saw Mrs Jones, standing alone a little to one side, holding Sir Nigel's head. Her veil as usual hid her face, but again he noticed how her stance had changed, an imperceptible slackening in the line of her spine and shoulders that showed deep inward thought, and, he guessed, an echo of Lung's unhappiness. He could almost feel her fear and uncertainty. This was so unlike her that without thought he led Bessie across towards her. She turned her head to look at him, stiffening her stance as she did so.

"It'll be all right," he muttered.

She reached out an arm, took him by the shoulder and drew him close against her side, holding him there while the wind flapped her cloak round him in swirling folds.

"Let's hope," she whispered.

Beyond the stone lake the track was better than any they had travelled for many days, sometimes steep but always reasonably smooth, twisting its way around rock outcrops that covered all the long slope between the two pincer-like ranges that ringed the stone lake. The Lama rode Albert, sitting sideways across his haunches like a peasant and seeming to control him as easily as Mrs Jones controlled Sir Nigel, without visible signal or command. He hurried them on, apparently impatient for the first time in the whole journey, though the horses gasped and stumbled with the steadily increasing height until Mrs Jones insisted on dismounting and leading Sir Nigel up the steeper stretches. Once or twice, looking over his shoulder, Theodore caught a glimpse of the yak-train, already ant-like with distance, and beyond that the stone lake, which from this height seemed to glimmer and shift as if it were indeed a lake of water.

At last the ground levelled and the track swung east, dipped, and began to sidle steeply down along the far side of the right-hand range. Now below them opened another precipitous valley, wider than most they had seen and splitting into several side-valleys. Beyond it stood a single massive peak, not rising to any dramatic points but topped by a long smooth snow-ridge which made the whole slab seem solemn and tremendous.

"Now that's something," said Mrs Jones in an awed voice.

"In our language it is called the Dome of Purest Light," said the Lama. "Its contemplation brings self-knowledge. Tell the Mother of the Tulku that henceforth she shall gaze on it every day."

"I wish he wouldn't keep calling me that," grumbled Mrs Jones, who had learnt by now to recognise those particular syllables. "Counting chickens, that is."

They rode on down the twisting track. All along its length the little shrines sprouted on every small level, like a field of weird stone fungi. Slowly the snows of the great mountain changed their colour and the shadows on it, which had been a brighter blue than the sky, darkened and grew as the sun westered. There were pinks and golds among the glittering white, and the depths below were already heavy with dusk, when the track reached a point where it seemed about to lance out over empty space. The Lama rode unhesitatingly to this dead end and swung out of sight round a pillar of sheer rock. Theodore followed Mrs Jones round the bend and reined to a halt beside her. All three sat perfectly still, as if transfixed by the shock of vision. Then the Lama flung out his arm in a wide gesture.

"Dong Pe," he said.

Mrs Jones and Theodore sat and stared.

The buttress they had just rounded had concealed the way in which the dark cleft of the valley widened suddenly to an enormous bowl ringed by the towering ice ramparts, flanked with steep forests and floored with little meadows. The Lama was not pointing at any of that, but at the mountainside ahead. There, clinging like the hive of wild bees to what seemed almost vertical cliff, was the monastery. Its walls were white. Many of the roofs were flat; others were shallow curves of hummocky tiles, ending in wide-spreading eaves. In several places the roof-line erupted into pyramids topped with spiky onion-domes, and the largest of these, near the middle, seemed to be covered with a dull yellow metal. The monastery spread apparently endlessly along the cliff, as if it had grown there, section by section, wherever a ledge or cranny gave the builders foot-hold. The flat roofs and the sharp lines of buttresses and the heavy-lintelled deep-set windows along the upper storeys made this growth seem more like that of a crystal, which increases by angles and facets, than that of a plant.

Above the main buildings the cliff was pocked with the mouths of caves, and below lay a huddle of small squat huts and exotic shrines. The whole site faced east and was already deep in the shade of the mountain behind it, so the faint glow of lights at many of the windows added to the sense of a huge, mysterious life born out of the very mountain.

"I have been to Lhasa and seen the great Potala," intoned the Lama in his clanging Mandarin. "I have travelled in India and seen the mighty shrines of that land. I have seen even the sea. But in all this world of illusion I have seen no illusion that can compare with Dong Pe."

Chapter 11

For only the second time since the destruction of the Settlement Theodore was suddenly convinced that his prayers were being listened to. Once, at the top of that far-away rock pillar, when he had tried to pray for Mrs Jones; and now, here, in the guest-house below the gates of Dong Pe monastery, with the bitter mountain air fingering his shoulder-blades as he knelt on the rug beside his cot, while his lips moved as usual through the automatic phrases and his mind roamed helplessly.

He had been thinking, as it happened, about Lung. Two images had floated side by side into his head—that last morning in the valley, Lung lying with his head in Mrs Jones's lap, drifting in love; and his arrival at the guest-house last night, snarling with sulky suspicion. Theodore liked Lung; at the start of the journey he had seemed at least half-absurd, but slowly Theodore had discovered some of what Mrs Jones had seen in him, humour and intelligence, and a kind of exulting innocence which he occasionally let gleam from behind the fastidious façade. But Theodore, despite that liking, had not been able to grasp the depth and strength of Lung's love for Mrs Jones, and so had found it hard to bear the apparently childish fits of sulks that had followed its ending. Now, in his half-dreamy state, self-hypnotised by the empty repetition of words, he found himself laying the two images side by side, the exultation and the misery, as if they were two pieces of cloth he was comparing. He was swept with a wave of sympathy for poor Lung, as sudden and powerful as the scent of honeysuckle come upon at dusk.

As the wave ebbed he knew he was being listened to—not the movement of his lips, but his thought. It was as though, wandering round the deserted chapel of his soul, he had found a footprint in the dust that was not his own. He stopped praying, opened his eyes and stared around. Opposite him hung a shimmery cloth woven with a picture of the Buddha cross-legged on his throne and surrounded by grimacing warriors and monsters and calm, bare-breasted women. The guest-house was a gaudy tunnel, sharp-lit by the morning light through small square windows. Lung lay curled on his cot. From behind a partition of blue and scarlet hangings came Mrs Jones's light snore, contented as the purr of a cat. Neither of them had been the listener. The Buddha was only a picture, smiling that sweet inane smile. And the listener was fading now, fading, gone—frightened, as it were, by the sudden concentration of Theodore's thought. That first morning he rose, smiling self mockingly at the sudden whimsy that his visitor might have been the Siddha Asara; he could not then know how many times, morning and evening, he would find the same nameless presence waiting to pray beside him.

As they breakfasted he became aware that the relationship between Mrs Jones and Lung had changed again. She had spent a full hour last night, coaxing the poor young man out of his sulks, and when Theodore had dozed into sleep they had still been sitting side by side by the stove, talking in low voices. She must have told him about the child she might be carrying, his child. He seemed very uncertain how to react—shy, puppyish and strangely clumsy. It was as though the idea that the love-affair might ever result in offspring had not crossed his mind before. Mrs Jones found his behaviour irritating and was sharp with him, but instead of lapsing back into sulks he tried to turn his clumsiness into a joke, which only made her crosser still. She was at a high pitch of irritation when they heard a soft knock at the door.

"Visitors I can do without this morning," she snapped. "Go on, one of you! Ain't you going to let them in?"

Lung scrambled to the door, almost colliding with the Lama Amchi who had chosen that moment to open it and enter. He was followed by a tall young monk, very thin, with a round smooth head too small for his body. Everybody bowed like dolls. Unasked the two monks settled cross-legged on the floor, completing a circle round Mrs Jones's stove. Mrs Jones produced two more of the steel mugs from her hamper and filled them from the tea-pot. They all sat in silence for a while, as if the stove were an object set there for them to contemplate. The steam drifted up from the mugs. Theodore wanted to fidget, but stayed still.

"I introduce to you the Monk Tomdzay," said the Lama Amchi suddenly. "He will come here each morning, so that if you have any wishes or needs you may tell him and he will see that they are met."

"I am honoured to be of service," said the young monk in very good Mandarin with barely a trace of the Tibetan twang.

"Delighted to meet his excellency," said Mrs Jones in her drawing-room voice.

There was another long silence, broken only by the smack and suck of the holy men gulping at the scalding tea.

"Oh, come on!" said Mrs Jones at last. "Ain't one of you going to ask what happens next? Is there any harm in me going botanising? When are they going to consult this here oracle they're on about? Lung, my love, you'll have to tell him I told you what's up."

Lung's embarrassment took the form of language so flowery and contorted that Mrs Jones became more and more impatient, and eventually cut Lung's translation short with an unmistakable gesture.

"What a bunch of idiots! You have a go, Theo, get it into their heads I got to know what's up."

But the Lama Amchi seemed to have understood both the gesture and the motive behind it.

"The time is not propitious to consult the oracle," he said smiling. "In some days, however, the astrological signs will change and then we will hold the ceremony. Meanwhile, go where you will. If you wish to journey in the valley, Tomdzay will arrange for an escort. In most parts of the monastery too you may come and go as you like—we are not a sect that forbids the presence of women. Indeed, many of our monks are married. You will not see me again until the ceremony of the oracle, as the time has come for me to retire and engage in meditation, but as I say Tomdzay will attend to all your wants."

While Theodore repeated the explanation to Mrs Jones, the Lama Amchi returned to his tea. Perhaps he was already half-withdrawn into his meditation, but his noddings and suckings made him seem much older and less commanding than he had been during the journey, like a gaffer mumbling by the hearth. Suddenly he rose to his feet with a single effortless movement that was almost as though he had floated himself upright.

Tomdzay copied him. They bowed. The Lama Amchi intoned a few words in Tibetan and they were gone.

"What a pair of beauties!" said Mrs Jones. "Each one as sly as the other. Now listen, I been thinking. First off, this oracle's going to say whatever old Amchi tells it. His idea is get the baby born and then tell everyone it's this Tulku they've been waiting for . . ."

"What when child is maybe girl?" interrupted Lung.

"They'll have a baby boy ready somewhere, mark my words. You see, it ain't only finding their Tulku and dishing the Chinese as appeals to Amchi—it's having the kid so young. F'rinstance, even if he'd managed to convince himself it was Theo here, like he tried to first off, that wouldn't of been half as good, cause of Theo being getting on for grown up. But if he starts with a kid aged nothing, that's another twenty years Amchi's got of running this here monastery before the kid takes over."

"But you said you weren't going to have the baby here," said Theodore.

"Course I ain't—I was just giving you a f'rinstance of how sly old Amchi is. And we got to seem to go along with him, what's more. One sign we're trying to scarper and he'll watch us like a cat at a mousehole. But we're going to, and we got to start thinking out how straight off, cause if we leave it too long all them passes will be blocked with snow, and besides I'm not going swinging across any of them bridges when I'm eight months gone.

"Now, listen, there's a lot of things we can try. First off do I tell old Amchi I'm not carrying, after all? I ain't so sure that'll work, 'cause I 'spect it ain't true and he's got a way of guessing—and once he gets it into his head we ain't on his side then he'll keep a tight hold on us—lock us up, I shouldn't wonder. So I think I won't say nothing about that for a bit.

"So, next, we start looking for a different way out. I can do that while I'm off botanising. I know he told you as the way we come was the only way into this here valley, but he's quite up to pulling a fast one over something like that, make us think we hadn't a hope of getting out. Next, you remember what he said about this Tojing bloke being scuppered by traitor monks? I'll bet there's one or two of them still about. You don't get a place like this run all of a piece. There's all sorts of splits and gangs under the holy surface. I reckon that's one for you, Lung—you hang around, keep your eyes open, see if anyone seems a bit extra friendly, keep your wits about you. You'll know him when you meet him, some bloke as asks a lot of little questions and then keeps shying away from the subject . . ."

"Why will this man help us?" asked Lung dubiously.

"Dish old Amchi, of course. There must be a gang here as don't want him to come up with the new Tulku, go on running things another twenty years. Now look, you won't have to go hunting around for this bloke, 'cause if he's there he'll come to you. All you got to do is be where he can find you. There's got to be a library, place like this, so why don't you go scholaring—you'll like that. Lot of 'em will be shy of you, 'cause of you being Chinese, so I think you'll know the right bloke when he comes along. Take your time. Act shy. Don't rush it . . . Now, young Theo, you've got to see if you can't pick up a bit of the lingo. That's important."

"Learn Tibetan? Me? Why?"

"Because we're going to need it whatever happens. I'm not

laying much odds on me finding a way out of here what we can manage by ourselves. Lung's got a bit better chance, finding a bloke what'll help us. But my bet is in the end we're going to have to buy our way out—find a gang of yak-drivers or blokes like that what's prepared to risk it, or even some of these escort wallahs that's supposed to keep an eye on us—that'd be favourite, 'cause they could pretend to take us off botanising and we might get a whole day's start—two days, if we make out we're going right over the far side of the valley so we've got to camp out ... but anyway, Theo, if we're going to do that we got to be able to talk the lingo. There's not many peasants as know Chinee, I bet. And even suppose we get out one of the other ways, we'll still have to do a bit of chit-chat, time to time. Now, I ain't no good at languages, never have been; and Lung here, well, he's had plenty practice in English but the way he's got on don't give me that much confidence. So it's up to you ..."

Her ill temper had gone. It was as though a sulky, dank dawn had been cleared by a driving north wind, lifting doubt and low spirits like dead leaves and making the blood sing. The lines on Lung's face had hardened and his eyes were sparkling —after the days of dejection this was his soldier-woman come back again. Theodore wanted to laugh, not with mockery but with the same sudden exhilaration.

"Sure," he said. "I'll learn Tibetan."

The mood lasted while they groomed the horses. They found an old man there who had brought some coarse feed and was now spreading dried fern over the floor of the shed they had been given for a stable. He treated Mrs Jones with awe and tried to prevent her grooming Sir Nigel, but she quickly bent him to her will and made him watch while she showed him exactly how she wanted everything done.

"Every comfort, you see," she said to Theodore. "Grooms, stable-boys—if we wanted footmen with white knee-breeches I bet they'd lay them on somehow. I won't be taking the horses, couple of days at least. They're fagged out, and it'll look lots more natural if I start my botanising close at hand, get the monks used to the idea that's how I spend my time, before I start off on proper expeditions ... Ta very much, Theo. Jorrocks here and me can finish off. You go and find some nice monk what wants to teach a kid his own language ..."

Theodore was hesitating just inside the main gate of the monastery when an old monk came shuffling along the inner wall, automatically twitching a line of little copper cylinders— another sort of prayer-wheel, Theodore guessed—into motion as he passed. They revolved with an erratic thin clinking. He ignored Theodore's Mandarin greeting, took him by the shoulder, and made gestures towards the southern end of the maze of buildings. Then he himself went shuffling out of the gate. Theodore shrugged, but obediently turned left and began his exploration. (Weeks later he found that the old man had been telling him that one is supposed to move around sacred ground in a clockwise direction—had he realised that at the time, Theodore might well have gone the other way.)

He walked at random through the maze. The monastery was a series of interlocking courtyards, mostly small and irregular, and often at different levels imposed by the under-lying mountain. Dark archways, ramps or stairs connected the

ground levels, and the upper storey was a second maze of
wooden galleries, where the russet-robed monks went to and
fro. It was all built of anything that had come to hand, whitewashed stone, flaking plaster stuck with cobbles, wood, woven
bamboo, tiles, with here and there billowing swags of creeper
clothing whole walls. Each courtyard had its own character,
like a village; one might be tumbledown and untidy, with a
yak tethered against a wall, a dung-pile in one corner, a couple
of women pounding something in a tub near by; then, through
the next arch Theodore would come out into a smooth-paved
rectangle, neat walls hung with banners and all freshly painted
since the winter, with a half-formal procession of monks
walking across the space, carrying ritual objects.

The exhilaration Mrs Jones had whipped up in him had
dwindled by now, but obediently he greeted everyone who
seemed free to speak to him. Some smiled, some made signs,
some ignored him entirely. He began to realise that the
sensible thing would have been to ask Tomdzay to find him
a teacher, rather than looking for one at random. Yes. And
that would put it off for another day. Perhaps Mrs Jones might
even have changed her mind by then . . .

He reached this conclusion just as he came up a shallow ramp
to a larger arch than most. Beyond it lay yet another courtyard,
but quite different from any he had so far seen. This one was
huge. On its further side rose the building with the gold-roofed
dome which had dominated the monastery on their first sight
of Dong Pe; below that glittering curve and spike was a
heavy, plain wall of pale stone, almost undecorated and with
no opening except for a pair of large doors which stood wide
open. This square black hollow and the slablike wall around it
contrasted strongly with the exotic dome, and indeed with all

of the rest of the monastery, which seemed to Theodore to have a frilly, tinselly, almost rubbishy quality about it, with the gaudy paintings and the flapping flags and the rows of battered prayer-wheels and the general lack of any obvious plan in its building.

Along the eastern side of this courtyard ran an arcade, supporting a balcony rather grander than most but otherwise quite in keeping with the temple architecture. Opposite it, however, was a surprise, for here the mountain suddenly showed itself, natural rock rising towards the snows in a series of shelves and inclines. The rock had a naked look, like the skeleton of a dead beast that has been scoured clean by birds and insects. It became steeper as it rose, and where the true cliffs began it was pocked with caves, some of them mere openings and some extended into walls and roofs. Stairs, hewn into the rock, zig-zagged up to these dwellings—if dwellings they were. Theodore saw three russet-robed monks moving among them, two carrying a large hamper-like basket from which the third took something when they reached each cave and passed it through a slot in the stonework or settled it on the floor of the opening.

Lower down the cliff, only a little above the roof-line of the monastery, was a wider shelf than most, and here was another oddity. Two houses occupied this site, side by side, each the mirror image of the other. A month ago Theodore might have thought they were perhaps shrines, or tombs, but he had slept in too many Tibetan villages to mistake them now. They were slightly plainer than Tibetan farms and more solidly built, and the upstairs windows with their heavy yellow shutters were much bigger than a farm would have afforded, but they were clearly houses. The steps between them and the courtyard were wider and more ornate than the ones that climbed on up to the caves.

Like a mouse creeping round the skirting of a room Theodore walked along below the rock wall and round the far side to the big doors. Peering into the dark he found it was, as he had suspected, a temple. The air here was full of incense and the heavy, greasy smell of the butter lamps. He didn't cross the threshold, partly from fear of doing anything that might offend these pagan worshippers, and partly from a deeper-seated fear of being in any way involved with the powers they worshipped; but he stood for a while at the door, gazing at the enormous statue of the Buddha which dominated the twinkling dark. There must have been some cunningly arranged skylight to cause the gold mask, with its too-calm and too-sweet smile, to glow as if with inner light, making the dark around it seem thicker than ordinary dark, so that the flames of the hundreds of lamps were weak yellow spots and the clutter of idols and ritual objects were veiled as if by smoke, their true shapes undiscernible, but showing themselves here as the glimmer off a jewel and there as flash of a staring white eyeball. The darkness and the richness and the closeness seemed to reach out into the mountain brightness infecting it in the same way that the smells of incense and burnt grease infected the clean thin air with their sick weight. Theodore would have turned away at once, but that would have been to acknowledge the power, to accept that it was something he was not prepared to face; so he stood there, staring bluntly at the Buddha.

As he turned at last, feeling that he had neither acknowledged the powers nor refuted them, his eye was caught by a movement. The arch through which he had entered the courtyard lay towards the mountain end of that side, and so far he had never really looked at the rest of it. Now he saw that it was mainly occupied by another temple, smaller and much more ornate than the one on whose steps he stood. There was a frivolous little dome and spike, also covered with gold; a pair of closed doors painted with red and orange and green demons; several banner-like streamers hanging from poles along the parapet; and two rows of large prayer-wheels on either side of the doors, the ones on the right still but the ones on the left twirling vigorously, though there was no monk near enough to have recently spun them. At roof-level, behind the banners on the left, a small windmill was turning, but on the right the sail of a similar mill pointed monotonously at the sky. It was something to look at, a change from Buddhas and idols, a mystery which reason might solve. Almost eagerly Theodore strode across the courtyard to inspect the mechanism.

It turned out to be as he had guessed. The windmill drove the prayerwheels through a series of cords and pulleys. Each of the pulleys was itself a miniature prayer-wheel, but despite this there was something about the whole device which struck Theodore as oddly un-Tibetan. It was so ingeniously simple, and also efficient. With a very little adaptation it could have been made to do something useful. It was just the sort of thing Father might have invented, with its use of native techniques and western ideas to achieve something which neither could do alone.

The thought of Father shook him with an appalling, savage pang, as if the healing of the past weeks had been all suddenly ripped away, and the wound was yesterday's. He stood dazed and sick, swaying to the steady tinkle of the prayer-wheels, thinking *The Buddha did this to me. The Buddha did this to me.*

He shook his head violently, trying to drive the nonsense notion away, and for further distraction turned to climb the temple steps in order to cross and find out why the other set of wheels wasn't turning. He was still dazed, and perhaps staggering slightly, for though he must have seen the monk come out of a small wicket in the main doors he still managed to bump into him. The monk appeared not to have noticed him till the collision.

"Oh, I beg your pardon," he muttered automatically.

"Not at all, not at all," said the monk. "Ought to have been looking where I was going—not that I can very well these days."

It took Theodore a moment or two to grasp that they had both spoken in English. The monk was peering at him with pale, opaque blue eyes. His head was quite bald, but a frizz of stiff white beard stood out all round a reddish-brown face. He was only an inch or two taller than Theodore, and looked as though nature had designed him to be plump, which he was not.

"How d'ye do?" he said. "Fine morning."

He was smiling with great sweetness, almost eagerness, which contrasted with the snappy bark of his voice.

"Yes, it's lovely," said Theodore. "Uh, my name's Theodore Tewker. I came here yesterday."

"Good. Good. Excellent. My name's Achugla. Used to be Price-Evans."

"Pleased to meet you, Mr Price-Evans."

"Major Price-Evans. Not that it matters. You're American, by the sound of you. Care for a cup of tea? Come in. Come in."

Without waiting to hear whether his invitation was accepted, the old man turned and led the way through the wicket.

Theodore followed him into the near-dark, into the reek and richness, where the face of another Buddha gleamed half way to the roof. Left to himself Theodore would have backed out, but the monk who called himself Major Price-Evans was shuffling away to open a door into a small bright cell. Following him Theodore found that this was lit by a skylight. There was just room in it for a cot and shrine and a stove. The walls were covered with gaudy hangings, some of them showing pictures of the Buddha, others what might have been demons or might have been gods, and yet others which were merely patterns of huge letters.

"Sit down, sit down," said the Major, waving a hand at the cot. "Come here to study under the Lama Amchi, have you? Sound a bit young for it—none of my business, of course."

"We came here by accident. The Lama Amchi helped us to escape from some brigands, and brought us here."

"If Lama Amchi's in it, it's not an accident."

"Anyway, I'm a Christian."

"Are you now? Good. Good. Excellent."

The Major beamed at him as though this was the most interesting news he had heard in years, then turned to the stove and before Theodore could think of a polite way to stop him had ladled out two mugs of tea from the pot that stood murmuring there. The smell told Theodore what it was.

"First-rate brew, this," said the Major happily. "Nothing like it for keeping you going in the mountains. Often strikes me that if we could have persuaded Thomas Atkins to drink the stuff we'd never have had all that trouble getting him to Kabul and back. Hey?"

"I guess you're right, sir," said Theodore, taking the copper mug. He had little idea what the Major was talking about, but there was a warmth, an eagerness, an innocence about the old man that made you want to please him. Even, it turned out, to the extent of drinking Tibetan tea and getting it down without gagging.

Meanwhile the Major talked. His story was difficult to follow because he rambled to and fro in time and space, and because the people and campaigns he had known forty years ago seemed no more and no less real than the pagan demons he now served. At one moment he would be talking about a miraculous fast achieved by some Lama, and the next he would have slid into an account of getting a famine train through southern India, only to find the people he had come to save lying dead in their tens of thousands round the railway head with the kites wheeling above the almost fleshless bodies. As far as Theodore could make out he had been a soldier in the British Army in India, an engineer concerned to build the bridges and roads for the campaigns of the British Empire.

He seemed to have dabbled in a lot of religions and superstitions but had gone on with his soldiering until something had happened ... "Just came to me, me boy, like Paul on the road to Damascus—not so sudden as that, quite, didn't fall off me horse or anything—been brewing up inside me for a long while without me knowing—but there I was, one week sitting at me desk, supervising me coolies, dining in mess, all that, and next week I'd chucked it all up and was tramping along a dusty red road, barefoot, with nothing in the world but me begging bowl." He seemed to have wandered right down into Ceylon, where he had finally been converted to

Buddhism, and then come rambling back towards the hills, further and further, settling at last in this final cranny in Dong Pe. It didn't seem to him at all extraordinary—nor had Theodore's sudden greeting on the temple steps in a language he hadn't spoken for twenty years, nor did anything else that had happened or could possibly happen. He was almost blind.

"Finished your tea?" said the Major suddenly. "Come and have a look at the temple, hey? Worth seeing, you know. Well worth seeing."

It didn't cross Theodore's mind to refuse. The dark was no longer ominous in his company, the pagan powers no longer dangerous. At the cell door the Major slipped a pair of thick felt pads onto his boots and began to walk with a movement like a skater's.

"Might as well give the floor a bit of a polish while I'm going my rounds," he said.

"That's clever," said Theodore.

"Not my own idea. Copied it from a lama I met at Ghoom."

"Did you make the windmills that drive the prayer-wheels outside?"

"Yes, yes indeed. Lamas weren't all that keen on it. Wheel's sacred, you know. Never see a barrow in Tibet. Bit uneasy about *using* wheels, even when it's to drive prayer-wheels, and some of them not that keen on having the prayer-wheels turn of their own accord—can't acquire virtue by turning them yourself, hey?"

"One side has stopped turning."

"I know, I know. Storm last winter, you know, and my old eyes aren't up to mending it. Never mind. All material endeavour must fail, you know. It's all illusion. Not that I wouldn't like to get it mended. Dear me. Now this fellow here, he's one of the *chos-skyong*—that means Spirit Kings . . ."

The temple was quite small, and filled with the presence of the gold-faced Buddha. The gold was real gold, Theodore decided, and the glitter of the idol's ornaments sparkled from real jewels. Though the temple was packed with objects—so much so that there seemed little room for worshippers—these all had the air of being precisely placed in relation to the central statue and became part of the Buddha's presence. Even the line of hideous, grimacing, weapon-waving demons in front of which the Major had halted were part of the grammar of the place, with a meaning of their own in the context of the smooth metal face and the eternal smile. Theodore could sense that, though he didn't know the grammar in question and didn't want to.

"Could you teach me Tibetan?" he said.

"I don't know about that," said the Major. "Why do you want to learn it?"

"Oh . . . well . . . I like to be able to talk to people, I suppose."

"Much better keep silence. Much better. Still, I daresay I could. Started writing a dictionary when I first came here . . . Tell me something, me boy—have I got this fellow clean?"

Theodore inspected the Spirit King with different eyes. Parts of the monster gleamed with steady polishing, but elsewhere a cranny held a cobweb or the whole surface of a dishlike object which the monster carried in one of his several hands was mildewed with ancient dust. There had been a note of anxiety in the Major's voice.

"He's fine," said Theodore. "Just a couple of places . . . would you like me to give them a rub?"

"If you would," said the Major, gruffly. "Don't mind telling you I've been fretted about this since my eyes began to go. Worked out a routine, you see, a system of work so I can keep everything spick and span as a gun-carriage, but I'm not such a fool that I don't know I'm bound to miss places. Oracle-priest, he's very nice about it, pretends not to notice . . ."

"Aren't you the priest in charge?"

"Dear me, no. Dear me. I'm not the oracle-priest. Shouldn't care to have that happen to me. No, no, I'm only the cleaner . . . Now, you'll find a ladder under that hanging on the back wall and I'll get you my brush . . ."

For an hour or more Theodore climbed about among the idols brushing and polishing, while the Major pottered around on the floor, muttering prayers, commenting on the attributes of the idols, filling the innumerable little lamps that glowed on almost every flat surface, or pulling from a shelf a loose-leafed sacred book to show Theodore its intricate strange pictures and patterns. Far off, like a clock striking, a gong began to boom with a steady beat.

"We'll pack it in now," said the Major. "He'll be here any moment and I like things shipshape when he comes."

"Who?"

"Oracle-priest. First rate young man—would have made a good soldier, I sometimes think. Can't say how grateful I am to you, young fellow."

"Shall I come back tomorrow and do some more? And you could start teaching me Tibetan."

"Have to think about that. Now, stow that ladder where you found it and come and give me a heave on the other door . . ."

The sun did not shine into the temple, but the mid-morning

brightness was strong enough to lay a gleaming path across the polished floor as the doors opened. The gleam darkened with a shadow, and through the widening gap paced a monk wearing the usual russet robe and a tall pointed hat made of silvery cloth. The monk knelt before the Buddha and bowed till the tip of his hat touched the floor. The Major and Theodore, each standing by a leaf of the doors, watched him in silence for a full two minutes until he rose, removed his hat and turned. He gave some sort of blessing to the Major, who answered him in Tibetan, beaming and anxious; then he turned to Theodore.

"Welcome to my temple," he said in Mandarin.

He was a square-built man of about forty, smooth-faced and athletic-looking.

"Thank you for letting me see it," said Theodore awkwardly. "It is very interesting."

"Of course. But there are times when I'd be glad to be somewhere else. I hear you were attacked in the valley of the Jade River. There are notorious bandits all along that way—Lolo, very unreliable. We never travelled through there in groups of less than ten, all armed. But that track leads up to Starve-all Pass and through the ranges well north of here. How did you come to be right down on the Jade River gorge again?"

Theodore explained. The priest nodded and asked more questions. He spoke Mandarin in a quite different way from the Lama Amchi, with a better accent but much more erratic grammar. The Lama Amchi spoke as though he had learnt the language systematically, from books, whereas this man had evidently picked it up in a series of smatterings. Once or twice he used earthy idioms, or words that didn't belong to

Mandarin at all but to Miao or languages Theodore didn't
know. He was very friendly and easy to talk to.

"How do you know the country so well?" asked Theodore.
"Were you born there?"

"No indeed. From the monastery wall I could show you
the house where I was born, on the far side of the valley. But
my father kept a team of yaks and used to trade into China,
and he brought me up to that life. I would be at it still if I
hadn't been chosen to become the oracle."

"The oracle?"

Theodore had guessed that he was talking to the oracle-
priest, but had assumed that his function was to perform some
special sort of mumbo-jumbo with an idol. There was something shocking about this bluff, earthy man's casual announcement that he himself was that idol.

"Yes indeed," he said. "That's me. You wouldn't think at
it to look at me, would you? And I'll tell you another thing
that might surprise you—it's a lot harder work than driving
yaks."

Mrs Jones was in a bad temper that evening, and took it out
on Lung. Theodore had heard a little thunderstorm grumbling
away below the monastery during the afternoon, but hadn't
realised that Mrs Jones had been lower down still. Her escort,
none of whom spoke any language she knew, had insisted on
keeping to well-worn paths and on coming home the moment
the first drops fell.

Lung endured her malice very well and teased her gravely
in return. They were both very interested in Theodore's
meeting with Major Price-Evans.

"He might give us a hand," said Mrs Jones. "It ain't as surprising as you might think, finding him here. Lot of sappers go bats in the belfry. Ask him to tea, Theo, and I'll see if I can't wheedle him."

Lung refused to say anything about his own adventures during the day. He looked smug and knowing, but Theodore guessed that this was only a way of teasing Mrs Jones and concealing the fact that he had achieved nothing at all.

Chapter 12

The visit from Major Price-Evans was not a success. He came eagerly enough; Theodore met him at the door of the temple of the oracle and led him down to the guest-house. As they passed through the main gate of the monastery he said, "Last time I set foot outside Dong Pe, why, it must have been sixteen years ago." He sounded like a child being taken on a long-promised outing, but as soon as he was introduced to Mrs Jones his manner began to change. Though Theodore had told her the Major was blind she had made herself up with extra care and was wearing the lacy pink blouse and red skirt she had used to impress P'iu-Chun. Her manner was more formal than usual, and she spoke all the time in what she called her drawing-room voice, level and grave and a little throaty. Theodore was amazed. He had heard her acting this part for a sentence or two, but he had no idea that she would be able to corset her extravagant personality so easily into this constrained and tasteful style. The thought struck him that supposing her story had taken a different path and she had married the man she called Monty, this would have been her normal appearance, and the woman he knew as Mrs Jones would only have been allowed to erupt at odd and secret moments.

Her conversation was exactly right too, Theodore thought. She seemed to know India quite well, and claimed to have travelled along several of the roads the Major had helped to build; and she had been to Ceylon and most of the other countries he had visited on his pilgrimages. She talked about these, asked questions, very gently tried to draw him out. But for all her care he seemed to retreat further and further into his shell, and to shrink his slight body into the folds of his russet robe. His answers, which had begun as the rambling untroubled flow that Theodore had heard on their first meeting, became shorter but even less coherent, and he began to have trouble with his breathing, wheezing heavily in the silences until it seemed an agony to draw each breath.

This gasping eased quickly as Theodore led him back up the hill, and he was perfectly happy and cheerful by the time he reached his cell.

"Well, that weren't much cop," said Mrs Jones when Theodore got back to the guest-house. "Shy as a schoolboy, poor feller. You'll have to try and handle him, Theo—but don't ask him for help till he's got over the shock of meeting me."

Next day the Major never mentioned Mrs Jones and seemed to have forgotten the incident. Theodore had already evolved a routine for his visits: the Major would be waiting for him at the wicket—on the third day even in one of the rare thunderstorms which rose high enough along the mountain wall to drench the monastery; then they would have tea and talk; then clean the Temple; when the oracle-priest came Theodore would gossip briefly with him; and when he left they would retire to the Major's cell for a lesson in Tibetan.

Provided the Major was there Theodore enjoyed the cleaning and found it helped him master his horror of the convoluted heathen mysteries which the idol symbolised for him. It was a thoroughly mundane process, picking loose fluff out of a demon's snarl; the grimace lost all its meaning and became only

an awkward pattern of crannies which let Theodore think more
about the sculptor's stupidity in producing such a shape than
about the myth he had tried to embody. In a quite different way
the Major helped make the monsters ordinary. The old man
accepted them, as he accepted everything, with the same
innocent delight. He accepted the meaning behind the grimace,
but seemed to drain the nightmare into himself and remove
its terrors in the process, so much so that Theodore found
himself beginning to think that anything the Major believed in
or approved of must have something to be said for it. He knew
this was a dangerous idea, but he couldn't help it.

Only once did something happen which broke this pattern.
Theodore had his ladder up against the idol of the Buddha and
was using a soft brush to dust among the crannies of an intricate
jewelled shoulder-piece when it struck him what a contrast
this was with the almost appalling smoothness of the face. He
paused and looked up. This particular statue had the eyes closed
in contemplation, but from where he was standing on the
ladder Theodore could see that the lids were not completely
shut, and that through the slit between them and the gold
underlid Someone might be watching him.

As if to prove that the face was nothing but gold and stone,
Theodore climbed the last two rungs and deliberately scuffed
the dust from its smile. He had been going to rootle with his
brush into the inch-wide nostrils, but suddenly he felt ashamed
and returned to the jewelled shoulder-piece. The gesture
seemed to have worked, and the idol was inanimate once more.

Conversation with the oracle-priest was untroubled.

"Don't tell him nothing," Mrs Jones had said. "He only
wants to use it for his oracling. My Auntie Rosa, she was a

fortune-teller at all the fair-grounds, so I know the tricks. She said that all you got to tell a feller is one true thing about him which he doesn't think you could of known, and he'll believe everything else, no matter what."

In fact the oracle-priest seemed as happy to answer questions as to ask them. The Lama Tojing Rimpoche had chosen him— "recognised him" was what he said—as the new Dong Pe oracle soon after the old one had died. One day he and his father and his brother and his uncle had been leading a train of yaks across the Stone Lake when they had found the Lama Tojing, all alone, waiting for them on the near shore. The Lama Tojing had simply beckoned him out from among the other three. He hadn't wanted the job, but he'd been chosen, hadn't he? There was no escape from that. Next he'd been sent on a four-year training course in Lhasa, and by the time he'd come back to Dong Pe the Lama Tojing had vanished. No, he'd no theories about where he'd got to—of course the other Lamas had kept asking him when he was performing his duties as oracle, but apparently he'd never given answers that anybody could understand. Of course he didn't remember any of that himself—he was only telling Theodore what the others had told him afterwards.

"It must have been very difficult getting trains of yaks across the Stone Lake," said Theodore.

"Not as bad then as it is now. Since Lama Tojing vanished the Guardians have got a lot worse, throwing the stones about and that. We used to be able to keep the causeway in much better shape—the Guardians seem to know we haven't got a Siddha here, and they do what they like."

The Tibetan lessons seemed to go off the rails almost at once.

Major Price-Evans had learnt the language mainly in order to understand the prayers and chants of worship, and the sacred books stored in the temple. It was difficult for him to remember that there might be any other reason for learning the language. His Buddhism was just as intense as Father's Christianity, but in a quite different manner; Father had been, so to speak, an athlete of faith, funnelling all his energies into his worship, consciously driving himself on to further attainments and endurances; the Major seemed to make no effort at all—he was like some natural creature, it might be a grass-hopper, which can flick itself across a space a hundred times its own length because that is what it was made to do. So he tried to teach Theodore by chants and ritual, which Theodore's mind refused to accept, even when his tongue mouthed the incomprehensible syllables. Learning went slowly.

Theodore did learn, though. On about the fourth morning he was able to give an adequate greeting to a group of women who had dragged a communal loom out into a courtyard and were weaving a patterned piece of cloth too long and narrow for a blanket, too fine for a rug. They laughed as they answered him and tried to explain what the cloth was for, but he understood very little of their quick chatter. He got the impression that they knew who he was and why he was there, and were excited but a little wary of him, as though he might bring ill luck on them if he said or did the wrong thing.

In the afternoons Theodore would have a drawing-lesson from Mrs Jones, and then help her clear and prepare the patch of earth she was planning to use as a garden for her finds—or at least pretending to plan. "Nothing like a bit of garden to make it look like you're meaning to stay," she said. On days when her expeditions took her further afield Theodore would draw for a while, and then wander by himself through the steep, many-tracked wood below the monastery, with its pockets of clustered shrines and groves of prayer-flags.

Sometimes Lung joined Mrs Jones on her expeditions—she had her escort thoroughly tame by now, of course, so that they did what she said without question—but often he spent the day in the monastery, where the Lama Tomdzay had introduced him to the Librarian. Most of the sacred books were kept in one of the two temples, but the monastery over the years had amassed a weird collection of other volumes; one evening Lung produced a collection of Latin sermons, printed in Madrid in 1743—heaven knows how it had wandered, almost like Major Price-Evans, to this last nook. Theodore, who to Lung's disappointment knew no Latin, feigned interest but took it back to the Library next day, and found Lung there sitting with a middle-aged Lama, drinking tea Chinese-fashion, and discussing the exact meaning of an ancient Chinese Buddhist hymn with a scholarly absorption that seemed to show he'd completely forgotten why he was supposed to be there.

On the seventh evening of their stay Tomdzay came to the guest-house in the dusk and told them that the stars were propitious for the oracle ceremony to be held next morning, and that the Lama Amchi had finished his period of contemplation and would appear. The three foreign guests were expected to be present.

"I'm not going," said Theodore in English.

"Oh, I think you better," said Mrs Jones.

"I will not attend a ceremony in a heathen temple."

Theodore would have liked the words to come out with

heroic firmness but all he achieved was a feeble mutter. The Lama Tomdzay looked at him enquiringly. Lung translated what Theodore had said into Mandarin, toning down its bluntness with polite twirls.

"The ceremony will not be held in the temple," said the Lama Tomdzay.

"That makes no difference. I'm not going," said Theodore, still speaking English and leaving Lung to translate. The Lama Tomdzay stood for a moment, nodding his head gently, then took Lung by the elbow and led him to the door, where they spoke for a while in low voices. Lung came back looking embarrassed.

"Tomdzay say this," he said in English. "If Theo not come gladly to oracle ceremony, then monks bind him and carry him to temple."

"No!" said Mrs Jones. "I won't have it! If they're going to do that to Theo, they'll have to do it to me as well!"

"I say this," said Lung. "I tell him Missy fight for Theo. He say monks bind and carry Missy also."

"Let 'em," said Mrs Jones grimly.

"No," said Theodore. "I'll come."

Lung looked immensely relieved, but Mrs Jones shook her head.

"It's all right," said Theodore. "They can't touch me."

"Course they can't," said Mrs Jones with one of her sudden, marvellous smiles. "Only it just shows how far they're ready to go, don't it?"

Next morning she appeared from behind her screen wearing a long black dress, padded at the hips, narrow at the waist, with a double row of pearl buttons running up the curve of her bosom to her high lace collar. She took half an hour to coax her hair into a tall structure of curling swags, and grumbled about her hat, a little black nonsense which she pinned to the front of the hair-pile so that its two bright blue feathers curved up over the top and its fine veil just covered her eyes.

"If only I hadn't left that other hat-box behind," she said, "where that first lot of beggars had a go at us. I had a lovely hat in there, just the job for getting me fortune told in church."

Theodore thought she looked extremely striking, and he could sense Lung almost shivering with pleasure at the sight of her—indeed, the dress had about it a hint of military uniform, with its stiffness and formality disciplining her bouncy curves. She had painted her face several layers thick and her eyes flashed with excitement behind the veil.

When the Lama Tomdzay led them out of the guest-house Theodore saw that the paths of the mountainside were covered with little processions, as if the whole valley was emptying itself up into the monastery. A crowd jostled at the main gate, but Tomdzay headed further west to a narrow dark door which Theodore had always seen closed before now. Inside it they climbed a steep stair to the series of open galleries which linked the upper storeys of the courtyards; below them the crowd moved and bustled at random, and even up in these apparently private areas they came on several groups of gossiping peasants, usually with a monk or two among them. Once they picked their way through a full-blown family meal with children scampering round while adults sucked noisily at the reeking tea.

"A big ceremony is also a time for visiting," explained Tomdzay. "Every family has a son or two in the monastery."

Again, despite all the strangeness, Theodore felt a powerful sense of familiarity, of a community all of whose activities centred round the main business of worship, as they had at the Settlement. Here belief was not a frill or decoration on the structure of life, not something that happened on Sundays as a change from everyday affairs, but something that happened all the time, so that it too was everyday. He felt an urge to linger, to lean on a railing and watch the steady gathering, but Tomdzay led them briskly on till they reached the long gallery which ran down the eastern side of the central courtyard.

"Here we will wait," he said.

"Hi! Look at the orchestra!" said Mrs Jones, craning over the railing.

Below them, on the steps of the temple of the oracle, a throne had been placed. In front of it was a table, or portable altar, bearing several swords, a mace, and two objects like fire-irons, all ornately jewelled. In front of the altar, below the steps, two chairs faced each other, the nearer one quite plain and the further much larger with an immensely high back carved to represent the sacred wheel. Now a group of monks was filing in and parting to stand behind the chairs. In addition to the normal russet robes, they wore hats, or rather helmets, of gold with immensely exaggerated crests, like coxcombs. They carried various instruments, the most impressive of which were a pair of twelve-foot horns, quite straight but widening to a bell which one monk supported on his shoulder while the monk who was going to blow the instrument followed four yards behind, carrying the mouth-piece end. Others bore smaller horns, and flute-like pipes, others gongs and bells, and others strange twisted objects which it was hard to imagine producing any sound at all.

More monks followed, massing in rows facing the temple

steps but split by an aisle down the middle, so that now the steps and the space with the two chairs in it was surrounded on three sides by a russet phalanx. Beyond this more people came crowding in to the courtyard, peasants and monks mingling in a much less organised fashion, like spectators at a fair. The Lama Tomdzay, as if he had received a signal, gave a little nod and led the way along the gallery, walking behind a double row of monks who were now lining the rail. At the far end he turned down a steep and narrow stair and brought them out at the back of the courtyard, near the steps of the other temple. Here his pace slowed, and the four of them began to move with a drifting motion, first along a path that had been kept open by the crowd near the courtyard wall, and then down the central aisle towards the altar. As they passed they seemed to create a moving patch of silence among the muttering bustle.

"Like getting married," whispered Mrs Jones. "Here comes the bride."

At last they reached the space in front of the altar where the two chairs faced each other, and at a sign from Tomdzay Mrs Jones settled onto the smaller one. Lung and Theodore stood behind her. There was a longish pause. The line of prayer-wheels tinkled monotonously. The crowd stirred and muttered until, at no noticeable signal, a noise began, a heavy, continuous groan at so deep a pitch that each vibration was a separate pulse. Theodore saw the monk at the back of the vast horn opposite blowing fat-cheeked into the mouthpiece, but when at last he drew breath the sound continued, rumbling on from the horn behind Theodore, rising in volume like a slowed wave; as it began to dwindle the first monk put his lips to the mouthpiece again and started to blow, creating another wave. It was impossible to imagine a deeper note that would be a sound at all.

When a bass drum began to thud, its boom seemed light by comparison. Now cymbals clinked and flutes twittered. There was no tune, but the noise was not formless, because the underlying vibrations from the big horns held it together, as if the other sounds were building themselves out of that groundswell and dying back into it. Theodore thought it was somehow like the noise you hear when you hold a sea-shell to your ear, but enormously louder and richer, the hum not just of the distant ocean but of the whole universe, purring along its unimaginable nerve-lines.

At the peak of the music a monk danced out of the temple swinging a brass bowl on a chain. Pale blue smoke poured up from the bowl, swirling into wreaths as the monk pranced and postured round the altar, but before he had finished his dance Theodore was aware of the focus of the crowd's attention shifting towards the back of the courtyard. The music throbbed into silence. The dancer disappeared through the temple doors, but at the same time two other monks appeared carrying a long, pale robe and a tall forward-curling hat. As they came round the altar to the steps the Lama Amchi glided out from the aisle between the massed monks. He let one of the men put the robe round his shoulders, then walked up the steps, round the altar and up to the temple doors, where he stood for twenty seconds with his hands above his head, palms together. Slowly he knelt, bowing to the invisible idol until his forehead touched the stone.

A monk began to chant in a bass monotone which echoed the wave-pattern of the now hushed horns. Bells clinked. The massed choir of monks in the courtyard answered with a booming swell of voices, and as that sound died the monks lining the gallery took up the chant. The pattern of solo, bells, response and echo continued while the Lama Amchi rose and disappeared into the temple, then reappeared, had his tall hat placed on his head, and settled into the chair opposite Mrs Jones.

Now the huge horns started their droning and the other instruments joined in, working up to a surge of sound at whose climax four soldier-monks carried a man out of the temple and placed him on the central throne.

If Theodore hadn't been expecting to see the oracle-priest he wouldn't have recognised him. He was wearing a gold helmet rising to three spikes, a breast-plate covered with jewels and ornate fretwork, under the breast-plate a heavy brocade jacket reaching to his knees and with full long sleeves, and boots of orange leather, very massive, with enormous soles. He lolled on the throne, inert, eyes closed, like a clumsily manufactured doll.

When the roaring of the horns ceased the choir-leader began another chant, interrupted as before by bells and responses. At the clink of the second lot of bells the oracle's eyes opened and for a moment he was the man Theodore knew, staring around but not seeming to see anything. The muscles of his face bunched into a grimace, making him unrecognisable again. He sat quite still, staring pop-eyed over the heads of the congregation, while the rhythm of the chant increased and horns and drums and cymbals joined their sounds. Slowly he began to quiver, as if he too was an instrument vibrating to the beat of the universe. Shaking more and more violently, but with his massive boots rooted to the stone, he rose to a standing position. The soldier-monks who had carried him out moved forward to hold him by the arms and prevent him from falling, and an old monk hobbled out from behind the Lama Amchi's chair and started to wave what looked like a folded sheet of paper in

front of the oracle's face. The noise increased. People all over
the courtyard were shouting, even screaming. The group
round the throne convulsed. The oracle seemed to toss aside
the four men who were holding him so fiercely that one of
them fell flat on his back with a thud which Theodore could
hear through the uproar. He dashed towards the altar, snatched
up a sword and stood there, his face dark purple and snarling,
like the rabid ape that had once attacked the Settlement and
bitten two people before Father had shot it. Now he darted
from the altar, swinging the sword in both hands, slashing with
definite aim as if at targets only he could see. The boots and the
clothes bulked him out, but even allowing for them he seemed
to have grown both taller and broader than the calm and
unremarkable man who had chatted with Theodore about the
tracks into China.

All the while the uproar in the courtyard rose. The screams
of the people steadied to a shrill and wavering wail which wove
through the unvarying chant of the monks and the boom of the
big horns, rattles and thunders from the drums, the clink and
clank of bells and other hoots and twitterings. Theodore discovered his throat was sore because he was yelling with the rest.
He clamped his mouth shut and shook his head in violent
refusal, breaking the hypnotic tendrils that had begun to bind
him into the ceremony.

Thus freed he could see that the soldier-monks were advanc-
ing on the oracle-priest in a wrestler's crouch, ducking under
the whirling blade, scuttling away crabwise when a darting
lunge came their way. The priest charged suddenly down the
steps, causing one of the retreating soldier-monks to stumble
against the Lama Amchi where he sat impassive on his throne,
but the other two seized their moment and leaped like tigers at

the priest's back and clung there, each gripping an arm. The sword clanged to the stone. The priest spun round. One of the men lost his grip and was hurled against the steps, but at the same time the first two closed in. In a series of convulsions they forced the priest up the steps, round the altar and back to his throne where they held him, one at each arm, one at his legs, and one using both hands to clamp the priest's head to the back of the throne. The spasms that shook his body dwindled. The purple flush left his face, fading like a healing bruise through vivid yellow to chalky grey. Theodore realised that the shouting had ceased some time back, and the chant and the music were now softening towards silence.

The old monk who had waved the paper came hobbling up the steps again, this time carrying what looked like a writing-slate with a jewelled frame. He stood beside the throne and bent his body forward so that his ear was close against the priest's mouth. In total silence and steadily increasing tension the whole courtyard waited until the monk with the slate nodded his head a couple of times and started to write; then a low sigh of release breathed into the mountain air. Theodore couldn't see whether the priest's lips were in fact moving because the old monk's head screened them. Less than a couple of lines had been written when the monk straightened, backed away, bowed and returned to his place. A murmur of comment rippled round among the watchers and then the horns began their boom and the chant of invocation rose once more.

Incredibly the ritual repeated itself six times in all. Six times the chants began the pattern, and the people shouted, and the priest convulsed on his throne, threw off his attendants, seized a weapon from the altar, fought with invisible powers and was wrestled back to his throne. Theodore kept his mouth shut now, but he noticed Lung beside him yelling like a demon. He couldn't see more than the side of Mrs Jones's face, but she sat as still as the Lama Amchi and seemed to be smiling slightly, as though she was watching a play. The fights were not always the same. The next four times the priest stayed at the top of the steps, and once climbed onto the altar and made his fiercest lunges upward, as if battling with a giant; but there were enough repeated elements—particular strokes and charges by the priest and feints and scuttlings by the attendants—for Theodore to tell himself that the whole ritual had been re-hearsed, and that was why nobody was really hurt. On the other hand there was no doubting the appalling effort that went into each fight. Even the spasms that shook the priest when he was sitting on his throne seemed as much as a man could endure just once, let alone six times.

Sometimes the monk with the slate wrote only a word or two, and once several lines.

When the sixth episode began Theodore knew it must be the last because there was only one weapon left on the altar, a stubby mace whose shaft twinkled with crusted jewels but whose head was a plain ball of spiked iron. This time, when the noise in the courtyard seemed enough to shake fresh avalanches from the mountains the priest came staggering round the altar and down the steps. The attendant in front of him ducked clear and he rushed straight at Mrs Jones, whirling up his mace as he came. She rose, calmly, as if to greet or confront him. He seemed to see her, a visible enemy for the first time, and halted with the mace poised two-handed above his head. She stood her ground, gazing up into his contorted face. The noise in the nearer part of the courtyard had snapped short at his rush, but there was still some shouting in the distance from people who couldn't see what was happening. Theodore stood terrified as the mace hung there, but couldn't move a muscle to help her. He heard a grunt and a threshing noise beside him and was aware of Lung struggling in the arms of two large monks. The priest gave a long, rattling groan as though something other than air was being forced or torn from his lungs. The mace fell with a clatter to the paving. He swayed, shrank, tottered. The attendants caught him as he collapsed and carried him back to the throne.

During the business with the slate, Mrs Jones stood quite still. Any flush was hidden under the layers of make-up, but Theodore could sense the excitement that throbbed through her. As the old monk came hobbling back to his place by the Lama Amchi's chair the attendants picked the priest up, throne and all, and carried him back into the temple. The music began again, and then the chanting—solo, bells, responses—without any of the untamed yelling that had accompanied the performance by the oracle priest. Mrs Jones turned and spoke to Lung, who smiled and hung his head. She patted his hand and made motions to the two monks still holding him to let him go.

"Dead brave he was, wasn't he?" she whispered to Theodore. "Stone me if I could of moved a finger . . . Hi, look at old Amchi rigging the vote!"

Theodore followed her glance and saw the group round the Lama Amchi's chair—the monk with the slate and two other dignified old men—poring over the slate itself. The Lama Amchi was running a thin finger down the written lines, pausing here and there and tapping, as if to emphasise a point.

Theodore found he was shivering. Just as the throb of the big horns had seemed to set up the vibrations of the other instruments, so Theodore's shudders felt like an echo of the violent

convulsions that had shaken the priest. He tried to force his
muscles still, but it was no use. He knew that he had not merely
witnessed a pagan ceremony from the outside. He had taken
part—he had *been* part of it. He had accepted the powers which
had occupied the body of the priest. He stood, shivering,
shaking his head, aware that Mrs Jones was watching him, until
the group round the Lama Amchi's throne broke up.

The monk with the slate moved up the steps. The Lama
Amchi rose to his feet. The other two disappeared among the
chanting ranks. The music swelled to a climax, then faded to a
single voice, each monotone phrase followed by a thick drum-
beat. Soon those sounds stopped too and the priest with the
slate raised his arms for silence.

At first he chanted his words, like any priest following a
known formula, but after a minute his voice changed to something nearer speech and as it did so the reaction of his audience
also changed. Now he was telling them something they had not
heard before, and they were listening with taut attention.
Between each phrase he paused to let the twanging syllables
echo off the further walls. First he would read from the slate,
then look up and speak at greater length, as if expounding the
meaning of what he had read, and then he would slip back for a
sentence or two into the tone of prayer, and be answered by a
short response from the monks. Theodore, calmer now, guessed
that this would happen six times, and then Tomdzay or somebody would perhaps tell him what it all meant. He was quite
unprepared for what happened as the final phrase ended.

The horns were still booming when the nearest monks broke
from their ranks and rushed toward him. Theodore was
dragged aside and almost fell among the crush of bodies. He
heard Lung shouting angrily, some yards away. He stumbled

backwards against something hard, the lowest of the temple steps, and scrambled up clear of the crowd. Once there he turned and looked out over the heads of the struggling mob.

Below him the monks were crowding to a focus like bees at swarm-time clustering round their queen. At the thickest centre of the mass a slow eruption began, an upwelling of arms with a dark object half-hidden among them. Jerkily it took shape as it separated itself from the jostle of russet robes and became a black, high-backed chair with carrying-poles at either side. The monks, a dozen to each pole, were holding it not shoulder-high but at arm's length above their heads. At first its back was towards Theodore, but then it swung sideways like a boat at tide-change as the monks began to carry it through the press, and he could see Mrs Jones sitting up there, smoothing her skirt down with one hand and with the other tucking a loose whorl of hair back into place under the silly little hat. A low, baying hum rose all round the courtyard.

The crowd was too thick-packed for the monks to carry her through, so they passed her from hand to hand above their heads. The arms rose round her chair like waving wheat to take the load, or to touch chair or skirt, or simply to stretch towards her. Her face was stiff and calm, her back straight as a soldier's. She came quite close to Theodore at the beginning of the wide sweep she was to move in, and even through her veil he imagined he could see the electric energies flashing from those huge eyes. The hand on her lap moved as if to begin a gesture, then stilled, so he guessed she had seen him, but she didn't smile. They had that chair ready, he thought. They knew it was going to happen. They knew what the oracle would say.

As the crowd jostled to follow her the crush below the steps eased and Lung came panting up to stand beside Theodore. He looked pale, drained, furious. For a while he stared at the retreating chair where it bobbed and wallowed above the threshing arms, then he sighed and struck his fist into his palm.

"She thinks there is nothing in the world that can out-face her," he muttered. "She does not understand what she has met today."

Chapter 13

At once the routine of days changed.

Theodore had intended to visit Major Price-Evans immediately after the ceremony, to find out what it all meant and how it affected him and his friends; but he was too shaken to resist Lung's demand that they should return to the guest-house, so now he was kneeling on the floor and pumping the primus stove, while Lung sat withdrawn and brooding on his cot. In theory Theodore was getting ready to welcome Mrs Jones after her adventure, but really he was trying to restore his own centre of balance by contact with things he knew, by handling a western gadget and making tea the way Mrs Jones liked it. He had just got the flame to roar and steady when Tomdzay came striding through the door with no warning at all. He beckoned to Theodore.

"Come," he said. "You are needed."

"Where is Mrs Jones?" said Lung and Theodore together.

"The Mother of the Tulku is in the house of the Lama Amchi Geshe Rimpoche. It is there that we go."

As Lung took a pace towards the door Tomdzay barred his way.

"Only the Guide is needed," he said. "The much-honoured Father of the Tulku may stay here."

He made a slight movement, not enough to let Lung pass but enough to make sure he could see the three soldier-monks waiting beyond the door. Lung took a half-pace towards them, hesitated and turned.

"Not permit Missy think she strongest," he muttered in English.

Theodore smiled bleakly at him and followed Tomdzay out of the door.

This time they entered through the main gate of the monastery. The crowd was still streaming out, but whatever the crush they jostled aside to let Tomdzay pass; it took Theodore a little while to realise that their eyes were turned not on Tomdzay but on him. He was used to being stared at on his wanderings through the monastery, by eyes inquisitive but wary, but these stares were different, open and respectful—they might have stared at one of their idols in much the same way.

When the little procession he was now part of reached the main courtyard there were still plenty of people about, who behaved as though they had been waiting to see him, not pushing close as they had round Mrs Jones but forming a wide clear path between two packed lines of watchers. Tomdzay led the way down the centre of this space to the flights of stairs that zig-zagged up the rock towards the two houses that stood there. One of these, Major Price-Evans had said, belonged to the Lama Amchi and the other was kept in permanent readiness for the return of the Lama Tojing or the arrival of his successor.

The escorting monks stopped at the bottom of the stair, but Tomdzay led the way up to the door of the left-hand house where he paused and whispered a brief prayer or incantation, then held the door open for Theodore.

"Enter," he said in a low voice. "Be reverent."

Automatically Theodore returned his solemn bow and crossed the threshold. As the door closed behind him his immediate impression was of yet another temple, not of stone but of wood, all polished to gleam in the near dark, and cluttered with jewelled idols and ornaments, and hung with garish cloths. Butter lamps glowed in front of some of the idols and the still air prickled with incense, but not so heavily as it did in the temple—the smell was thinner, or perhaps finer.

"Coo-ee, Theo," called Mrs Jones's voice. "We're up here. Come and look. I never seen such a view."

Theodore followed the sound up a flight of stairs, polished till they were as slippery as an ice-fall. At the top was a little vestibule, beyond which he found a large airy room which ran all across the front of the house with its windows looking out over the monastery roofs to the tremendous range beyond. This room too glistened with polish and twinkled with knick-knacks and idols.

In the many hours he was to spend there with Mrs Jones and the Lama Amchi, Theodore never became used to the nudging presences of the idols, whispering in his mind, *You have felt us. You have known our power. We are real.* He could look at a particular statue and perceive that it was mere stone, lacquered and gilded; its staring eyes had no mind behind them, its expression was whatever the sculptor had thought proper to carve there; that was all it consisted of. But out of his direct line of vision the idols were never quite empty; behind each half-seen mask a power brooded. Most of the Lama Amchi's statutes were of the Buddha, and so were the innumerable pictures in the hangings and paintings. All these seemed to express a strange multiple being; it was as though Theodore was being watched by an eye, many-faceted like an insect's, but turned not outward but inward, inspecting through all those facets the object—Theodore—at its centre. Furthermore the silver or brass bowls and the butter lamps and the bright-patterned rugs and cushions and the hundreds of other garish or glittering objects, each with its own meaning and use and all bright with jewels and gold, served to increase the feeling of light refracted and splintered so that the eye could watch not only from all possible angles but in all possible hues. Sometimes Theodore could close a facet off, as if drawing a blind across a window. He might learn, for instance, the symbolism of an object or the myth behind a particular pose of the Buddha, and by refusing to accept them he could rob a presence of some of its power; but it would still be there, and much as he longed to he was never able to deny the whole vast system of beliefs and myths and symbols. Even if he had had the knowledge and intelligence to understand it all—and there was so much of it, so sharp and intricate in detail, so vague and ungraspable in outline—Theodore knew he would not have been able to argue it out of existence. You needed more than understanding for that. You needed a sort of spiritual energy, a soul-force, such as Father had possessed. The Lama Amchi possessed it too, and so did Mrs Jones, but not Theodore.

He found Mrs Jones sitting on a wide, low stool with her back to the windows; she was still wearing her hat and veil and had managed to rearrange her hair and dress after the wild ride through the courtyard below. The Lama Amchi sat facing her on a great throne-like chair of black wood with sides as tall as its back and a rainbow-coloured canopy above. The back of the chair was deeply carved with the sacred wheel, whose spokes and rim framed the Lama's head like a dark halo. He sat cross-legged on the plain wood seat, a pose which made him look like a toy neatly folded into its box. Later Theodore learnt that whenever he was not occupied with some other duty he spent all his time in this position on this chair, and slept in it too.

The Lama greeted Theodore with a face that seemed to smile, though his lips did not move, and pointed to a smaller stool beside Mrs Jones's. Unlike the great wheel-throne, this was comfortably padded, a point which Theodore hardly noticed at the time but became increasingly grateful for as the weeks went by. They sat in silence for some time, the Lama gazing into distance beyond the mountain-tops, and Mrs Jones staring at him as though she were about to paint his portrait. Theodore glanced uneasily from one to the other wishing that Mrs Jones would say something in English so that he could begin to tell her of his determination not to be tricked any further into the maze of heathen fantasies.

"How weak is the intellect of man," said the Lama suddenly. "When I met you in the pass I was given sure signs that my search had ended, but I was blind to a full half of them, or saw them in a mistaken light. Because I thought at first that you, child, might be the Tulku, I believed that your companion, the Chinese, must be the guide of whom the oracle spoke. And though I soon discovered that the Tulku is yet to be born, I was too blinded by my first perceptions to see that it is you who are the guide. It is you who are to guide the Mother of the Tulku to me."

"I don't understand," said Theodore. "Mrs Jones is here."

"Not all journeys are across space. Two consciousnesses may be far apart in the dimensions of earth and yet side by side in the dimensions of the spirit; two bodies may share one room, while their consciousnesses are separated as if by many mountain ranges. Now say this to the Mother of the Tulku. I will

speak slowly and pause often, so that you may make my meaning sure. The oracle confirms that she bears a child, and that he
will be the Tulku of the Siddha Asara, who in his last incarnation wore the body of Tojing Rimpoche. That much is certain,
though the Ones who speak through the oracle use shadowy
language. The oracle also repeated the signs that were to assure
us that we had found the Tulku, and when it confronted the
Mother of the Tulku it recognised the presence of Asara and
shrank before him. It warned, too, in dark language, of dangers
and betrayals to come—these will become clear as the wheel
turns. And it gave us a further sign, which is not for us but for
the Mother of the Tulku, that she may know whose body she
bears. We interpret certain words as meaning that the Siddha
Asara willed the death of the body of Tojing Rimpoche at a
propitious moment, only a moon and a half gone by, and chose
for his new incarnation a child that was newly conceived at the
foot of a pillar beneath a foreign shrine. Was it so?"

Theodore stared at the Lama, felt his face go red and half-
opened his mouth to say that he couldn't ask Mrs Jones a
question like that.

"You are the guide," said the Lama gently. "You are, as it
were, the bridge between us. We travel to and fro upon you,
but our coming and going does not change you by a pebble or
a grass-blade."

Theodore turned his protest into a cough, and translated.
Mrs Jones gave one of her throaty little chuckles.

"Wonder how he knew that," she said. "I s'pose it might
be right. I mean, that's the first place it could of happened,
ain't it?"

"Where?"

"Oh, don't you remember, that great lump of rock with the

cave in it, where I told you my life history. That was a pillar, sort of, and it had a shrine at the top, too."

Theodore explained in Mandarin. The Lama nodded.

"You see?" he said. "The oracle gives clear assurance to the Mother of the Tulku, so that she may know that all we ask of her is rightly asked."

"Tell him to come off it," said Mrs Jones. "No, I s'pose you better not. Just like my Auntie Rosa said, ain't it? They tell you one true thing and expect you to swallow the rest because of it. Still, I wonder how he knew."

"I talked to the oracle-priest about the way we came," said Theodore. "I think I said we camped by that pillar. Of course I didn't say anything about . . . about . . ."

"Lucky guess, then," said Mrs Jones. "Perhaps old Lung's been boasting a bit too. You'll have to be careful what you say to His Reverence, Theo. We got to make him think we're proper impressed."

There was a long pause, during which Theodore became aware of something else in the room beside the three of them and the vague presence of the idols—a very faint, half-regular wheezing, whose source he couldn't identify. He was too occupied with the struggle to translate to pay much attention to it, but decided there was probably a large dog asleep behind one of the several screens, snorting and wheezing through its dreams.

"Thus it is yet more certain," said the Lama suddenly. "Now comes our task to prepare, that the Tulku may be born in an appropriate manner. It has happened sometimes that the Dalai Lama himself has been born in the hut of a serf, just as an offering at a shrine may if necessary be made from a common butter-bowl. But where we have choice we use more seemly implements, and thus it seems proper to us that the Mother of the Tulku should have knowledge of our faith, that she may compose herself into harmony for the birth of the Tulku."

"Oh Lor'," said Mrs Jones.

There was no need to translate the muttered moan. The Lama smiled at her with innocent sweet charm.

"I must explain that this is the reversal of normal procedure," he said. "Normally a person who wishes to learn how to set his footsteps in the Way of Enlightenment will seek out a teacher, whom we call a *guru*, and ask him to accept the applicant as a student, whom we call a *chela*. The *guru* will consider the applicant's worthiness, and set him harsh tasks to test his faith, and only then perhaps accept him. Now it is I, the *guru*, who am asking you, the *chela*, to accept me as your instructor. All instruction will be useless unless you are willing. If you refuse you will be in no way punished, but will be honoured through-out Dong Pe as the Mother of the Tulku, and when the child is weaned and able to leave you you will be rewarded with gold."

"Gold!" said Mrs Jones. "What does he think I am?"

"But hear me," said the Lama, speaking ever more slowly. "All the gold we can give you—and Dong Pe is famous for its wealth—is nothing beside the riches of instruction. You have a great soul. It has passed, perhaps, through the bodies of many princes who have fought great wars and given laws to empires. But for all their power and fame they were lashed fast to this world of things, which is not the soul's true home, but is all illusion and folly. You cannot remember these past existences, but I perceive that as I speak of them your soul acknowledges their truth. And now the wheel of your being has turned, as it can do only once in many thousand years, turned to the point where you can begin to free yourself from illusion and seek the soul's true home. The child is a Christian, but you have no beliefs."

"I got married in church, of course," said Mrs Jones, "but I can't say as I ever took religion very serious."

"Then you are, so to speak, a blank slate, waiting for the writer's hand. What will he write there? Let it be my hand, and I shall write truths which will set you on the path to enlightenment, to the bliss which is beyond being. Or keep the slate blank and let the wheel turn on, to carry you through countless more existences until perhaps it reaches a point where such a chance comes again."

"Stone me," said Mrs Jones. "I've had some funny offers in my time . . ."

Her last two comments had been flippant, but the tone behind them had been at odds with the words. Theodore, used to her moods now, had sensed the change while the Lama had been speaking. At first she had listened to the talk about *guru* and *chela* with wary politeness, nodding at the end of each phrase to show she had understood; but when the Lama had begun to speak of her supposed past existences—an idea which Theodore thought too absurd to take seriously—her pose had stiffened and her eyes had flashed behind her veil, and each nod had been more decisive than the last, as if she not only understood the nonsense but accepted it. In the silence that followed her muttered comment Theodore heard once more the thin wheezing sound he had noticed earlier.

"Tell him it's a deal," said Mrs Jones suddenly. "Tell him I've always known, since I was a tiny kid, I wasn't here only this time. I couldn't of become me, bang, like that, out of nowhere. There'd got to be something before."

"It is a mighty spirit," said the Lama. "Blind and bound it has yet groped towards the way. Tomorrow we shall hold the ceremony of initiation in which I accept you as my *chela* and you accept me as your *guru*. Till then I must prepare myself with meditation."

He rang a small bell. Mrs Jones rose, smoothing her skirt, and curtseyed. Theodore rose too and contrived a bow which was little more than a stiff nod, but the Lama had his eyes closed. A strange monk came in and stood by the door. Still with his eyes shut the Lama intoned a Tibetan blessing. They left.

The courtyard at the bottom of the stairs was still crowded, but an escort of half-a-dozen monks formed up and led them through. This time the people pressed closer and a strange cooing hum rose and fell. Mrs Jones strolled through the mass as though it was all perfectly normal.

"Notice your pal the Major snuffling away behind that screen?" she said.

"Oh! Yes, I heard . . . I thought it was some sort of dog . . . Why . . ."

"Check on what we was saying in English, of course. See if we was trying to string old Amchi on."

"Do we have to do what he wants?" said Theodore. "Look, the Lama said you could tell him no and it would be all right."

His misery must have sounded in his voice, because Mrs Jones stopped in her tracks and stared at him.

"You poor mite," she whispered. "I never thought . . . You see, I wasn't just having him on. I want to hear a bit more, 'cause nothing anyone's said has ever made sense to me quite like that—and I never even bothered my head about you having to sit through it all . . . I know, tell you what—the Major, poor old beggar, no reason why he shouldn't do it, if he's to be there anyway. Better than sitting snuffling behind that screen. We'll get him to do the interpreting and that will let you off. How about that?"

She spoke softly, almost pleadingly, as though she longed for him to be comforted. There was nothing Theodore could do but smile and nod, but in his heart he knew it wouldn't work. This was something he was doomed to endure.

There was a visitor in the guest-house, a strange monk whom Lung was entertaining to formal Chinese tea. Theodore would have expected Mrs Jones to insist on a proper brew-up after the long morning, but she settled onto her knees and accepted a beaker of the straw-coloured water with a camellia petal floating on it. The monk, a square-faced, sturdy man called Sumpa, made conversation in good Mandarin, asked Mrs Jones about her plant-hunting and suggested areas of the valley that were worth exploring. He stayed a good twenty minutes but mentioned neither the Lama Amchi nor the morning's ceremony with the oracle.

Next morning Major Price-Evans was waiting as usual on the steps between the prayer-wheels, smiling his welcome as Theodore walked across the courtyard.

"Well, me boy, that was a marvellous thing to see, wasn't it?" he said. "All six powers coming into the oracle, one after the other, hey? I've only seen that happen once before—four or five's a very good score in the normal way."

He spoke with the enthusiasm of a sports fan who has witnessed some remarkable performance and wants to re-live the moment with a fellow-spectator.

"Now, come in, come in," he went on, taking Theodore by the arm and almost thrusting him into his tiny cell. "Poor old oracle's going to be a trifle sore this morning, I can tell you—sometimes takes him a week before he can get along without a stick after a show like that. All six powers, hey?"

The cell had changed. There were new hangings on two of the walls, and a stool for Theodore to sit on, covered with a brilliant little rug. A dish of orange cakes stood beside the tea-urn, and the drinking mugs were different, with ornate handles.

"Like that mantra?" said the Major, waving a hand towards the more garish of the new hangings, which showed an elaborate pattern constructed from a few Tibetan letters. "Wish I had my eyes to see it properly—stunning bit of work, hey?"

"It's very striking," said Theodore. "These aren't the usual mugs."

"No, no, me boy. Somebody guessed you might be looking in and sent a few things along. Cakes, too. Nice of them, don't you think?"

It was difficult to show enough enthusiasm for the changes, but Theodore did his best for the old man's sake and not for any mysterious "them". It was a comfort that the Major's manner hadn't altered—if the Buddha himself had materialised in the little room Theodore felt he would have been greeted with the same smile of delight, the same barking questions and cries of "hey?" The cakes were sweet, pungent and slightly warm. Theodore nibbled one and tried to plan a tactful approach, but in the end he blurted his question out.

"Major Price-Evans, couldn't *you* do it?"

"Do what, me boy?"

"The interpreting. The Lama Amchi wants to explain about

enlightenment to Mrs Jones, and because the oracle says I'm the guide, or something, I've got to sit there and turn it all into English for her, and . . . and . . ."

He wanted to say that he loathed not just what he was being asked to do but the whole pagan system of gods and Buddhas. He guessed that the Major would accept such an outburst perfectly calmly, in the way he accepted everything else, but Theodore couldn't bring himself to say it.

"Don't fancy it, hey?" said the Major kindly. "Can't say I blame you. Not the sort of offer I'd have jumped at meself when I was your age. I would now, though. I would now."

"Well, why don't you? You could do it much better than I can, because you understand what the Lama Amchi's talking about."

"Me understand the Lama Amchi! My dear boy, you don't know what you're saying! When I first came here I had a notion he might take me on as a *chela*, but he said it was no go. Disappointment at the time, of course, but now I can see he was right. I'll have to plug on through a lot more existences before I'm up to that level."

Ruefully the Major shook his head.

"But . . ." began Theodore.

"Don't talk about it any more, there's a good chap. Out of the question. You are the Guide, you know."

"No I'm not! I'm a Christian, and I always will be. I'm not going to help with any of these heathen ceremonies! I don't believe in any of it!"

"Don't you?" said the Major, not at all put out, but leaning forward and trying to peer at Theodore with his bulging, nearly sightless eyes. "Used to think a lot of it was nonsense meself, you know, even after I settled in here. But bit by bit I've begun

to see how it all fits in. You wait and see what the Lama
Amchi's got to say."

"Isn't there anyone else in the monastery who speaks
English?" cried Theodore.

"Not so far as I know. Quite a few speak Pali, of course, and
Sanskrit. Lot of Chinese. Mongolian dialects. Couple of fellers
came up from Burma and stayed on—they must speak something . . . But in any case, me boy, it's no go. You *are* the Guide,
you see. A child of a foreign faith, bearing symbols of the lower
creations—that's what the oracle said. I heard him with my
own ears, and it's as plain as the nose on my face that the powers
mean you."

"You didn't hear him," said Theodore. "You heard that
other monk reading out what he said the oracle had said."

"But that is the way it is always done. The powers only speak
in the barest whisper."

"So you never know if the man with the slate is telling the
truth."

"My dear boy," said the Major, still not seeming at all
shocked, "why shouldn't he? They're not fools, these monks.
The Master of Protocol—that's the fellow you saw with the
slate—he's a long way on to enlightenment, almost free from
the illusions of the world. Think what he'd do to all that if he
started perverting the word of the oracle!"

"He might think he was doing the right thing. I mean, he
wants to keep Dong Pe out of the hands of the Chinese, doesn't
he, and that means getting in first before the Chinese produce
somebody they say is their own Tulku. And anyway, people
do do things like that—Christians too, famous ministers, and
bishops, and cardinals, although they know they'd go to hell
for it."

"I dare say. I dare say. There's nowt so queer as folk, as my poor batman used to say—good example meself, some people might think. You'll just have to take my word for it that the Master of Protocol was telling the truth, and we won't talk any more about it. It won't get us anywhere and it will only make you miserable."

"But . . ."

"I think we'll drop the subject. No? Well, I suppose I'll have to show you I mean it. I hadn't meant to tell you this, but I see I must. Now listen. Even if the Lama Amchi himself were to come and beg me to do what you want, I'd turn him down. He might threaten to throw me out of Dong Pe, but I'd still turn him down."

"But why . . ."

"That woman . . . I've been fretting about this, because I didn't care to tell you, but as a matter of fact I'll be glad to get it off my chest. Lama Amchi asked me to go along yesterday morning—never set foot in his house before—sit behind a screen, listen to what you and Mrs Jones were saying. I've told him I won't do it again. Remarkable character, Mrs Jones, don't you consider? Here I am, past seventy and good as blind, and yet . . . I've known quite a few women in my day—nothing like an Indian Army station for hot little intrigues—and yet there was I, tucked in behind that screen, listening to that voice, and she brought it all back—the glances across the dinner table, the squeeze of a foot as you helped some other fellow's wife into the saddle, dusk beneath the deodars . . . Can't have that, you know, just when I'm starting to free meself from the wheel, all those memories coming whistling me back, hey? Not much help to you, me boy. I'm telling you partly to get it off me chest, and partly to show you that there's

no question at all I'm going to do what you ask. I'm sorry,
but there it is."

"I see," said Theodore dully. "Shall we go and clean the
temple?"

"Been round already. All done. Can't have the Guide doing
that sort of work, you know. What would the other monks
think of me?"

"I like cleaning the temple. It's something to do."

"My dear boy . . ."

"I'm going to start over where I left off, and nobody's going
to stop me."

The Major's protests were short and feeble. He liked company while he was doing his chores and was glad to be over-
ruled. Encouraged by this success Theodore determined to
refuse to be present at Mrs Jones's ceremony of initiation as the
Lama Amchi's *chela*, whatever anyone said or threatened.

He was brushing out the intricate crown of a female god
called Tara when the big doors opened and the oracle-priest
came in to perform his morning rituals. His face had a huge
bruise all down one side, and he limped along, supported on
one side by a young monk and on the other by a crutch.

"How do you feel?" asked Theodore, in answer to his
croaked greeting.

"Like a thrashed yak," said the oracle-priest, with a rueful
peasant grin.

Chapter 14

The tussle over the initiation ceremony was nothing like as fierce as Theodore had expected. He told Mrs Jones beforehand, and she pleaded with him with surprising earnestness, then suddenly shrugged and said, "Ah, well. You'll just have to tell old Amchi it's against your religious principles. I'll back you up, if you really feel that way."

The Lama Amchi on the other hand accepted Theodore's decision almost as though he had been aware of it already.

"It is not necessary that the Mother of the Tulku understands the ritual," he said. "It is only necessary that she has faith in it. But tomorrow, when her instruction begins, it will be necessary for you to be present."

"All right," said Theodore reluctantly.

The Lama Amchi was a teacher very like Father in some ways, patient, systematic, stone-certain of his divine right to teach. At the school in the Settlement Theodore had been neither the best pupil nor the worst. At Dong Pe there was only one pupil, Mrs Jones. Theodore was a piece of class-room equipment—a blackboard, so to speak, on which the Lama Amchi wrote for Mrs Jones to read. Theodore deliberately chose this role, rather than become a second pupil in the class. He tried to learn nothing, to let only the surface of his mind become engaged and then to wipe it clean as soon as Mrs Jones had understood what was written there. The job was both tiring and tedious, and though Theodore was perfectly at home in both languages, after about half an hour his mind would go numb, so that he was unable to find the right words for even the simplest phrase. The Lama seemed able to guess when these moments were coming, and would often tell him to rest just as he felt the blankness coming on him. Then Theodore would rise and bow and go to one of the windows, prop his Bible on the sill and read for a while with his fingers stuffed in his ears to shut out the sound of Mrs Jones practising the throbbing and humming mantras which the Lama was teaching her. Or else he would take a pencil and a sheet of the fibrous Tibetan paper and make one more effort to sketch the majestic bulk of the mountain called the Dome of Purest Light, which composed all the far horizon of the valley. After a while, as if at an unperceived signal, he would fold his paper away or put his Bible into his pocket, turn, bow to the Lama, and become a blackboard again.

But even as a blackboard he learnt something. Certain marks, so to speak, could never be quite rubbed out. For instance, he was startled out of indifference by discovering that the Lama didn't believe in God. Gods, yes, but all bound like men to the world of illusion, beyond which lay something which wasn't God, but was what the Lama called enlightenment, the only not-illusion. All life yearned towards that state. Souls were like fish struggling towards their spawning-ground against the rush of a great river; they were born again in many forms on that almost endless journey, until they reached their goal. But some, reaching it, turned back to help the others. The Buddha himself was not God, or even a god, but a soul who had chosen to be re-born into the world of illusion when it could have

escaped, in order to show others the way. The Siddha Asara
was another such teacher.

Theodore paid attention to what the Lama said about the
Siddha Asara, because he thought it might affect their escape,
but he could make no sense of it. The child in Mrs Jones's
womb both was and was not the Siddha Asara, just as in his
previous life he had been Tojing Rimpoche, who was himself
and not the Siddha, and yet he was the Siddha . . . Theodore
gave up, but the mark was there on the blackboard.

At other times a mark would come and remain indelible in
spite of him. The Lama, explaining what he meant by saying
that Mrs Jones had not needed to understand her initiation
ceremony, but only to have faith in it, had told the following
story: some three hundred years before, the fifth Dalai Lama
had noticed the goddess Tara walking every day along the
pilgrims' path round his palace. He made enquiries and found
that one old man among the pilgrims made that journey every
day, repeating the mantra of the goddess as he went. Only the
old man got the mantra wrong each time, so the Dalai had him
taught the correct words. Immediately the goddess ceased to
walk the pilgrims' way, and did not re-appear until the old man
was allowed to say her mantra in his old, meaningless way.
Theodore hated this story but couldn't forget it. It embodied
so much he disliked and distrusted about the Lama's religion—
the empty repetition of syllables, like the automatic rotation of
prayer-wheels, as if nonsense was more holy, more worth
while, than honest, wholesome intelligence striving for the
meanings of things . . . and yet at the same time Theodore
himself acknowledged a presence that listened morning and
evening to his attempts to pray but gave no other sign. Were
his prayers, like the old man's mantra, nonsense too?

What did Mrs Jones make of all this? Theodore never asked
—as soon as he was out of the Lama Amchi's room he tried to
forget everything to do with it, and Mrs Jones, quick as usual
to perceive his needs, normally spoke about other things. But
occasionally she would forget, and almost as if talking to herself, would make some comment. One day, for instance, as
they were walking—or rather processing, for she was never
allowed to move anywhere within the monastery without her
own ritual escort—across the main courtyard she said, "Funny,
that, about my spinal column."

"What do you mean?"

"Just it comes in a lot. Don't you remember, him telling me
to form the shape of it in my mind, and then dream up a lotus
growing out of the top of my skull? That's not the botanical
flower what you and I know, *Nymphaea lotus*, what I always
have a bit of trouble getting out of my mind—it's his holy
lotus, of course. You remember that?"

"No."

"Oh, I won't bother you with it . . . only I keep thinking,
some of what he tells me, I ought to of worked out for myself
long ago. Spines, for instance—I've always had a fancy for
back-bones."

She gave a silent chuckle, reached out and ran her hand from
the small of Theodore's back up to his collar; it was the sort of
half-thinking caress one might give to a dog that settles along-
side one's chair, but it made him shiver as though energies were
flowing from her finger-tips into his marrow. They walked on,
four monks before and two behind, but he had to restrain himself from shaking himself as a dog does after such a touch.

That must have happened quite early in the course of her teaching, because she was still wearing her hat and veil, and all her make-up, and was carrying a frilly parasol over her shoulder. But as week added itself to week and then month to month, she changed. There was no particular day on which she discarded her hat—instead she spent a couple of evenings remodeling one, twisting and steaming and punching and stitching the tolerant felt until, though it was the same hat in all essentials, it now had a curious upward-pointing peak vaguely like the caps worn by Tibetan nuns when they came from the nunnery, two miles along the mountain, to attend one of the ceremonies.

A few days later the veil vanished. Mrs Jones also took to wearing her dark russet riding-cloak, experimenting with its clasp, taking up its hem, devising a loose belt, until she had a garment that fell in much the same folds as a monk's robe. She gave the parasol to a peasant woman who admired it. And by unnoticed stages she abandoned her make-up. This change was so slow that there was no certain morning on which Theodore realised that her skin was rather coarse—not pocked, but large-pored—with a delta of wrinkles at the corner of each eye, and that a line of dark down ran along her upper lip. The blue-black shadows faded from round her eyes, making them seem less enormous, but they were still the same eyes, large, sparkling with life and full of secrets. She might spend half an evening in her screened nook in the guest-house, quietly humming her mantras or sitting in total silence, cross-legged on her cot, staring at one of the patterns of Tibetan letters which she had hung there; but then she would emerge and begin to tease Lung and Theodore, or touch up her plant-drawings or look at Theodore's latest work and show him how the emphasis of a line or the deepening of a shadow might give a picture body. They would eat supper, and then she would sit beside Lung on his cot with her head on his shoulder and his hand clasped in her lap and sing his favourite song . . .

The boy I love sits up in the gallery,
The boy I love is looking down at me . . .

and Lung would smile and fondle a tress of hair with his free hand and pretend to be happy, but often the tears would stream down his cheeks as she sang. Theodore was neither shocked nor embarrassed by these scenes. It was like watching an old couple, grandparents of many children, sitting by the hearth and remembering their courting days.

Lung, of course, noticed and resented each alteration in Mrs Jones. Sometimes he argued, but more often he would try and do things to draw her attention back to earlier days: fuss over her plant collection, or try to get her to organise her sketches; strip down her rifle and clean it; unpack and repack the baggage, on the pretext that everything had to be ready for the escape; and so on. One morning Theodore and Mrs Jones returned from the Lama's house to find that Lung had hammered nails into the wall and hung there, like a military trophy, the sword he had taken from the dead bandit. The rifle was slung across it.

"That looks real handsome," said Mrs Jones. "Mind you, you'll have to keep cleaning it, or it'll get the rust. It'd be better off in its case, honest."

"Will not be there long time," said Lung.

"Oho! What's up, then? You onto something?"

"I find friend who help us escape."

"Have you now? Sure? Who is he?"

"You see him long time back, drink tea with me. Lama Sumpa his name."

"Ah, that fellow! What's in it for him?"

"Not say, but perhaps he think if help Chinese, then Chinese make Sumpa Abbot of Dong Pe."

"Now you be careful, my love. He'd help the Chinese just as much by pushing me into the first ravine we come to."

"No, no," said Lung, smiling confidently. "Sumpa say perhaps Lama Amchi find wrong Tulku, but Sumpa not sure. If this maybe true Tulku, Sumpa afraid to kill Missy, see. But take Missy far from Dong Pe, then baby is born. If he is true Tulku, Sumpa says, he find way back to Dong Pe."

"Now, that's amazing!" said Mrs Jones. "Just what I been thinking myself. I'll know, won't I? He'll tell me, somehow, if he's . . . what the oracle said he is, and then I can bring him back."

"So you *are* coming," whispered Theodore.

"What do you mean, ducky?"

"I've been scared to ask, and so's Lung, I guess. You've been taking Buddhism so seriously. I mean, your clothes, even."

She laughed, and her fingers flicked dismissively at her habit.

"You're forgetting I'm an actress," she said. "I like to get myself into a part and play it proper. Not that I ain't serious about what old Amchi's been telling me—fact, it makes more sense to me than anything I've heard from all the other holy bodies what have tried to make a decent Christian of me. But look at it another way—I've got to take it serious, haven't I? Old Amchi would spot at once if I didn't."

"But you're coming, all the same?" insisted Theodore.

"Course I am. I told you as I nearly died having my other kid. I'm not risking that again, any more that I can help. I'm getting myself to where there are proper doctors, whatever old Amchi says."

"Good," said Lung. "Now, Sumpa make this plan . . ."

"No, don't tell us, love," interrupted Mrs Jones, "or Amchi'll smell it out. Don't you think so, Theo?"

Theodore nodded. In the glimmering room at the top of the Lama's house the odour of conspiracy would have reeked about them like incense.

"I guess you're right," he said. "Only how long have we got to wait?"

"Five weeks," said Lung. "Then is big festival. Plenty people come to Dong Pe. Everybody most busy. We go then."

As those weeks dragged by Lung and Theodore discussed this conversation many times. Mrs Jones usually managed to turn the subject aside, but when Lung tried to insist on talking about the escape she refused to listen.

"You know," she said once, "I'm like an old hank of wool what's got itself all of a tangle, and now I'm sorting myself out and rolling me up into a proper ball what I can knit with."

She seemed to find the days of waiting no trouble at all, and Theodore endured them well enough, but they were a trial for Lung. He took to visiting Major Price-Evans with Theodore, helping to clean the Temple and arguing, very formally and politely despite his inadequate English, for Confucianism against Buddhism. Theodore paid little attention to these debates, which were not very satisfactory even to Lung, because the Major was such a difficult opponent, tending to agree with everything Lung said and then somehow to incorporate it into his own side of the argument. One morning Lung, exasperated but still needing distraction, offered to mend the little windmill which was supposed to drive the second line of prayer wheels. The Major was delighted, and Lung set about the job with his usual self-mocking competence, borrowing tools from somewhere and then—as if to spin the project out through the weeks of waiting—cutting every strut and joint as if he were making fine furniture.

So, slowly, the moment for escape neared, with increasing tension, like the felt approach of thunder. The monastery began to pulse with a sense of quickened life as the time of the great Festival came nearer. To Theodore's relief the Lama Amchi announced a holiday from the lesson-periods, as it was his duty to meditate for three days before the start of the Festival, and first he wanted Mrs Jones to take part in the next ceremony of her initiation. He paused when he had made this announcement, and after Theodore had finished translating continued to stare at her with his misty but luminous gaze. She nodded.

"Fair enough, she said. "If that's the form, I'll do a bit of meditating too. Ask if he can find me a cell or something, where I'll be alone."

"The cell is already waiting," said the Lama. "Tomorrow morning we will hold the ceremony, and then the Mother of the Tulku can retire to her cell. For six days after that we will meet here each morning, so that I may teach her the exercises to follow when she is alone, and then we will both withdraw into silence."

For a moment Theodore was horrified. This seemed to end all hope of escape. Then the thought struck him that perhaps Mrs Jones knew what she was doing—if she was supposed to be shut in her cell, and in fact they started their escape on the first night, then with luck it would be three days before she was missed. If that was in her mind, she gave no sign, but when

Theodore looked at the Lama he found the old man watching him with an intent, half-amused stare, as though he had read every detail of his thought.

Next morning Theodore came out of the temple of the oracle with the tang of the Major's greasy tea on his lips, and heard the tinkling bells on his right echoed by a new set on his left. He looked and saw that the line of prayer-wheels that had been motionless were twirling like the others. He wondered whether it made any difference that Lung, who had brought them back into meaningless motion, didn't believe in them at all. Presumably not. His function was like the wind's function—it didn't believe in them either. Still, Theodore was glad for Lung's sake that his work had been successful so he went back into the temple and climbed through the series of rooms at the back to the roof. The rooms were tiny, and empty except for the one on the ground floor. They were connected to each other by ladders like the one he used to clean the Buddha and the taller statues. He found Lung out on the roof, making final adjustments.

"Well done," he said in English. "You've got them turning faster than the other lot now."

"Perhaps I mend that also," said Lung. "Happy you come, Theo, for you help me. This rope not good, fall off in strong wind, and my arms not long to hold two end." ·

His readiness to talk English showed he was in a cheerful mood, but he slipped into Mandarin to give more detailed instructions. Theodore held, pulled and twisted as he was told, but when they set the windmill going again it turned out that this latest adjustment had unbalanced other elements, so that it now quivered alarmingly at each revolution.

"The thing is full of demons," said Lung with a laugh. "No wonder in this place. Now how shall I exorcise them?"

He slipped a cord from a pulley and stopped the juddering, then paced around the mechanism, fingering struts and ropes. In the silence a bell clanked and was answered by another, sounds that made Theodore aware of a noise that he had heard for some time without noticing, the deep drone of temple music, joined now by the fluting and tinkling of lighter instruments. He moved to the parapet and looked over the edge.

The doors of the main temple opposite were open, but the mountain brightness was too strong for him to see anywhere into the dark, square hole from which the music came. Now he could distinguish the deep gargling chant of the choir-leader and the boom of response from the choir. He thought he could see the blue shimmer of incense streaming below the lintel and up into the glistening air. The courtyard itself was empty.

He was about to turn back to the trap-door when two monks, wearing the ceremonial gold cockscomb helmets, emerged from under the right-hand arch, followed by Mrs Jones and then four monks. It was a tribute to the vigour of her personality that he knew her at once, because she was wearing the full costume of a Tibetan nun, the heavy, belted robe and the ungainly pointed cap, even the yellow boots. Theodore must have gasped or made some movement that showed his surprise for in a second Lung was at his side, silent at first, then speaking in a voice that was like a groan of anguish.

"She is shameless! Look how she walks, and yet she is but five months pregnant! It is my child, my child!"

He made a movement, as though to rush down into the

courtyard and confront her, but then turned back to the parapet and stood quivering, whispering to himself or groaning aloud, while Mrs Jones, escorted by her small procession, crossed the courtyard. At the temple door she knelt with all her usual grace and touched her forehead on the paving, then rose and was swallowed by the dark square. Lung was in the middle of a long, relaxing sigh when he stiffened again and pointed at the mountainside. The Lama Amchi, unescorted and wearing his plain russet robe, was coming down the stairs from his house.

"He is a sorcerer," said Lung. "Look, he is flying!"

Of course it wasn't true, but even to Theodore's eyes it seemed that the Lama was coming down the zig-zag flights in a series of slow swoops with only the hem of his robe touching the steps. Once he was on level ground they could see his feet pacing beneath the robe, but still that sense of supernatural gliding remained.

"He is a sorcerer," repeated Lung. "He is stealing her soul!"

"No one can do that," said Theodore. Not against her will, he added to himself.

They watched while the Lama performed the same ritual of prostration at the temple door and, welcomed by bells, floated into the dark. Lung groaned again.

"She is not coming," he said.

"She promised she would."

"Then why all this?"

"She's acting."

"She believes."

"What did she tell you last night? I woke up once, and you were still talking."

"She said she will come with us, but only because she is frightened about the birth of the child. If it were not for that she would stay."

"Well, that sounds certain enough, doesn't it? And she hasn't much time to change her mind."

"Six days," said Lung.

Chapter 15

The festival was due to last for several days, during which the monks performed a series of dances, or plays—Theodore found it hard to tell which—acting out different bits of their faith. As usual it was difficult to get a coherent account from Major Price-Evans, because his enthusiasm kept reminding him of extra details, or of other parts of other ceremonies which could be compared with what he was describing. For instance he was trying to explain a dance in which somebody wearing the mask of a three-eyed bull and carrying a sword and a bowl of blood attacked an image made of coloured dough and cut it to bits, which were then scattered among the spectators, who ate them.

"He's the Lord of Death, of course," explained the Major. "Used to be a real human sacrifice, I shouldn't wonder—lot of that sort of thing in Tibet before the Buddhists took over. Never seen a human sacrifice meself, though I've seen some rum things in my time. Suppose I would have had to try to stop it, in any case—British officer can't just sit through a thing like that. All a bit like Communion Service, hey?"

He had sounded so far off and wistful, discussing the proper behaviour for a British officer who found himself in the audience at a human sacrifice, that it took Theodore a moment or two to grasp the meaning of the last sentence, especially as the Congregation's name for the central Christian ritual was "The Lord's Table".

"No!" said Theodore explosively, "it's nothing like."

"Oh, I don't know . . . but I didn't mean to put you out, me boy. My fault for describing it badly, hey? Wish I could tell you how stirring it all is, with the music, and the colour, and the masks and all that. No set places for the audience—not like a theatre, hey—happens right in among you, and suddenly you find it's happening inside you—see what I mean?"

"No. Don't the people watching get in the way?"

"Not at all. Fact I've seen 'em join in once or twice, become part of the show. Seen a scrawny little chappie stalk into the middle of a dance with a dagger stuck through both cheeks— no blood, of course—and tell them he was some demon they'd affronted, somehow. Not invited, I dare say, like the witch in Sleeping Beauty. All they did was put a bit into the dance apologising to the demon, and the demon would leave the chappie, who'd take the daggers out of his cheeks and go and sit down and watch the rest of the dance as though nothing had happened. You can't get away from it. The Gods are very close to us up here. Don't you feel that, hey?"

"Yes," said Theodore.

The energy of his own assent shocked him like a blow. The single syllable had exploded out of him with even more force than his rejection a minute or two ago of the Major's idea that sacrifice of the dough giant had anything to do with the Lord's Table. He startled the Major, who tried to peer at him, blind-eyed, then nodded thoughtfully in silence before he broke once more into rambling talk.

Theodore barely heard. He was thinking *God is very close. He does not answer me, but he is very close.* He felt a strange sense of movement towards a crisis, like the silky tension in a river's surface as it flows into the last still reach above a fall.

During the next few days the memory of this almost violent moment of assurance came and went, but the sense of coming crisis endured, fed not only by the approaching flight but by the feeling of excitement that filled the valley, like a liquid brimming up to the jagged rims. The preparations for the festival produced a tauter rhythm in daily life, full of sudden little turbulences. The very day of his talk with the Major, Theodore came into one of the minor courtyards to find a team of monks there, prancing like frogs to the beat of a small drum. Evidently the Major was mistaken when he said the dances were performed without rehearsal.

Later still Theodore was passing along one of the balconies when he looked over the rail and saw that the paving of the small courtyard below was covered with monstrous faces, fresh-painted and laid out to dry, snarling or grinning, staring at the sky with huge, round, unwinking eyeballs. Most of them were much more than masks, structures like the shell of a lobster, made to cover the performer almost to the ground; eye-slits cut in their chests showed that when they were worn they must stand nine or ten feet high. Largest of all was a three-eyed monster, dark blue, crowned with a ring of little white skulls. Its mouth was made to move, and now it hung open at its widest, displaying clashing white teeth and a scarlet gullet. Theodore could just make out that it was supposed to represent a bull, presumably the one who would cut the dough-giant to pieces in the dance the Major had described. He told himself it was only a mask, stupid and ugly, but all the same he shivered. As he turned, a monk came and leaned on the railing beside him as if to see what he had been looking at, then grabbed his arm and drew him away from the railing. It was Lung's friend, Sumpa.

"You must not look at that one without due preparation," he muttered.

"What is it? Why?"

"Yidam Yamantaka. Death and slayer of death. That he should encounter one at the start of an enterprise . . . walk with me, and if we meet anyone I shall be expounding to you the meanings of Yama and Yamantaka . . . in two nights you must leave."

"I know. Lung told me. I don't know if Mrs Jones knows. I only see her now when we're at the Lama Amchi's house. I don't even know which is her cell . . ."

"I will show you. But you are fully ready?"

"Some other people have moved into our guest-house, so we've had an excuse to pack most of our things away."

"Good. Now listen. At dusk the day after tomorrow the Steward of the Guest-houses will send fresh guests to your house. The honoured Lung will protest that there is no room, and the steward will say that there is nowhere else available. I will then come and suggest that you and the honoured Lung move to a cell in the monastery, and you will accept this. Thus your disappearance from the guest-house will be accounted for. You must tell some story to your friend Achugla."

"Major Price-Evans? All right," said Theodore reluctantly. Deceiving the old man would be unpleasant.

"What about the horses?" he asked.

"It is arranged. Your guide, whose name is Tefu, will take a paper to the groom who has looked after them, authorising him to buy them. He will give the groom, who cannot in any case read, some money for himself. All that is not important, or if it is I shall have taken care of it. There is no time to discuss it now. Lean on the rail here and listen."

They had reached by this time the gallery on the south side of the courtyard, and a little way along it Sumpa halted and leant his elbows on the rail. Theodore fell in beside him, as casually as he could.

"You see the hermit-caves?" said Sumpa.

"Yes."

Major Price-Evans had told Theodore about the hermit-caves. In each of them lived a monk who had vowed to endure total isolation while he performed spiritual exercises. Most of them were walled in, with only a slit left open through which food could be passed. At the end of his time the monk would emerge purified, and gifted with strange powers. Apparently the Lama Amchi had achieved this, living alone, walled into one of the caves, for seven years. It was to this he owed his spiritual authority. Seven years!

"Follow the left-hand stair up, then," Sumpa muttered, "and you will see a ledge branching off to left and right. Three caves on the right-hand branch and one on the left. The woman is in that single cave on the left."

"Walled in?" whispered Theodore.

"Of course not. There is a token stone at the entrance. Now, immediately we have left the guest-house I will take you to a side-door to the monastery—the one you used when you came to the ceremony of the oracle. Go there on the night and behind the door you will find a monk's robe, folded. Take that with you and go to the cave. You will meet no one of importance. All the senior monks will be in the temple for the ritual that starts the days of meditation before the festival. The woman

will be there also for a while, but at a certain point in the
ceremony she will leave and return to her cave. She will find
you there and not be alarmed. You will explain what is
happening. She must dress in the robe you carry and raise its
cowl, so that in the dark she may pass for a monk. You will
lead her back by way of the door through which you entered
the monastery, and turn west, along beneath the wall, until
you come to the place where there are many shrines on either
side of the path, above and below. You know it?"

"Yes."

"At the third shrine turn left and climb straight up the hill.
In thirty paces you will come to a platform which was made
for a shrine not yet built. Tefu will be waiting there, with the
honoured Lung, and your horses. He will have yaks and men.
If you leave at once, travelling in the dark, you will be able to
camp by the edge of the Stone Lake and cross it next day at
dawn. You can do all this? It must be you, because you speak
the woman's language, and moreover you are the Guide, so no
one will question or stop you."

"I think I can do it. I don't see why not. I'll make sure I know
my way through the monastery so that I can find it in the dark.
I'm much more worried about the journey."

"No difficulty there, provided you leave unnoticed. You
will have three days' start, and before the end of that time you
will be among friends. I am only the furthest finger-tip of
the strong hand that will take you to safety."

A monk came pacing along the gallery. Sumpa started
telling Theodore the names of the demons who inhabited the
mountain peak, but as soon as the monk was out of earshot, led
him away to show him where he would hide the robe Mrs
Jones was to wear. Theodore by now knew the monastery well

enough to notice that they were making a longish detour to avoid the courtyard where Yidam Yamantaka—Death and Slayer of Death—stared at the sky.

There was one more meeting at the Lama Amchi's, and Theodore, despite his new nervousness, could not see that it differed at all from any of the other recent meetings. The pattern had changed from that of earlier days. Nowadays Mrs Jones wore her nun's robe and barely seemed to notice Theodore, speaking directly to the Lama in Tibetan, stumbling but happier to communicate like this. The Lama answered her questions in short, repetitive sentences, and only called on Theodore to amplify some idea that could not be treated in simple terms. So Theodore spent most of his time at the window, reading or drawing; and even when he was taking part in the lessons, the ideas he was asked to translate were so strange and rarified that there was no need for him to shut his mind to them—he could not have begun to grasp them, however hard he had tried.

This made the lessons less tiring, but he was distressed by the increasing gulf that had opened between Mrs Jones and himself. It was she, now, who treated him as a mechanical device, while the Lama became increasingly polite and kindly. At the end of one meeting he had said, "Theodore, a guide exists by virtue of the path he has to show. Once the journey is made and the path known, he is a guide no more. A bowl of life-giving food does not itself give life. Once the food is eaten, the bowl is only a bowl."

"Yes, I know. I didn't want to be anyone's bowl."

"But you have served honestly, my child. I think well of you, for what my poor thoughts are worth."

"Thank you."

An odd little part of Theodore's nerves rose from the prospect of resuming the old life with Mrs Jones, the songs and the teasing and the rush of energy flowing out of her which was now all turned inward. Would it be like that again? He didn't dare wonder. Luckily at that last lesson he was hardly called on to take part at all. It consisted largely of silences, repetitions of sacred formulae, hummings in the throat or single syllables exploding, while Theodore stood at the window and neither read nor drew, but stared at the majestic skyline he hoped he would not see again.

The scene at the guest-house went like a well-rehearsed play. For some days the over-decorated little room had become increasingly crowded and smelly and noisy as visitors began to gather for the festival. Tibetans seemed to have no sense of privacy at all, so wherever there was a spare patch of floor they thought it natural to spread out their flea-ridden blankets and bed down. Lung, now triply fastidious in his loneliness, fought against these invasions, using a screen and a barrier of baggage to mark out the area which belonged to him and Theodore, but even these frontiers of civilisation contracted daily under pressure from the alien horde. On the evening marked for the escape there were already eight Tibetans—two of them boisterous small girls—using the guest-house when the door heaved on its frame, the latch gave, and a squat woman backed in, dragging a loose pile of baggage. Two thin little men, so alike that they were certainly brothers and therefore probably her husbands, followed laden with pots and food. Several children seemed to be hovering in the dusk beyond the door-frame.

The woman, bewildered but cheerful, stared round the room, spotted the last empty space between Lung's cot and

Theodore's, and marched towards it. Lung rose to fend her off,
but her technique for getting through the gap between the
screen and the baggage was the same as the one she had used at
the doorway—she reversed, pulling her belongings behind her,
moving with enough momentum to knock Lung onto his cot
when she collided with him. By the time he was on his feet the
children—there were only two of them after all—were climbing across the baggage pile, the men were halted in the gap, and
three of the other inhabitants of the guest-house were crowding
behind them to watch the upheaval and explain to the woman
that the space between the foreigners' cots was sacred ground,
or something of the sort. At the same time the two little girls
came shrilling across to tell the new children about the wickedness of climbing on foreigners' baggage, a lesson they themselves had only learnt two days ago. In the end Lung had to
move the screen to reach the door where the Steward of the
Guest-houses, a middle-aged monk, stood gap-toothed and
blinking.

Lung began to argue. The Steward, who had acquired a
smattering of Mandarin in the course of his duties, answered
mostly with gestures, designed to show that the other guest-
houses were even more crowded. Angrily Lung took him by
the elbow and pulled him out of the door, so that it seemed
perfectly natural for Theodore to wriggle through the crush
and join the discussion outside. He reached them in time to see
Sumpa come strolling down the path from the monastery.
Lung turned to him in despair and fury.

Perhaps it was all a little too pat, but it seemed to Theodore
quite convincing. Sumpa and the Steward argued for a little in
Tibetan—perhaps for the benefit of the visitors now crowding
the doorway, or perhaps because Sumpa had somehow engin-

eered it that the Steward should bring the newcomers down, without letting him know the reason. But after a minute Sumpa turned to Theodore.

"If the honoured Guide will come with me," he said, "I will show him an empty cell in the monastery which he can share with the honoured Lung. Meanwhile the honoured Lung can supervise the packing of your belongings. These peasants will bring them up to the path below the monastery wall and I will arrange for their collection from there."

He spoke a couple of sentences in Tibetan and turned away, striding up the path with brisk small steps. Theodore caught him up.

"I went out to the shrine this morning," he muttered. "There was a camp among them, three tents and some yaks."

"That is Tefu and his friends," said Sumpa. "I will go there now and send them to fetch the baggage. You go to the small door. The robe is where I showed you."

When they reached the monastery wall he gave a formal little nod and hurried away, vanishing almost at once in the near-dark. Theodore followed the blank line of the wall in the other direction, noticing for the first time how noisy the evening was, with laughter and shouts from the guest-houses and the more distant throb and pulse of temple music. Below him, at the heart of the valley, a thunderstorm had brewed, and the continual flicker of its veiled lightning picked out the tree-tops and the spiky pinnacles of shrines below the path. When he came to the small side-door he found it wedged slightly open with a stone, and tied with a leather thong to prevent it from swinging in the wind. He slipped the knot by touch and slid through, kicking the stone away and latching the door from the inside. The robe was there, folded along the wall. He slung it across his shoulder and felt his way up the stair to the maze of galleries above.

This section of the monastery consisted mostly of the quarters of senior monks. Now there was no one about, and few lamps burnt in any cells; but from the direction of the main temple came the murmur and throb of horns and drums and the ocean-like rumble of the monks' responses, all echoed from the valley by the growing mutter of the storm. The building was like a vast creature, the rhythm of whose life at times draws all its living cells to the centre of its system, leaving its outer parts mere lifeless shell, untenanted. Through these veins and chambers Theodore stole like an infection. He felt totally safe.

"I am armoured in faith," he whispered several times.

Whatever happened God would not let him be harmed, but moved beside him now so that all the demons of the mountain could not touch him. This exaltation of certainty lasted while he walked silently above the courtyards, round behind the temple of the oracle, down a stair and out into the main courtyard through the arch from which he had first seen it.

It was full night now, with many stars, though they were smudged out to the north where the thunderstorm was rising and nearing. He picked his way along beneath the slope of natural rock to the stairs he had climbed so often, going to lessons at the Lama Amchi's house. Almost nonchalantly he started up them, reached the ledge where the two houses stood side by side, crossed it diagonally and began to climb the steeper, more irregular stairs to the caves. Stirred by the fringes of the storm, the night wind, icy cold, slashed and whipped at the mountain, snatching his panted breath from his lips and tugging at his clothes. He slowed his pace, taking care over each step, husbanding his energy as if he had the whole mountain to climb. When he looked over his shoulder he was astonished by how far he had come; the rock-face plunged down, seeming far steeper from above than from below, and the whole monastery was mapped out beneath him. The thought struck him that he should have come up here before and looked at the whole valley from this height. But mostly he kept his eyes on the individual steps, which were often no more than scooped footholds in the rock, no larger than a dinner-plate. At the steepest places a coarse rope, greasy with use, ran beside them.

At last came a change, a step that was wider than the others, and broader too, a place to rest and recover breath without feeling that the wind would scour him off the mountain. But it was too cold to stand still for long, and Theodore was about to climb on when his eye was caught by a dim yellow light to his left and he realised with a shock that he had reached the first line of caves. His eye was now trapped by that light and could see nothing else, so he had to feel his way, trembling suddenly with the knowledge of the sweep of rock below him, till he reached the cave mouth. Heavy curtain was stretched across it just inside. Eagerly he slipped through.

"Hullo, Theo," said Mrs Jones.

She was sitting cross-legged on a prayer-mat on the floor, opposite a place where the cave wall had been roughly plastered and then whitewashed. Elsewhere it was naked rock, but hung with the usual banner-like pictures and patterns that decorated all the monks' cells. The butter-lamp on the stool beside her cast slant shadows upward across her face. Her eyes were open but they looked heavy with sleep, and she was smiling dreamily, a smile that reminded Theo of the remote sweet smile of the Buddha in the temple.

"I thought you'd still be in the temple," he said.

"Gracious me! I've missed it! I was having a vision—'salright, you didn't interrupt nothing. I think it was finished."

"It's time to go. They've sent me to fetch you. Everything's ready. We couldn't get a message to you earlier, but . . ."

"I know, ducks. Listen, I'm afraid you'll have to go back and tell them I ain't coming."

"Not . . . But the baby! Proper doctors! India!"

"It wasn't never going to be India, love, not if that Sumpa had anything to do with it. He wanted the Tulku born where the Chinese could get their hands on him. But it's no odds either way, 'cause I'm staying here. We'll be all right, me and him—that's one of the things I seen in my vision."

"I don't understand."

"No more do I. I was just sitting here, humming one of me hums, when all of a sudden that wall there started a-glowing, all kinds of colours and shapes, real beautiful, like nothing I never seen, and I sat where I was with my eyes on stalks, and somehow the patterns became a lotus, and it opened and opened, and there he was at the heart of it."

"Who?"

"Tojing Rimpoche, the Siddha Asara."

"What did he look like?"

"I don't know. It wasn't that sort of seeing. The lotus was, but I seen *him* somehow different, in a way as won't go into words. But he was there, right enough."

"I thought he was supposed to be . . ."

She chuckled like her old self and slapped her belly.

"In here. Not really. It ain't like that, far as I can make out. Matter of fact, I don't think any of them's proper clear how it all works—you see they don't usually find a Tulku till he's four years old, about, when he can talk and tell 'em things about his old life, so as they can be sure they've got hold of the right kid . . . Do you know, couple of nights back he gave me a great kick from inside—funny how they do that—but it's early, innit? Shows the little beggar's going to be strong . . . bit of a shock for you, young fellow, climbing all the way up here and finding I'm going to cry off."

"No, ' said Theodore slowly. "I guess I've known for a long time that you weren't coming. I guess Lung's known too . . . Oh, Mrs Jones, won't you come and tell him yourself? I can't! I just can't!"

She nodded briskly.

"Quite right. 'Course it's up to me. I s'pose I wasn't proper come to after my vision, trying to put it on you . . ."

She had learnt the Lama's trick of rising so that she seemed to float to her feet.

"Sumpa gave me a monk's robe," said Theodore. "In case anyone tries to stop you."

"They won't . . . it'll be funny going out without my escort. Wonder where they got to. Probably they come to take me to the temple and found me having my vision, and they understood what was up and cut along without me. You go first, young fellow. Heavens, hark at that thunder!"

The storm had drifted closer now and was rubbing against the lower slopes of the mountain, the glare of its flashes making the landscape jump into being, sharp as cut paper, and then float dazingly on the retina when all was darkness again. The wind threshed among the many-faceted roofs below and thudded against the rock-face. If the monks were still singing in the temple, their voices were drowned by the voice of the storm. Clutching the hand-smoothed rope Theodore started down the first slant of steps, feeling for each foothold in the dark.

"You ain't scared?" called Mrs Jones. "Want me to go first?"

"No. It's all right," called Theodore.

He had in fact hesitated at the first step, full of a sudden horror of falling, but then he remembered the assurance of safety that had surrounded him as he had come up this way, and he went down confidently, flight after flight, until he reached the platform where the Lama Amchi's house stood beside the one that had belonged to Tojing Rimpoche. He was only half surprised to find that Mrs Jones had followed close on his heels, as if there were neither night nor storm.

"That's where he'll get born," she said, flicking a thumb towards the empty house. There was something not exactly false about the gesture, but still not quite right. Indeed, since she had first spoken her manner had jarred. If he hadn't come to know her so well in the past months he would never have noticed, but now he realised that she was play-acting. The role of Mrs Jones—the exuberant, warm, resourceful, crude-spoken horsewoman, who had worn her make-up so thick and her clothes with such an air—no longer quite fitted her. She had changed. She was somebody new and different, trying to fit herself back into the old role for the moment and getting it subtly wrong, too boisterous, too coarse-grained. He shook his head, unhappy at the distances that had stretched between them, and led the way down to the main courtyard.

As they reached the paving there came another change in her. She put her arm round his shoulders and held him close against her side, so that the folds of her robe flapped around him as they walked. Warmth seemed to flow out of her, and not simply warmth but a deep, quiet contentment.

"Mind you, that was some vision I had," she said, speaking

in a quite new voice, very soft and even. "I wonder if it'll ever happen again. I hope so. Or perhaps once is enough."

Still holding him she started to make the humming noise which the Lama had produced the night he had first told them about his search for the Tulku, a noise like the purr of a great cat, dreaming. She let go of him as they climbed the stairs, but was still humming as they moved through the network of galleries towards the little door. An old monk, tottering along with a lamp, met them, peered astonished through the dimness and stood reverently aside. Mrs Jones said a few words to him in Tibetan, perhaps a blessing, but didn't pause in her stride. Theodore noticed that she was actually walking in a different manner, as though she was conscious every instant of the treasure she now carried.

"Do you believe everything the Lama Amchi says?" he asked. "You used to say he was sly."

"Oh, he's that all right, sly as a coach-load of politicians. Everything we said about him at the start, wanting to keep his hands on Dong Pe and all that, it's true. But it don't make no difference to him being holier than all the saints in the calendar and wiser than the Three Wise Men. But I ain't doing what I'm doing for him, you know. I ain't even doing it for the Tulku. I'm doing it for me."

They met no one else as they crossed the final galleries, crept down the narrow stair in the outer wall and through it into the night. Theodore wedged the stone back into the jamb and lashed the door tight with the thong, then started along the path. The valley was like a cauldron now, boiling with thunder. The cloud-layer hid the lightning-flashes, but the glare of them filled its surface with sudden luminosities, so that a cloud-tower would glow white for a moment, seeming to float by itself in the dark, and somehow to belong for that moment to the same order of creation as the monastery, with its towers and spires and ramparts. Though it felt as if huge rain-drops should have been clattering down, the air was desert-dry, whipping to and fro in fierce gusts. Theodore discovered that he was still carrying the monk's robe, slung over his shoulder, and the wind flogged it against his ribs as though it held a wiry but boneless body. The thunder drowned any noise the wind might make, so that its violent movements came unheralded, like willed onslaughts.

Theodore led the way along the path until they reached the area of shrines. At the third one—he saw its spire, topped with a crescent, outlined against the higher clouds which flickered continuously with reflected light from the storm—he turned and began to climb the slope in paces only a few inches long. Mrs Jones came effortlessly behind him. Now a different light showed, faint but yellow and steady—a lantern. Theodore climbed panting over the rim of the platform and saw in the dimness men and horses and loaded yaks, but before he could advance a pace Mrs Jones seized his elbow.

"Why'd you bring me *here*?" she gasped.

"It's where Sumpa told us to . . ."

"But he must of known! This is the place where they're going to build his shrine—Tojing Rimpoche's, when his body comes home!"

Before Theodore could answer Lung rushed out of the group of men, no doubt having heard her voice.

"You come, Missy!" he said. "I think all these long days . . ."

"No, sweetie, I ain't coming," she answered. "Listen . . ."

The rest of the sentence was drowned in thunder. She led Lung aside, and in the next glare Theodore saw the pair of them outlined right at the edge of the levelled ground, Lung with his head bowed and Mrs Jones facing him, holding both his hands in hers and looking up into his eyes. Lightning came and went and came again, and each time they were still in the same pose. A man grunted close at Theodore's side.

"When we go?" he said in harshly twanging Mandarin. "This most bad night. Go soon."

"I don't know," said Theodore. "Wait. The woman is not going."

"Ho! Monk Sumpa say woman must go! Say if woman no want to go, then we bind woman and carry!"

"No ..." began Theodore, but the man—presumably he was the one called Tefu—turned and called to his companions. One of them was holding the lantern, so Theodore could see their surge across the levelled space towards where Lung and Mrs Jones stood. He called a warning, probably inaudible against a great bellow of thunder, but Mrs Jones turned and as the rumbles died started to speak in Tibetan. The men stopped in their tracks.

That last thunderclap was like a signal for the storm to end. Though it still muttered a little at its further fringes, and though the wind still hooted and flapped among the shrines, her voice rang clear. Theodore heard the word "Tulku" repeated several times. A man, perhaps Tefu, made a lunge towards her but the others caught him and dragged him back. One actually whimpered out loud. Mrs Jones didn't shout or rage, or even raise her voice more than was necessary to pierce the wind, but from her tone it was clear that she was telling them what penalties would be inflicted, by god and man and demon, on any who dared to touch the Mother of the Tulku. She faced them as confidently as she had faced her rebellious porters on the day Theodore had first seen her, though armed with other weapons. In some ways she had changed less than he had thought.

"Fair enough," she said, switching suddenly back to English. "I've told 'em to bring our clobber back down to the monastery gate, and we'll all go home and have a good night's sleep. I'll see as nobody gets into hot water over any of this."

Theodore never clearly remembered walking back along the path to the monastery. He retained a dream-like image of several monks, including Tomdzay, at the gate, courteous and unsurprised, and then at last he was sitting exhausted on a cot in a fair-sized upper room in the monastery and watching some junior monks carry in the baggage and stow it against a wall. And then Lung stood framed in the doorway, wild and unfamiliar in Tibetan clothes, with the bandit's sword stuck through his belt. He stared at Theodore, opening and closing his mouth as if trying to speak, but no words came. Instead Lung rushed suddenly forwards. Theodore tried to rise and dodge the attack, but had hardly moved before Lung's arm was swinging at him, snatching at the robe he still carried slung across his shoulder, dragging it free so violently that he pulled Theodore to his feet. Theodore began to edge towards the door but Lung glared round the room, moving his head in savage jerks, until his eye was caught by the beam running up the far wall. He strode towards it, holding the robe at arm's length in his left hand, while with his right he drew his sword and swung it back. The moment the robe touched the beam he struck, crying like a demon.

He stood back, panting. The russet cloth was pinned to the beam and hung limp from the blade, but the hilt still quivered from the force of the blow. Lung gazed at it, uttered a sobbing groan, flung his arms wide and collapsed face down on his cot.

Chapter 16

Who knew about the failed escape? Everybody? Nobody? It was impossible to tell. Sumpa had vanished—but had he run away? Was he hiding? Was he prisoned in one of the hermit-caves? Was he dead? Again there was no clue. Tomdzay came to their room next morning to ask if they were comfortable and apologise for their treatment at the guest-house. Then, still speaking as though it were an ordinary matter, he said that as soon as the festival was over Lung and Theodore would be given money for their journey and escorted to either India or China, whichever they might choose. Lung lay face down on his cot throughout the interview and gave no sign that he had heard a word, but Tomdzay didn't seem at all put out, though Theodore noticed that his eye was caught by the monk's robe, still pinned to the beam by the sword. An unreadable expression flickered across his face but his voice didn't falter. When he had left Lung groaned, raised his head and let it fall back again onto his pillow. His misery so filled the room that Theodore could not bear it for long, and left to wander round the monastery.

The whole great maze was humming with preparations. In the main courtyard the steps of the great temple were being extended to left and right with wooden staging at various levels; new banners and hangings fluttered from archways or dangled in gaudy streams down the fronts of buildings. It was all very well for Major Price-Evans to claim that the dances were unrehearsed, but now there was hardly an open space that didn't swirl with troupes of performers or echo with strange music; passing one of the kitchens Theodore saw through an open door a rickety scaffolding at whose centre was a weird grey bulbous mass, over ten feet high. Two men were perched on the scaffolding painting the object, which seemed to Theodore wholly out of place in a kitchen until, some time after he'd walked on, he realised that what he'd seen had been an early stage in the creation of the dough giant which in a few days' time Yamantaka, Death and Slayer of Death, would hack to pieces and fling to the attendant worshippers to eat. An echo of human sacrifice, Major Price-Evans had said, and also an echo of the Lord's Table. Theodore shuddered, not at the blasphemy but at the dough giant itself, cretinous, cold, grotesque, a parody of flesh. He decided to go early for his call on Major Price-Evans.

Usually Theodore didn't argue with the Major about Buddhism—it didn't seem polite, for one thing; for another, as Lung had found, there was no way of winning such arguments; and for a third, till now Theodore had felt ashamed to pretend he held his beliefs with the through-and-through simplicity of the Major's faith. There was always that numbness and emptiness at the centre, which had been there since the Settlement had been destroyed and Father had died. He was not in his heart sure that he had been doing any more than acting his belief, in the way Mrs Jones had said she was acting hers, or that his prayers and Bible-reading had been anything other than habits. But in the last week, since that spurt of faith when he had answered "Yes" to the Major's question about the gods, he had changed. He felt he was moving, just as the whole life of the monastery was moving, towards a turning-point. Of course until last night this turning-point had seemed to be the escape from Dong Pe, but though that had come to nothing the sense of movement was still there. Perhaps it was this which made him tell the old man not simply that he had seen the dough giant but what he had felt about it.

"See what you mean, me boy," said the Major affably. "You've got to remember that flesh is illusion, so old Yidam's only an illusion of illusion. Perhaps that's what you really felt."

"No it isn't. And anyway flesh isn't an illusion. My Father said that everything God made is holy, so how can it be illusion?"

"Ah, well, perhaps that's true too—only another way of looking at it."

"Something's either an illusion or it isn't. To say anything else is nonsense—the words don't mean anything."

"Now that's where we differ. I don't like saying anything's nonsense, because when you think about it a bit more it often turns out to be sense. A lot of what you're saying is just what I used to think, but then I found I was wrong about one thing, and then another thing, and so on, and now I've given up judging. Judge not that you be not judged, don't you know."

(The Major was a great quoter from the Bible, which he knew just as well as Theodore. But he also knew the Koran, and the Talmud, and a lot of other sacred books.)

"Jesus was talking about judging people," said Theodore.

"Quite right, me boy, but all these things mean more than just one thing, you know."

"Look, if you're not allowed to say something's nonsense —not allowed to think it even—it means you can believe anything you want to. The Earth's flat! The moon is green cheese! Pigs fly!"

"I heard about a lady the other side of Tibet who could turn herself into a pig. Abbess of one of the great nunneries. I don't know whether she could fly, but some of them can levitate, you know."

"Oh, sure!"

"I don't see why not."

"In any case, supposing it's true, what's it all for? These tricks they say they do are all so useless. Floating about in the air, or sitting by a frozen lake drying out towels with your body, just to prove you can do it!"

"Jesus walked on the water."

"He had to. His disciples were scared. They thought the boat was sinking. He didn't like doing miracles, and he didn't do them to show off. They were useful. He fed people. He healed people."

"Lot of Lamas do healing, you know. But it's interesting, isn't it—shows a difference in attitude. Wheels, now. In the west we talk about the invention of the wheel as a great thing because it's so useful. Here you aren't allowed to use it at all. Same with miracles—I don't think the Lamas would want to do them if they were useful. They are spiritual exercises, you know. They prove the Lama's mastery over illusion. That's one of the reasons we know we can believe what the Lamas tell us."

"My father saw men walking on live coals," said Theodore. "Do you mean he ought to have believed them if they told him the moon was cheese?"

"I don't know about that—seen that trick meself, you know, in Java. Wish I'd had the nerve to try it, too. But if a fellow like that started talking about the way the mind and the body fit together, I'd be interested to hear what he had to say, at least. Hey?"

The argument rambled on for a while, getting nowhere near any conclusion but covering all the amazing feats the Major had heard of Lamas achieving—prodigious marches over pathless country in impossible times, vast leaps, healings, trances—and then on to other countries, rope tricks, year-long burials, strange digestive feats, water-walking, and so on. The visit fell into its usual routine, and Theodore left as soon as the oracle-priest came to perform his morning ritual.

Having nothing better to do, Theodore took the trouble to cook the midday meal with special care, but Lung would not touch it; he lay huddled on his cot, groaning from time to time, and once or twice beating his clenched fist against his thigh. In the afternoon Theodore took Sir Nigel for a ride along the mountainside; the superb creature, fully rested now and used to steep places, moved with a sprightly energy and took Theodore further from the monastery than he had ever been, down among the tiny meadows where men and women toiled stripped to the waist in the surprising warmth, and right to the steep woods which clothed the lower flanks of the Dome of Purest Light. But all the time Theodore could feel Dong Pe calling him back; it was not safe to be so far away; something had still to happen.

Once back he longed to be away. Lung's fury and grief filled the little room like smoke, and that night the monster Yidam Yamantaka blundered through Theodore's dreams. At one point he woke, convinced that the dough giant was actually in the room, and saw a weird shape, dim in the moon-light, against the far wall. It took several frozen seconds before

he recognised the thing as the monk's robe which Lung had
pinned to the beam with his sword. He tiptoed across the room
and took it down, but when he returned from exercising the
ponies next evening he found that Lung had summoned the
energy to replace it.

The third day followed much the same. A visit to the Major
in the morning, a long ride in the woods in the afternoon. All
this time Lung ate nothing—didn't even stir from his cot while
Theodore was in the room, and appeared not to notice when,
that evening, two monks brought a large basket of food in and
explained in broken Mandarin that it would have to last until
the festival was over.

The fourth morning began with the steady beat of a slack-
skinned drum, parading through galleries and courtyards, a
noise more like the pulse of a large but bloodless creature—
Yidam Yamantaka, for instance—than any music. Voices
called, feet padded and scurried, and the drum thudded into the
distance, returning and fading as it wandered through the maze.
As Theodore lay and listened to it, he came face to face with the
fact that he was frightened. It was no use saying that he had
seen the masks being painted and the dough-giant being constructed, and knew quite well that they were only wood and
cloth, flour and water and coloured dyes. He also knew that at
times something breathed power into these stupid things, so
that their stupidity began to live and became horrible. He did
not want to be there when it happened, so he decided that this
morning, at any rate, he was going to stay in the cell. Even
Lung's misery would be more tolerable than the things outside.

He rose, lit the primus and started to make his breakfast. To
his surprise Lung heaved up on his cot and stared, hollow-eyed,
at the purring violet flame beneath the kettle.

"It is the day," he croaked.

"Yes. Did you hear the drum? I guess that means the Festival is starting."

"She will come down from the mountain. She has had three days to consider. All that time she has not seen the soul-stealer."

"Honest, I don't think . . ."

"No. If he had not been sure of her he would not have left her so. I must eat."

Lung seemed to have lost all his fastidious neatnesss. He slurped his tea so hot that it must have burnt him, spilling much of it but instantly gulping again. Crumbs of the dark, sour bread strewed his cot, but the moment he'd finished eating he threw himself back on the mess and lay staring at the ceiling. Theodore started to tidy the food away.

"Leave me, Theo," whispered Lung.

"I'd sooner . . ."

"I must be alone. Now. Alone."

Lung seemed to sense Theodore's intention to refuse, because now he half-rose from the cot, glaring at Theodore with a suddenly focused madness, as though Theodore were the cause of all his misery.

"Go!"

The word was like the grunt of a wounded animal. Lung was still rising when Theodore picked up his rough Tibetan coat and backed through the door. For a moment he stood hesitating, wondering what to do, how to get help. It was as though one of the horrible powers of Dong Pe had come and instead of giving weird life to a masked dancer had actually invaded the body of his friend. He moved a pace along the gallery and standing on tip-toe peeped over the sill of the small window into the cell. Lung was lying on his cot, face down now, apparently exhausted with the effort of driving Theodore from the room. Perhaps he was right, and all he needed was to be alone. The fact that he had eaten was encouraging . . . Theodore moved away, shaking his head. He decided to go and check that the old groom hadn't forgotten to feed and water the horses in the morning's excitement. Then he could weed Mrs Jones's garden for a while—a dreary and disconsolate task without her—and then come back in an hour or so and see whether Lung was all right.

The quiet courtyard where they lived was full of sudden life, as monks thronged through the arch that led towards the temples. Theodore turned against the flow of men hurrying in the same direction along the gallery and made his way to a stair that would bring him out in the courtyard by the monastery gate, but reaching the gallery above it he saw that he would not get out that way. The crowd at the entrance was like hunched waters pressing to pass a sluice; anyone trying to move against it would be in for a battering, and might even get trampled underfoot. So he turned back and, moving with the stream now, made his way through the maze of galleries towards the little side-gate; he had meant to avoid the gallery that ran along the east side of the main courtyard, but a door that would have let him through by a back way was for some reason closed and bolted, so he had to retrace his steps. To his surprise the gallery was almost empty. Monks were lined up along the balustrade, but there was plenty of room to pass behind them, and gaps through which it was possible to see the scene below. This was so amazing that despite his intentions Theodore stopped at one of the gaps to watch for a moment.

When the people of the valley had gathered in that courtyard for the ceremony of the oracle, Theodore had thought it an immense crowd, but compared to the crush he saw now it was little more than a sprinkling. It seemed impossible that there could be room for more, but still men and women, monks and peasants, were jostling in through several archways, setting up pressures in the mass below which made it move in ponderous eddies.

"You have come to watch?" said a voice in Mandarin beside him. "To be part of the ceremony you must be down there."

Theodore turned and saw the oracle-priest. He answered with a grunt—he was only watching. He was not part, and never would be. His eye was caught by a rush of movement on the staging at the temple steps to his right—a monstrous figure, surrounded by demons, was swaggering about while a dancer all in black and riding a black hobby-horse, came tittupping on. The dancer abandoned his horse, took a bow from his shoulders and began to perform his dance, moving in wide swoops, with arms stretched so that his black robes fluttered round him. The monstrous figure, who wore a green mask and a towering crown, came nearer to the dancer, who suddenly stopped his fluttering swoops, stood straight and mimed with the bow. Imaginary arrows sped towards the monster. At this point Theodore recognised the story, which Major Price-Evans had told him—it was about a King of Tibet a thousand years ago who had tried to suppress the Buddhists; and how a Buddhist hermit had appeared in front of the palace riding a black horse and wearing the dress of a black magician, and there had performed a magical dance, which the King had come out onto his balcony to watch; then the hermit had taken his ritual bow, shot the King dead and galloped off towards the river; the King's guard had rushed in pursuit, but no one on either bank had seen a black rider on a black horse because the hermit had turned his cloak inside out as he rode through the river, which had washed the black paint off his horse, so all any witness had seen was a white magician suitably mounted on a milk-white steed.

Theodore was inquisitive to see whether the dancer would change colour, and if so how, so he stayed, telling himself he was only watching. The monster-king danced his death; a line of men in blue-green robes, waving a long blue cloth to make the waves, appeared on the other side of the stage; the hermit picked up his hobby-horse and sped towards them, pursued by demons; the dancers in blue closed round him for a moment, hiding him completely, then opened out and there he was all in white on the far side, beginning to dance his triumph while the demons prowled for their prey, unable to see him. It was cleverly managed, but Theodore was surprised to notice that the crowd below scarcely responded—indeed many were not even looking in that direction.

"Why don't they watch?" he asked. "Isn't that why they've come?"

"They are waiting for the Lama Amchi to appear," said the oracle-priest.

"Is that more important than the dances?"

"To these simple people, yes. It was he who found the Lama Tojing Rimpoche, and now it is he who has found the Mother of the Tulku. He was already a great one in their minds, and now he is greater still."

"When will he come?"

"When the dance of Yidam Yamantaka is about to begin. First there will be some singing, then another dance, then more singing and then the dance of Yidam Yamantaka."

Now, knowing what to look for, Theodore could indeed perceive that the crowd was thickest at the foot of the steps that zig-zagged up to the two houses and the caves beyond. The sense of patient waiting, of adoration, of awe, struck him like a wave. All for this one man . . .

"But when the child is born . . ." he muttered.

"He will be a child for many years," said the oracle-priest. "A Tulku does not come into his powers at once, so the Lama Amchi will guide him. And even when the child is a man . . ."

He gave a cynical little chuckle, and shrugged as if to show he was not a monk through and through, but had once been a yak-driver and seen other lands. It was a relief to hear him speak so, to share a moment of disbelief at the centre of this factory of appalling faiths. Perhaps Theodore's feelings showed on his face, because the oracle-priest smiled and shook his head reprovingly.

"The Lama Amchi is a truly spiritual person, and of great wisdom and power," he said. "And the child that is born will be the Tulku. Through my mouth the oracle spoke."

"How do you know?" cried Theodore. "How do you know it isn't all made up? You can't remember anything you said!"

The oracle-priest looked at him for a moment with the same reproving smile and was just about to answer when a change came over him. He seemed to be having a fit. He shook. The smile became a snarl, and his coppery clear skin suffused red and purple, while the veins of his forehead swelled until they were like knotted roots of trees. He took one staggering pace towards Theodore and towered above him.

"Go to your room, Theodore," he whispered. "Go to your room and wait."

The voice was not human, a rasping sigh coming from a great distance, but it seemed to Theodore as he flinched back that the words were English. Once only in his life, when Theodore had offended, Father had used those exact words; and the voice, through all the distortion of distance, spoke with Father's exact tone.

Theodore's cringeing movement away from the swollen creature became a stagger and collapse as the shock struck him. He picked himself up and scuttled, cowering, until he collided with the back wall of the gallery. There he turned and ran, hunching his shoulders, not daring to look behind him; he twisted through a dark opening, scuttled down a corridor and out onto the gallery of a small courtyard, thronging with folk below him. Two more turns and he was lost. Yesterday he had known almost every winding of this maze, but suddenly all that knowledge was wiped away; his flight became like a journey in a dream, a panic rush through familiar country whose parts no longer fit together. He stopped at the entrance to another dark corridor and stood shaking his head, as though trying to clear the chaos from it, but all the time he heard the rasping whispered words. A monk glided out of the dark and spoke to him in Tibetan.

"My room. My room," whispered Theodore.

He spoke in English, but the monk seemed to guess his need and took him gently by the elbow and guided him like a blind man through the maze until they reached a familiar gallery and a familiar door. At the touch of the latch Theodore's wits came back to him, enough to make him mutter his thanks to his guide before darting through the door and heaving it shut. He drew a deep breath and turned to face Lung, but the room was empty.

Perhaps even in his terror Theodore had been unconsciously bracing himself to face his friend's snarl of fury and rejection, and now, finding there was no need, he let a long sigh shake his body as that strand of tension slid away. The process did not stop, but ran on and on all through the web of fear, and self-pity, and self-distrust, loosing first the tautness of the morning's nightmare and then ravelling on through ancient knots and cords that had shaped his nature.

The process was timeless, his whole life, two or three breaths drawn a pace inside the door. There had been a pool in the ravine in which Father baptised his converts. Out of a place like that Theodore stepped into the middle of the room, where he stretched and sighed, as if waking from a dream.

I am re-born, he thought. He said the words aloud.

"I am re-born."

Ideas came to him, fully shaped, not needing to be thought out but already solid in their rightness, things he could hold in his mind and inspect and accept like an object held in the hand. The words which the oracle had spoken had been Father's, but they had not been spoken in anger. He had been sent back to this place to receive this blessing. The whole prodigious landscape centred on this point, this hidden room. Mountain, forest, meadow, the packed maze of the monastery, the Lama Amchi, Mrs Jones—they were all waiting for a birth, and perhaps it would come. But for Theodore it had happened now and here. If only he had had more faith he would have known it would be so—he too had been given signs, but he had failed to read them, confused by his own fears and longings, and the passions and expectations around him. Only a few days back, when he had given that vehement "yes" to the Major's question about the gods he had at once felt that it had meant much more

than he could grasp; no wonder, since it had been a signal as
sudden and strong as the kick Mrs Jones had felt from the child
in her womb ... He remembered the many times in the past
weeks when he had been conscious of the hovering presence of
the expected soul, the being for whom the peasants and the
monks, Lama Amchi and Mrs Jones all waited. Perhaps it had
been the weight of their longing which had made him aware
of it; but all the time the soul had been his own. The birth had
happened here.

Theodore didn't for a moment think or hope or fear that he
might himself be after all the Tulku of the Siddha Asara. That
other birth might or might not happen, with results which
those who longed for it might or might not expect. That was
something else. But now, here, he was fiercely conscious of
himself as Theodore, of the central numbness flooding with
life, the broken roof re-built and the cold hearth glowing. He
had heard Lama Amchi talk of those moments on the path to
enlightenment when the soul seems to leave the body and soar
free, and of the agony of its return to clogging flesh. Theodore
felt the exact opposite. The return was the ecstasy. He was
whole, and body and mind and soul sang at their healing.

He sat on the edge of his cot, staring at a patch of brilliant
green and absorbing the greenness of it. There was no need to
say prayers—it was better to sit with mind and soul spread out
and relaxed, like a bather after a long swim who lies on a
smooth rock and lets the sun dry him while its warmth purrs
through nerve and muscle. Though he could have sat like that
for hours, he felt the nature of his inner peace altering as his
energies gathered to meet some as yet unknown need. The
green patch stopped being only an embodiment of green and
became a scroll-like leaf at the edge of a painting of the sacred

lotus; the room took shape in detail so clear that to look at any object was to accept a blast of vision. He found himself staring at a few crumbs and a still-damp tea-stain on Lung's cot, seeing them in a way that let him experience, without any pain but with total understanding, the depth of Lung's desolation. Lung's absence built itself into his vision, an emptiness as strong as if it had been a presence. With a shock of sadness he remembered that Lung needed help far more than he did. At the same moment he was aware of another absence. The hunched outline of the robe, pinned by Lung's sword to the far wall, was no longer there. The sword had gone too.

His mind accepted the meaning of this with the same clarity as that with which his eyes were seeing. Lung was wearing the robe and carrying the sword. He had eaten that morning for the first time for three days, and as if it were a duty. He had driven Theodore from the room. Then he had disguised himself as a monk, and now he was walking through the maze of the monastery with his sword hidden beneath his robe. He was going to kill somebody. The Lama Amchi? Mrs Jones? Himself?

So Theodore must find him. Where? How? Ordinary reason began to work with agonising slowness, but in his new calm Theodore accepted that there was no point in rushing from the room until he had made some plan. As if to appease his body's itch for action he rose and crossed the room to inspect the place where the robe had hung, but as he passed Lung's cot his foot touched something solid, hidden under the tumbled bedclothes; he scuffed them aside and saw the sword, and beside it the little embroidered cap Lung always wore.

Relief lasted only for an instant. He picked the sword up, and as he stood weighing the lean, dark blade in his hands an image

sprang into his mind—this blade hanging on the wall of the
guest-house, where Lung had hung it, with Mrs Jones's rifle
slung crosswise over it.

His calm was chillier as he turned to the pile of baggage. The
flat rifle-case was there beneath a blanket roll. It was fastened,
but as soon as he pulled it clear he knew by its weight that it
was empty. Yes. A rifle could be hidden under a robe almost as
easily as a sword. It was a much more dangerous weapon.
There was no question now of Theodore risking lives by
looking for Lung on his own. He must warn the monks. But
they were all busy with the festival. The oracle-priest . . .

Theodore hurried along the galleries and corridors. His
shock-trance was gone, his nightmare over, and the monastery
had reassembled itself into known shapes and routes. By now
the courtyards were almost empty as the promised appearance
of the Lama Amchi and the dance of Yidam Yamantaka drew
the inhabitants towards the central arena. He could hear drums
and bells without accompanying voices, which meant that a
dance or play was being performed. He had no way of measur-
ing how long he had spent in his room—the enormous change
had happened in a sphere in which time had no meaning—it
could have been minutes or hours. Singing, the oracle-priest
had said, then another play, then more singing, and then Lama
Amchi would come down the steps to watch the Lord of Death
slaying the dough giant.

The gallery above the great courtyard was fuller now, with
massed ranks of choristers lining the balustrade, but leaving a
narrow passage where one could pass behind them. Theodore
strode along, studying the robed backs, looking for a close-
cropped dark head which wasn't wearing one of the gold cockscomb helmets. It had been under this arch, surely. None of the

backs was right. He tapped a shoulder. The monk turned, patient and unsurprised.

"Where is the oracle-priest?" Theodore said in Mandarin.

The monk answered in Tibetan, then pulled at a sleeve beside him. An older monk turned and Theodore repeated his question. The monk frowned, shrugged and said, "I will ask." More heads turned. There was a brief discussion in Tibetan. "Gone," said the old monk. "That way. Down." His hands made the movements of feet descending a stair. The other monks were smiling and nodding and echoing the gesture when from the courtyard below one of the long horns began to snore, a chime of bells rippled along an erratic scale and a drum thudded. The monks turned from Theodore. He saw their backs swell as they drew breath for the first crashing syllable of the chant. So the play was over and the second lot of singing had begun.

Theodore ran now, down the gallery behind the chanting ranks, to the stair that circled down in the corner of the courtyard; he stumbled and almost fell down its dark steepness, but clutched at the railing and caught himself, then picked his way down to the hallway at the bottom. This space, lit only by the archway into the courtyard, was thronged with monsters. The dough giant, painted and grinning, towered on its sledge by the arch, surrounded by the team of black and scarlet demons who would haul it onto the stage. Beyond them the voice of the solo chanter gargled its strange deep note while the bells tinkled and clanked. The oracle-priest was not here. Urgently Theodore turned to a group by the foot of the stair.

"Who speaks Chinese?" he said. "A man is going to shoot the Lama Amchi."

A vast shape wheeled round and the monster Yidam

Yamantaka glared down at Theodore. He spoke his question again, almost shouting now, to the eye-slits in the chest. The creature took a pace towards him, making shooing movements with its arms, which protruded roughly from its hips. Several of the demons came crowding round, speaking in hissing whispers, no doubt telling him not to interrupt the ceremony but producing a noise both bloodless and furious, such as a brood of snakes might make if they could talk. Theodore retreated a couple of steps up the stair and made his plea again but was answered with more hisses and gestures of dismissal. Now, round the shoulders of Yidam Yamantaka and over the heads of the demons, he could see the solid crush of watchers in the courtyard—there was no possible way through there to warn the Lama.

As Theodore climbed the dark stair the image of the monster Yamantaka and the hissing demons was strong in his mind, not as creatures of terror, but as something else, a sign, a warning. He had been appealing for help to the wrong Gods. He must find Lung himself.

This was not a conscious decision, but as he strode back down the gallery, searching the heedless backs for one that might be the oracle-priest, his reason was asking, Where would Lung go? Where? The pulse of the chant was changing now, with the rise and fall of the deep horn-notes coming faster, like waves clustering closer together; the pitch of the voices and the other instruments held a tension, as if the outward discipline were about to burst under the pressure of the inner excitement and become chaos—a tingle like the fringe of foam that rims a wave just before it breaks. Soon, now, soon the music would end, and then the Lama Amchi would leave his house and glide down the steps to the last platform above the crowd. A perfect target.

From where?

The answer formed in the same pulse as the question. Theodore saw the image of the Lama moving down those steps as if floating an inch above them. He heard Lung's hiss— "He is a sorcerer! Look, he is flying!" The roof of the temple of the oracle, where Lung had turned from mending the wind-mill and seen the Lama on the steps. There!

Theodore broke into a run, racing along to the far end of the gallery and hurling down that stair and out into the courtyard. Here, at the furthest corner from the stage, the crowd was not quite so dense and it was possible to shoulder and twist a way through. The people, inured by now to jostling, seemed barely to notice him as they craned towards the steps that led down from the mountain. The soloist was chanting a phrase which Theodore recognised as the regular formula which came at the end of many different chants. In a few seconds the choirs would answer, echoing the phrase seven times, and the chant would be over.

He came to a barrier. The steps of the temple of the oracle were massed with watchers. They would not, or could not, yield at all when he tried to press through, though still they seemed not to notice him, drugged with the expectation of the Lama's appearance and the dance of Yidam Yamantaka. He got half onto the lowest step, slipped off and fell, then stayed at that level and squirmed through the forest of legs up the steps and at last to the temple doors. He had half expected to find them closed, but they were open and the pressure of the crowd had pushed a number of spectators right back into the familiar glimmering dark. They made room for him as he rose to his feet and pressed through. He couldn't see Major Price-Evans, but there was no time now for explanations—and if he could

deal with Lung alone, and not let any of the monks know . . .
He tried to move fast without attracting attention, reached the
door in the far right corner where the sacred books were,
opened it and slipped through into the little room beyond. The
trap door in the ceiling was open, but the ladder was gone.

He darted back into the temple and dragged out from the
hanging on the back wall the ladder he had used for cleaning
the idols; as he took it through the door the swing of the rear
end caught a great bronze dish and sent it to the floor, where it
landed with a clashing note like a struck gong. The singing in
the courtyard was over, and in the silence of expectation the
clatter made the people at the temple door turn and stare. A
monk among them frowned and started to stride across, but
already Theodore was into the little room and using the
momentum of his rush to swing the ladder straight up into
the trap.

He scuttled up the rungs, thinking that if Lung had taken all
the ladders he would have to pull this one up after him, but he
came through the trap and saw one ladder lying across the floor
and another still in place. He was already on it when a voice
called out in Tibetan and the ladder below rattled as the monk
tried it for safety. Then he was through into the third room,
rushing up the last ladder and out under the open sky, his lungs
gasping for the harsh thin air.

A solitary monk was standing at the parapet, his cowl over
his head, gazing out across the courtyard. The windmills
clacked in the silence, perhaps hiding the sound of Theodore's
arrival. But now, drowning all noises, a slow, rumbling gasp
rose from below, like the sound of the avalanches they had
heard when crossing the highest pass, but which he knew was
the sigh from unnumbered throats as expectation was answered

and the patience of waiting ended. The Lama Amchi had appeared.

The monk knelt, lifted the rifle he had been cradling against his robe and settled it into his shoulder, steadying his left wrist on the parapet. Holding his breath Theodore stole towards him. The kneeling figure tensed. Its thumb pushed at the safety-catch.

"Lung! Stop!" Theodore croaked.

The cowled head turned and Lung's face, drained grey with tension, stared at him for a moment, almost unrecognisable. It cuddled back to the stock.

Theodore launched himself at Lung's shoulders, reaching round at the same time to clutch at the trigger hand. As he struck he heard a shot snap through the humming silence, and then he was half off his feet, staggering against the parapet, grasping the gun-barrel now with the strength of panic as he felt himself beginning to tumble back into space. Lung was yelling and wrenching at the gun with both hands, hauling Theodore back onto the roof as his grasp was breaking. Theodore stumbled to his knees. He found Lung's leg in front of him, wrapped his arms round it and pulled. A shot banged as Lung staggered, steadied, and kicked at him with his other foot. A huge blow thudded into the side of his head, making the world black and full of whining pain. Far off he heard screams and yells, and nearer a voice shouting. He lay, conscious only of pain, and then of the slightly tacky surface of the tarred roof, and then he was fully aware, hearing grunts and thuds near by. Wincing at the mountain brightness he opened his eyes to see Lung and a monk wrestling near the parapet. The robes made them seem like a single, threshing figure, but suddenly the monk had the upper hand and was forcing Lung sideways towards the drop. Lung bucked and wriggled ineffectively. Theodore rose and staggered towards the pair, tugging at the monk's robe and shouting "No! No! No!" Vaguely he saw that the crowd below had changed colour, with every face now staring up at the fight. Distracted by Theodore's arrival the monk lost his grip for a moment. Lung twisted sideways and clear, then flung himself flat on the roof and lay there, sobbing.

Chapter 17

The monastery had a hospital. Theodore lay on his cot there with his eyes closed, relaxed and waiting for whatever might happen next. His headache was not so bad since he had persuaded the hospital monks to stop saying mantras over him and send somebody to fetch the medicine-tin from the baggage-pile. He had taken two of Mrs Jones's headache-powders, which seemed to have worked, though their sour-sweet taste hung like vomit in the back of his throat. But in any case he now seemed to have the power to push the pain outside himself, and let it ache away in the void without troubling him. Footsteps shuffled by his bed.

"Are you awake, my friend?" said the voice of the oracle-priest.

By the weak light of the butter-lamp at his bedside Theodore looked up at the solemn, sturdy features, half-expecting them to contort into the monster of the morning. The prospect didn't frighten him any more. He waited.

"They wish you to come to the Council," said the oracle-priest.

"Why?"

"How should I know? I am not a member of the Council. They were questioning me, because I had been speaking with you at the start of the Festival. But I do not remember what was said. Perhaps a power visited me . . ."

"Yes."

"Then it is vital to know what the power said. They seldom come uninvoked, and when they do, it is for matters of great importance."

"It told me to go to my room. That's all."

"You must come. We must know the exact words, so that the Master of Protocol may interpret them."

"I don't know the exact words. When it happened I thought you spoke to me in English, but now I'm not sure."

"In any case you must come. Are you well enough to stand, or shall I send for a litter?"

"I can walk. What's happened to Lung? Is he all right?"

"The Chinese? I do not know."

Theodore sat up carefully. The movement filled his head with a shrill whine, and his shoulders were very sore. He seemed to have a big, wincing bruise on his left thigh. Watched anxiously by the hospital monk who had been looking after him he eased himself free of the blankets and into his boots. The oracle-priest put a strong arm round his shoulders and led him limping out into the night.

The Festival was still going on as if nothing had happened. A group of performers was swirling through the small courtyard below the hospital gallery, carrying orange-flaring torches which made the shadows dart and flicker across their masks—these were of animals, mostly lions and deer. They swept in silence out under the further arch, from beyond which came the endless throb and tinkle of Tibetan music. The oracle-priest led the way towards the gallery above the main courtyard. The air was full of sharp smells, something like scorched hair mixed with bitter spices. From the corridor before the long gallery Theodore could see that something was burning on the courtyard floor, throwing an unsteady, bluish, chemical light through the long vista of arches; the light glinted off pillars and the watchers along the balustrade and cast their shadows waveringly on the wall behind. There seemed to be still a huge crowd watching. Theodore heard, and almost felt, their response of horror and excitement as the animal-dancers burst with demon-screams onto the stage, but he never reached a point from which he could see into the courtyard because the oracle-priest stopped in the darkness of the corridor and tapped at a door on the left. It opened a crack. A password was exchanged, and it opened fully.

Inside was a fair-sized room containing several idols and hung with Buddhist symbols and pictures. A dozen monks were standing around in patient silence. The two who were guarding the door wore their rosaries wound round their arms to show they were soldier-monks, and carried ornate swords which looked like ritual objects but could clearly be used as weapons. Two more of them guarded a larger door in the left-hand wall. Without a word to anyone the oracle-priest led Theodore to this second door. One of them opened it a crack, and waited. A voice was murmuring beyond. Another voice joined in, arguing against the first, then two more. A bell rang sharply, followed by instant silence. The guard swung the door open and the oracle-priest led Theodore through, still with his arm round his shoulders.

For a moment Theodore thought he had walked into another temple. There, at the far end of the longish room, was the idol of the Buddha, twice life-size, gilded and jewelled, gazing at him out of the gloom with its blank eyes and uninterpretable smile; the room was heavy with glitter and richness and mystery, all made stronger and stranger by the light of the erratic little lamps. Two of the wheel-backed thrones stood in front of the idol; four benches, two on each side, faced each other across a central aisle—these were occupied by about thirty monks, mostly elderly. The Lama Amchi sat on the left hand throne. The other was empty, waiting as it had waited these past twelve years, for the Tulku.

The Lama Amchi gave an order in Tibetan, and the monk who had let them in brought a stool and set it in the middle of the aisle between the benches. The oracle-priest eased Theodore gently onto it.

"Welcome to the Council Room of Dong Pe," said the Lama Amchi. "Are you fit to answer questions?"

"Where is Lung?" said Theodore.

"The Chinese? That need not concern us now. He is well guarded. He cannot harm you."

"What have you done to him? Is he all right?"

"We have more important matters to consider. It seems to us that as the Festival began this morning the oracle spoke to you. We must know what he said."

"I won't tell you anything till I've seen Lung."

Most of the monks in the room must have understood Mandarin, for Theodore heard a murmur of anger from the benches. The Lama Amchi seemed unmoved. His eyes turned towards the oracle-priest, who spoke for a short while in Tibetan. Theodore caught the word for "room".

"Is this so, child?" said the Lama, gentle as ever. "The oracle, speaking in your own tongue, told you to go to your room?"

"When I've seen Lung," said Theodore.

There was a short silence. A monk rose on one of the benches and started to speak in tolerable Mandarin, no doubt for Theodore's benefit. Theodore thought it was the old man who had held the slate at the ceremony of the oracle.

"If this word is true," he said, "it could be interpreted simply. Only this child, who is the Guide, could recognise the signs to show that the Chinese had gone into the monastery, taking a weapon with him. Only he could know where to look for him and prevent the crime. But he would need to go to his room to recognise the signs. But this is mere speculation without the exact words."

"This is unimportant," said someone else. "The most necessary thing is to know what the Chinese in Pekin are planning for Dong Pe. They have sent this agent to attack our great Lama . . ."

"That is not known for sure," said someone else.

"Then let us ask the oracle."

"The oracle ceremony cannot be held for at least ten days. First there is the Festival, then the stars are ill-placed."

"Yet the oracle spoke only this morning. The child must be made to tell us . . ."

The acid note of the bell cut through the clamour of voices and silence fell. The Lama Amchi said nothing but sat gazing at Theodore with that strange half-seeing gaze, as though all the solid material of the room—flesh and bone, wood and stone— were so much mist, through which he was gazing on something more truly there. Theodore stared back. He was aware of a web of tensions around him, a network which quivered to the touch of a hundred different motives and impulses; he could hear in the whispered exchanges at one side something that was more than mere discussion, something which held a challenge to the Lama Amchi's authority; he guessed that Sumpa had not been the only monk willing to help the Chinese, and that some secret sympathisers might even be present in this room. But for the moment none of those complexities mattered at all to

Theodore. He had one clear and simple aim—to find out what had happened to Lung and to do his best to protect him.

"You don't even know that Lung fired the shots," Theodore said suddenly. "Perhaps it was me. I'm a Christian. Perhaps I wanted to stop the dance of Yidam Yamantaka, because I think it's wicked."

He could hear the disbelief in the murmurs around him. The Lama Amchi smiled.

"You do not have such a thought in your soul," he said. "You are a friend. You are the Guide. Against your own inmost wish you have striven to help us, and now you have fought, as if with demons, to preserve my poor life. You have done well, and more than well, and our blessing is on you . . . No, it was the Chinese who fired the shots, though one indeed struck the shoulder of Yidam and one broke a lamp in front of the Buddha in my own room . . . Now I am at a loss. I do not see which way to turn if you will not help us."

"Let me see Lung."

"No."

Before the silence could really settle again a new noise rose, a voice from beyond the doors, quiet but urgent, its owner, even through the muffling timber, unmistakable.

"It is the Mother of the Tulku," said the Lama Amchi. "Do we admit her, my brothers?"

"A woman? In the Council Room?" said an appalled voice. Grunts of agreement followed the protest.

"She is the Mother of the Tulku and no mere woman," said the Lama. "And besides, she will come in whether we like it or no."

Without waiting for further argument he gave an order to the guard at the door, and at the same time rose to his feet. The door swung open and Mrs Jones came quietly through. Theodore realised that everyone else in the room was standing. He rose swayingly to his feet, turning to watch her come. She had the monks' walk to perfection now, and glided just far enough into the room to let the doors shut behind her, then knelt and bowed her head to the floor. Rising again she came forward in silence until she stood beside Theodore.

"What's up, Theo?" she whispered. "I heard a couple of shots this morning, and I knew they must of come from my gun, but no one won't tell me what happened. I been looking for you and old Lung all day, and in the end I got it out of someone as you was here. I was going to wait till you come out, but then I got it into my head as how you needed me, so I went and argy-bargied my way in."

"They won't tell me what they've done with Lung," said Theodore.

"Why should they of done anything with him?"

"He tried to shoot the Lama Amchi this morning. I stopped him. On the roof of the temple of the oracle. I got knocked out in the fight. They've been trying to make me tell them what the oracle said to me this morning, and I've been saying I won't tell them till they let me see Lung. I'm afraid . . ."

The clink of the bell cut him short.

"Let us do everything in order," said the Lama. "Child, we must now talk in Tibetan, so that the Mother of the Tulku can answer us."

Theodore nodded. At a sign from the Lama another stool was brought for Mrs Jones. Everybody sat. The Lama spoke for a short while. Theodore, from what Major Price-Evans had taught him, picked out enough of the words to guess that the Lama was asking Mrs Jones to persuade him to answer the question about his meeting with the oracle. He was preparing himself to refuse when instead of turning to him she replied to the Lama in Tibetan. She started easily enough, but then, to his surprise, stumbled and faltered, searched for a word, got going but almost at once came to a halt once more.

"This won't do," she said in English. "Trouble is, all the Tibetan I've learnt is about chants and meditation and such, which ain't much cop for talking about this kind of thing. I'll have to do it in English, and you put it into Chinee for them. All right?"

Theodore nodded, remembering his own difficulties with Major Price-Evans. Mrs Jones turned once more to the Lama Amchi.

"Now see here," she said earnestly. "Things ain't been going too bad this far, spite of old Lung trying to take a pot-shot at you this morning—not that he had a hope in heaven of hitting you at that range. But apart from that, I done everything you wanted, and more. When I first come here my idea was to scarper, soon as poss, and we set it up and four nights ago we was all ready to go, and you'd never have caught us, neither, with three days' start. Only who stopped it? I did. I'd changed my mind and decided I was going to stick it out here, and have the baby here whatever happens. And what's more, I been doing my level best to do it all the way you want, so as your Tulku can have a proper start in his next life, with a Mum what's really up to the job. I been meditating like nobody's business. I been learning every blind scrap I can about the sort of thing he's got to know—all right, I been doing it for my own sake, much as his, but you can't say as I've done one thing what you didn't want. Now you look like mucking it all up. Lung's the Father of the Tulku, ain't he . . ."

She was speaking at a slower pace than her usual rush, and had dropped into the slurred and twanging accent which Theodore had heard only once before, when she had been talking in the cave in the rock pillar about her childhood in the Thames-side slums. It was as though the years of her life between those old days and this had been an almost meaningless interlude. She spoke quietly but with great emphasis, and paused at the end of almost every phrase for Theodore to translate. When he reached this point there was a gasp and a mutter. Clearly most of the Council were not aware that Lung was the father of the unborn child. The Lama Amchi must know—yes, of course, Mrs Jones had told him very early on when they were discussing the signs announced by the oracle—but presumably he hadn't told the others. They wouldn't quite so easily accept a Tulku of half-Chinese parentage, perhaps.

"Is he still alive?" said Mrs Jones.

"His body lives," said the Lama.

"I want to see him."

"It is better not."

"Now, look here. This is what I mean when I say you're beginning to muck things up. For a start, it ain't right if the Father of the Tulku don't get proper respect, whatever he might of done in a moment when he was a bit off his rocker. And next, I am very fond of that young man. I ain't fond of him in quite the same way as what I was four months back, but I want to see as he's all right. I want that almost as much as I want to see that you get your Tulku born proper. Matter of fact, the one goes with the other. If I start thinking as how Lung got into trouble 'cause of what I did, then I won't be able to do my meditating and all, will I? That bit of guilt will be like a ruddy great mountain, bang in the middle of my road to enlightenment. I'll put it stronger. Unless I see as Lung's all right, and going to stay all right, then I'm going to turn round. I'm going to walk all the way back down the road as I've come so far along, and be what I was before I became your *chela*. Cause of why? Cause you'll of shown me, by the way you treated my friend Lung, that none of what you been teaching me matters. Perhaps it's true—fact I still think it is—but it still don't matter one blind bit if it lets you do that to a fellow like Lung. No, wait. I got something else to say. It's no use you thinking fair enough. She can go back and be what she was before, and have the baby, and after that it don't matter what she thinks or feels. It ain't true. I'm old for child-bearing. What's more I've only had one kid before, and that time I wasn't happy and I near as a toucher died, spite of the best doctors in England, and so did the baby. And I can tell you now it'll be worse this time. Oh, I can have your Tulku, soft and easy, with hardly a pang, spite of my age, 'cause of what you've taught me. But you know as well as I do it'll only work if I've got faith in it. Absolute, stark, unquestioning faith, body and soul. And if you ain't careful, that's not going to happen. So, now, let's have him up here and see what you done to him."

"He is a profaner of holy things," said the Lama. "He cannot come to this place."

"No he ain't," said Mrs Jones. "He was off his rocker, so it don't count. And what's more he's the Father of the Tulku. So this is where we start. If you say he's a profaner of holy things and I say he ain't, that means I'm turning back along the road you shown me. Don't it?"

"It is strange when the *chela* begins to teach the *guru*," said the Lama, mild as ever.

"I'm not teaching you. I'm just stating facts. And I'm not

threatening you neither. If any of this happens, it won't be because I want it. I don't. I want the Tulku to be born, here in Dong Pe, safe and sound. I want to follow on the path you shown me. But it looks like you're not going to let it happen."

There was a short silence.

"Let us ask the Council what it thinks of this matter," said the Lama.

Theodore had been aware, during all this exchange, of other voices straining to speak, but held back by the two powerful personalities at the focus of the argument. Now the pent waters burst. One monk started to argue sedately enough, but almost at once three others joined in. Angry shouts rose. An old man was on his feet, yelling the same short phrase over and over until his neighbours pulled him down. There was no mistaking the surge of intense hostility and hatred, not for anybody in the room, but for poor Lung, an invisible presence, at whom the monks shook their fists and screamed as if he had been standing there. There was a terrifying note in the tumult, as though the demons whose roles were being enacted outside by the masked dancers had been summoned to this room in their real selves, invisible powers of cruelty and rage and ignorance, occupying the bodies of the Council members in much the same way as the other powers had occupied that of the oracle-priest. Not all those present were shouting for vengeance on Lung. Perhaps almost half of them seemed to be arguing on the other side, but it made no difference—the contorted faces were the same, the gestures of violence, the bellows and screams. They were all possessed, beyond reason, whatever their original impulse.

The Lama Amchi waited with his bell poised, judged his moment and shook it vigorously. The noise was like a whip-lash, but the shouting barely faltered. He had to shake the bell twice more before the yelling diminished into a tingling silence. Theodore saw for the first time how thin was the old man's control, for all his prestige. Perhaps he was right. Perhaps only he could command and save Dong Pe. Perhaps it was not only love of power which had forced him into some of his actions.

"The Council is divided," said the Lama with a smile.

"So it's between you and me," whispered Mrs Jones.

This time the silence was longer. Mrs Jones and the Lama faced each other, as they had in their first meeting on the mountainside, and energies flowed between them as they had seemed to then, like the lines of force between the poles of a magnet. The other souls in the room were constrained and held in place by the flow of energies until the Lama smiled again, raised his head and gave a longish order in Tibetan. One of the soldier monks at the door left the room.

"It will take a little time," said the Lama. "Perhaps now the child will tell us what happened in his encounter with the oracle this morning."

"Fair enough," said Mrs Jones. "I think you won your point, Theo. You might as well let 'em see you mean to play fair by them."

"All right," said Theodore in Mandarin. "I'll tell you what I thought happened, though later I wasn't so sure. It began after breakfast, when Lung told me to leave our room because he wanted to be alone . . ."

He told the story carefully, in the right order, leaving nothing out, not even the fact that he had thought the oracle spoke to him in Father's words and tone, nor the fact that he had to all intents and purposes accused the Master of Protocol of cheating over the oracle's messages. They listened closely, but questioned him only about the exact words he had used before the oracle-priest became possessed and the exact words of the reply. These the Master of Protocol wrote down on a slate which he drew from the folds of his robe. As Theodore finished he heard a shuffle and murmur at the door.

"We will consider these meanings later," said the Lama Amchi. "Let the Chinese be brought in."

Theodore twisted on his stool in time to see the doors swing open and a shape outlined against the light from the further room. Though the shape was clearly composed of three people standing close together there was something inhuman, something monstrous about it. The shape split as the two men on the outside let go of the central figure and pushed it forward. It came at a slow, dragging walk, which still had that inhuman look, as though the figure were an automaton which would walk like this for ever. Even when it reached the area lit by the lamps in the Council Room Theodore was unable to recognise it as Lung. It was not just that the side of the face was puffy with a huge bruise and that dried blood had dribbled from the corner of the swollen lips. The face was not a man's face at all. It was expressionless. The eyes stared like an idol's, round as marbles, unfocused and unblinking. The head was unnaturally stiff on the neck, and the arms, held close to the side of the body, looked as though they were clamped rigid.

As this figure came up the aisle between the benches Mrs Jones rose from her stool, took two paces towards it and clutched it to her side. For a moment its legs tried to continue walking, but then they stilled. Lung, if it was Lung, showed no sign of knowing her.

"Oh, what have you done to him? What have done to him?" she cried.

"If we hadn't protected him from the crowd in the

courtyard," said one of the monks, "they would have torn him to fragments as we tear the dough giant."

"That ain't what I meant," she snapped. "And you know it. What have you done to him?"

"He was questioned and he would not answer," said the Lama Amchi. "That accounts for his having been beaten a little. Then, while we are considering the proper punishment for a breaker of idols, we locked his soul within him, as you see."

"Can you unlock it?"

"It can sometimes be done. But the Mother of the Tulku must understand that the Chinese is not now, so to speak, a person. He is in abeyance. Once he is himself again, with his soul guiding his body, he becomes again responsible for all that he has done. It is impossible that such a one should remain within the holy valley of Dong Pe, at the height of our great festival. He would be as it were a corruption, infecting all our rituals and ceremonies."

"All right," she said. "Give him his soul back and he can leave tomorrow morning. First thing. Theo can go with him."

The Lama seemed about to agree when somebody spoke angrily from among the monks.

"He cannot go back to China," explained the Lama. "There are those here who still believe that he is an agent of Pekin."

"It'll have to be Inja then. You can cope with that? They'll need an escort as far as the border. I've got enough money to see them through . . ."

"We will provide for such needs," said the Lama.

"It won't be cheap," said Mrs Jones. "Theo'll need a ticket to England and then to America, and Lung'll want a bit too . . ."

"Dong Pe is rich. It will be done. Now let us perform the ritual, for the longer a man's soul stays thus locked up the harder is his return."

He gave orders in Tibetan. The monks rose and rearranged themselves. A pair of small drums and a silver incense-lamp were fetched from a curtained niche. The butter-lamps were collected and lined up in a single row at the feet of the Buddha, making the statue seem to float, gold and warm, in the darkness of the rest of the room.

"Theo," whispered Mrs Jones. "Come here a tick. I want a word with you."

She was still standing, clutching Lung to her side as though he would fall without her. Theodore rose achingly and joined her.

"When this palaver is over," she whispered. "Come up to my cave. Nobody won't stop you. We'll have a bit of a chat, say good-bye, like. And there's something important I want you to do for me."

"I'll do anything," said Theodore.

"Sorry to make you go all sudden like this," she said. "But I 'spect you'll be glad of it, really. You'll see Lung's in good hands in Inja, won't you?"

"If I can."

"Course you can. Then there's this other thing. It won't be easy, but it's got to be done. Laying a ghost, like. And I shan't have the baby easy unless I know . . . shh, they're starting. Tell you after."

To Theodore's surprise it wasn't the Lama Amchi who performed the ceremony, but a gaunt, middle-aged monk wearing a black scarf across his shoulders and a black hat shaped like the prow of a ship. The small drums beat in the dark with a slow rhythm. The monks began to hum, a deep, throbbing note, enough of them keeping it up while the others paused for breath to make the hum continuous. Mrs Jones led Lung forward till she stood with him at the edge of the circle of light, but at a sign from the monk in the black hat she moved a little to one side. The smoke that rose from the incense-burner was not blue but orange, and had a heavy but acid smell that hung dazingly in the air. Now the noise from the monks' throats seemed to be throbbing through the solid stones of the walls and timbers of the roof, waking in them stone and timber voices which answered with the same vibration. The monk in the black hat picked up a small drum and beat a pattering roll on it, which he echoed with a sort of chant, a monotonous rattle of syllables all on one note but ending with an explosion of breath as though the air had been forced from his lungs by a violent blow from within. This—drum-roll, rattle and explosion—happened several times, and as it did so the monk visibly changed, becoming taller and yet more gaunt until his face in the upthrown light of the butter lamps was a skull with no gleam of any eye in the black sockets. When he had completed this change he put the drum down and became as still as the Buddha, though the rest of the room was now quivering to the vibrations of the noise made by the monks. Even the floor seemed to be trembling—Theodore could feel it through the soles of his boots—and Lung's silhouette, which had before stood sharp against the smoky globe of light in which the monk was working his magic, was now shadowy in outline as though the vibrations were centred on Lung, making him quiver like a tuning-fork.

Theodore concentrated his energies. He willed the magic to succeed. He did not hum with the monks, but for Lung's sake he joined his soul to theirs, letting it shudder to the same harmonics, so that there was nothing in the room that was not part of that single purpose. Perhaps he was praying, but if so it was not in any fashion that Father had taught him. He became pure prayer—not a boy praying to a separate God, but a single process in which boy and prayer and God were the same thing. He joined the ritual.

And now the globe of light seemed to contract, as though the magician were using the energies in the room to gather the light into himself. The shapeless hum also gathered to a focus, which was Lung. The walls became still and the floor no longer tingled beneath Theodore's feet, but the noise rose in pitch and came from a single point above Lung's head, and still rose and narrowed till it reached a tension where it had to disintegrate or become a new mode of sound. At that moment of breaking the magician, motionless for so long, suddenly spread his arms wide, threw them forward at Lung's body, and at last drew them slowly and heavily back. The noise had stopped. The globe of light widened and was ordinary. The magician, a skull no longer, stepped a pace back and said a few quiet words. As he spoke the rigid creature in front of him lost tension, slackened, became human, and at the same moment started to fall. It was Mrs Jones who caught him and eased him to the floor in front of the Buddha.

Surfacing from the daze of effort Theodore had run forward as Lung fell. He was too late to help, but stayed looking down at his friend. Lung's eyes were open. He had his head in Mrs Jones's lap and lay there, gazing up into her face, much as Theodore had once seen them in the valley of the lilies.

"Missy," he whispered, with a smile of painful joy, and closed his eyes.

Chapter 18

Theodore waited in the small room to which he had been shown by a servant wearing a black jacket and striped trousers —the butler, he guessed. The room smelt strongly of many things, especially damp dogs. A row of waterproofs and great-coats hung along one wall. The two chairs were upholstered in shiny red leather, padded with horse hair, and crackled angrily when one sat down, as if they were not used to such treatment. The pictures on the walls were of men in tall hats galloping on stretched-out horses under a moonlit sky. Outside the single sash window a pale sun shone, but the morning's rain still dripped from trees onto the gravel of the driveway where Theodore's cab waited. The cab-horse had a vague look of Albert about it.

Sooner than Theodore had expected the butler returned.

"This way, if you please, sir," he said.

His manner had changed. When Theodore had been trying to persuade him to take the note to his master at once, instead of leaving it to lie with the letters on the sideboard in the hall, he had been very stiff and in his cold way hostile. Now, though still stiff, he was respectful and even faintly inquisitive. Theodore followed him across the hall, with its polished floor and Persian rugs and cases of porcelain and trophies of animal heads along the walls, then down a short corridor to a door which the butler opened and held for him.

"The young gentleman, sir," he intoned.

"Ah. Come in," said a man's voice, light, musical, tense.

This room was quite large. Tobacco smoke mingled with the powdery scent of chrysanthemums which, with a number of plants Theodore had never seen, stood in large pots around the floor. Two large windows with heavy stone mullions looked out over a valley towards bare hills. The sweep of wood Mrs Jones had told him about—"just right for his lilies"—curled down the slope to the left, dark cones of pine spiring among the last tattered golds of autumn. Theodore knew that the house was less than ten years old, but it felt as though it had stood here for a long time and housed many generations of rich men. He could only guess that most of the objects in the room were expensive, just as most of the plants in the pots were exotic and rare, but that was not the reason why they were there. They were there because they suited the taste of the man they belonged to, and so the room felt as though it had taken shape round a single personality. In the hearth a couple of logs smoked in thin blue streams on a pile of white ash, and over the fireplace was a portrait of a woman, painted in profile to show the richness of her red-gold hair and the almost bird-like fineness of her profile. The picture fitted the room too.

Not much to look at, Mrs Jones had said, a little bloke, trim, something about him made him look like he's just been polished, even in the middle of a jungle . . .

Nothing about the description was wrong, but there was something else which Theodore felt he should have been prepared for, but wasn't—a vitality, a quickness of glance, a sense of hard intelligence poised cat-like behind the façade of this small neat man in his quiet tweeds.

"I'm Monty German," the man said. "I believe you are Theodore Tewker. How do you do?"

"Pleased to meet you, sir."

"How is she? When did you see her? Does she need help?"

"She was fine four months ago, sir."

"That sounds a bit final. Are you sure she's all right? You're telling the truth? She's not dead?"

"No sir. She's become a Buddhist . . ."

"Daisy! What else? There's something else."

"Yes sir. I said she was fine when I saw her, but she's going to have a baby . . ."

Mr German's face went white. He had been standing in front of the hearth, but now he took a quick step towards Theodore and stopped.

"When?" he whispered.

"In about six weeks, I guess."

"Has she good doctors?"

"No, sir. She says she doesn't need them. She's in a monastery in Tibet, and a monk called the Lama Amchi has been teaching her how to control her bodily functions. She told me to tell you that she'll have the baby as easy as rain in April. She told me to use those words. I think she's right, sir."

"Are you a Buddhist too, Mr Tewker?"

"No, sir. I'm a member of the Congregation of Christ Jesus."

"You'd better sit down and tell me a bit more. I must say I don't understand much of what you're talking about—in fact I can't make head or tail of it. I wasn't certain at first, but I've decided that you haven't come to try and get money out of me."

"No, sir. Mrs Jones made the Lamas give me enough money

—I sailed first class from India, and I have enough to pay my passage to the States, and then some."

"All right, but if you need any more . . . sit in that chair."

Unlike the chairs in the room where Theodore had first waited, these had been designed to make the sitter comfortable, and felt as though they had often done so; but Theodore perched on the edge of his, leaning forward with his elbows on his knees, concentrating on telling his story as exactly and unemotionally as possible. As he spoke the sense grew in him that by telling the story to the one man who was entitled to hear it all he was somehow disposing of it, detaching it from his life and setting himself free. Mrs Jones had asked him to lay a ghost for her, but he found he was also doing something of the sort for himself. Though he would always remember these last months, henceforth they would no longer haunt him.

Mr German didn't interrupt. At one point he rose and tugged at a wide embroidered ribbon which hung down the wall by the fire, and a little later the butler came in carrying a silver tray with two glasses, a green bottle and a silver jug. He opened the bottle with a pop and poured a glass of pale foaming liquid, which he handed to Mr German; then he fetched a low table to beside Theodore's chair and poured him a tall glass of orange. Theodore, who had stopped talking at a nod from Mr German as soon as the butler had entered, sipped his drink while he made up the fire and as soon as the door closed resumed his story.

It was all there, waiting to be uncoiled like a hawser running smoothly off a deck—the burning of the Settlement, Mrs Jones riding Sir Nigel down the rain-soaked track to stare at the broken bridge, the rout of her treacherous porters, Mrs Jones riding between the smoking huts, the journey's start,

P'iu-Chun's house, the ambush in the woods, the night at the rock pillar, the idyll in the valley of lilies, the flight to the bridge, the Lama Amchi, and all the slow accumulating change in her, right down to Theodore's last talk with her in her mountain cave. The only things he left out of the story were his own doubts and fears and miseries. Otherwise he put it all in. Things which he would have been embarrassed or ashamed to say to anyone else seemed necessary and therefore easy.

When he'd finished he looked up. Mr German was lying stretched out in his chair with his glass beside him, barely touched. There was a long silence.

"This fellow Lung?" said Mr German. "He's all right?"

"I liked him, sir."

"So did Daisy, evidently, and that's recommendation enough for me. But that's not what I meant. Does he need any help?"

"He was still very weak when we got to Darjeeling, sir, but we met up there with Professor Lockwood and his wife . . ."

"Yes, of course. Daisy told you to call on them?"

"Yes, sir. They said they would look after Lung."

"I'll cable Lockwood. My bank's got a branch in Poona. I'll cable them too. I could get him a job with our people in Hong Kong . . . but I should think the first thing he'll do is try to get back, wouldn't you?"

"To Dong Pe? Yes, sir. But they won't let him into Tibet.'

"Well, we'll do the best we can for him, one way or another. What about you?"

"I'm going home, sir. I have my passage booked from Liverpool on Thursday."

"Sure that's what you want? We can cancel the passage. You're welcome to stay here as long as you like."

"Thank you, sir, but I'd better be getting back to Bluff City.

I must tell the the Congregation what happened to Father and the Settlement."

"Yes, of course. And then?"

"I will finish my schooling and wait God's will."

"You won't go back to China?"

"If He guides me . . . but . . ."

"Yes. After what you've seen and felt it must be difficult to be so certain about things."

That was true, but it was only partly true. If the foundations which Father had given him had been shaken, Theodore had discovered other foundations beneath, broader and more enduring. The thought of Father nudged his mind.

"I guess I'd like to go back to China, sir. I want to see if I can rebuild that bridge."

"Good idea . . . And you won't forget me, will you, wherever you find yourself. I might be some use some day. The business I work for has a lot of connections in most parts of the world. And if ever you need money for what you're doing . . ."

"Thank you, sir. I'll remember."

"I hope you do."

There was another pause before Theodore felt in his jacket pocket and pulled out a long, thin envelope from which he took a sheet of fibrous Tibetan paper, folded in three. It was a picture of Mrs Jones he had drawn one afternoon, quite early in their time at Dong Pe, while she was working in her little garden. Because of the steepness of the ground she and Theodore had terraced the patch with rough stone walls, so that it was possible to stand at one level and work, barely stooping, at the next level up. Mrs Jones was in just such a pose, wearing her riding-cloak and travelling hat. Her face was hidden, but of the dozen or so pictures Theodore had made of her this was the only one he liked. He had brought it, but had not decided till this moment whether to show it to Mr German.

Mr German leaned across and took the paper, unfolding it with precise small fingers. He stared at the drawing for some time.

"Yours?" he said at last.

"Yes, sir."

"I would know her on the dark side of the moon," said Mr German quietly.

"You may keep it if you want, sir."

Mr German's glance didn't falter, but Theodore was aware of the portrait above the fireplace, a presence in the room.

"No," said Mr German. "No. But seeing her digging away like that reminds me—we'd better take care of this lily you've brought me. I wonder whether it's still all right. Where is it?"

"In a box in the cab, sir."

"Cab? Of course. We'll have to see your cabbie's looked after—we'll be some time yet."

They were standing on the rain-glistening gravel by the front door—Theodore holding the precious box while Mr German explained to the cab-driver how to find refreshment for himself and his horse—when a boy on a bicycle came swirling down the slope and stopped in a scatter of small stones by putting both heels to the ground and letting them slither. It was the first bicycle Theodore had seen close to. The boy was about nine, dressed in a stiff tweed jacket with sharp-stitched pockets, and knickerbockers of the same material.

"Hello, Dave," said Mr German.

"Hello, Uncle. What've you got there? Early Christmas present?"

"All the way from Tibet. This is Theodore Tewker—my nephew David. Mr Tewker brought me the present."

"How do you do?" said the boy. "Is he telling the truth? Miss Tancred says nobody is allowed to go to Tibet."

"I went there by accident," said Theodore.

The boy looked at him doubtfully, not sure whether he was being teased. He was slight and small-boned like Mr German, but with long-lashed large eyes under heavy black brows. The eyes were much greyer than Mrs Jones's.

"Since you are so conveniently mounted," said Mr German, "you might perhaps be kind enough to ride your machine down to the Heather Garden and find Mr Bancroft. Ask him to meet me in the greenhouses."

"Yip-yip-yip-yip," shrilled the boy, and sped away, still yipping. Mr German turned and led the way through an arch into a walled garden. Two men in sacking aprons were digging a trench round a small tree in the central lawn, and Mr German strolled across to watch them.

"She'll move all right, sir," said the man at the bottom of the trench, rubbing his hand along the inner wall and caressing a few brown root-fibres. "No more'n a few roots come out this far—she's a slow starter, ain't she? Six years she been here."

"Don't be too sure, Tom," said Mr German. "I've never moved one before but I have a fancy she'll sulk. Sure you can handle a ball that big?"

The three men discussed the problem of lifting the tree out complete with the earth it had grown in while Theodore waited dreamily in the soft and sighing air. At last Mr German turned away.

"One of my mistakes," he said. "Putting a *eucryphia* in a place like that—too tame, too tame."

"She said you had chosen the place for your *eucryphia*."

"Ah, that one's all right," said Mr German with a sudden astonishing smile. "I wish you'd been here two months ago to see it. Gardeners always say that, don't they? Best thing in the garden. Daisy and I walked all round here one sopping morning, talking about that sort of thing. I still thought she was going to share it with me then . . . ah, here's Mr Bancroft."

They had come out on the far side of the walled garden into an area of sheds and glass-houses. A stout little man was waiting there. He was dressed in black trousers and a black waistcoat, a blue striped shirt and white collar, with a black tie. He wore a curious black bowler hat, which he doffed to Mr German. His hand when Theodore shook it was as rough as sandstone.

"Mr Tewker's brought us a lily, Mr Bancroft," said Mr German.

Mr Bancroft grunted unexcitedly, as though he had heard better news in his time.

"I think it's the first one to be collected," said Mr German. There was an odd note in his voice, both anxious and humorous, as though he thought it desperately important to please this sombre gnome, and at the same time was amused by his own need to do so. He succeeded, to the extent that a gleam came into the gnome's bloodshot eye.

"Ah," said Mr Bancroft. "Let's have a squint at un, then. Travelled a good bit, I'll be bound."

He took the box from Theodore and led the way into the nearest glass-house. Moving very deliberately he opened the lid, drew out the inner package and with a thin-bladed ancient pen-knife slit the sacking away. Theodore began to feel nervous, remembering all his care on the journey, his reading and re-reading Mrs Jones's instructions, his dreams while he lay in the near-delirium of fever in Calcutta, waiting for the boat to sail, and kept imagining monstrous rots attacking the frail bulb.

"I'd have brought you seed," he said. "Only it wasn't ripe when the bandits attacked us."

Mr Bancroft answered with his normal dull grunt; bandits were no excuse for failing to bring ripe seed. The glass-house was warm and still, smelling of rich earth and the remains of grapes. Along the ranked shelving azaleas were coming into flower, and lower down innumerable small pots each bore a white label and a wisp of green growth.

"This is Mr Bancroft's workshop," said Mr German in a stagey whisper. "I'll show you the ones with all the flowers in later."

"Ah," said Mr Bancroft, probing at last into the packing of moss around the bulb. The backs of his hands were covered with coarse black hair. His fingers moved like creatures of the soil, tender and firm, nudging their way through the loose stuff to ease the bulb free. He brought it out and held it up, pressing with short, broad thumbs against its unfolded scales.

"Dried out a morsel, her has," he said. "More'n a morsel. Ah. But there's life there still. Yes, Mr Monty, we'll get a bloom out of her yet. Yes, there's life there still."

Dazed with the mild warmth and the sense of ending, Theodore watched Mr Bancroft's fingers fondle the crabbed root. The universe seemed to hum around this centre. The panes of the walls and roof were the facets of an inward-watching eye, focused not on any of the three humans but on the lily-bulb. Yes, perhaps there was life there, a soul there, a soul being watched at the very start of its almost endless journey up the river, its struggle through life after life, against the rushing current of created things, until it reached the source of its being, which would also be its ending.

Now Mr Bancroft was bending to scoop dark fine earth out of a bin into a red clay pot. Carefully he settled the bulb into the earth, spreading its frail remaining roots around it, and then began to dribble more earth down the gap between the bulb and the wall of the pot. While he worked he murmured.

"Ah, yes, my beauty," said Mr Bancroft. "Yes, yes. There's life there, aren't there?"

Peter Dickinson was born in 1927, in what is now Zambia, within earshot of the Victoria Falls. His father was a colonial civil servant, his mother the daughter of a farmer. He remembers very little of Africa, since the family moved back to England when he was small.

He went to a prep school, then Eton. Despite bad patches, he enjoyed Eton, especially towards the end when he became rather good at games.

Two years in the army finished with a commission in the Royal Signals, stationed on Golders Green, which was the result of a novel-like experience: he was given two numbers, and therefore two identities, when he joined up. From the army's point of view, he was two people, one of them a deserter. He was training in Northern Ireland when two seasick Military Policemen turned up and arrested him for not being in *their* camp on Salisbury Plain. The error took months to sort out – hence Golders Green.

The army was followed by Kings College, Cambridge. He read Classics for a year, then switched to English, and while doing research there, was offered a job on *Punch* – where he stayed as literary editor for seventeen years, though he did most of the jobs on the paper and at one time was simultaneously Beauty and Agriculture editor. He wrote a lot of verse for *Punch*, and some prose too.

Whilst reviewing thrillers, he had an idea for one which was new. He toyed with it awhile, then one night sat down at the kitchen table after supper and began to write. He got stuck half-way through the book, had a nightmare and used this for the first chapter of a children's book, which he then wrote to unblock the thriller. That worked, and both books were published in 1968. The thriller was *Skin Deep*, which won the Crime Writers' Association Golden Dagger for that year. The children's book was *The Weathermonger*. He also won the Golden Dagger for *A Pride of Heroes*, and wasn't off the short list with any of his first five thrillers. He has three times been runner-up for the Carnegie Medal – *The Devil's Children*, *The Dancing Bear* and *The Blue Hawk*; he won the Guardian Award for *The Blue Hawk*, and the Whitbread Award as well as the Carnegie Medal for *Tulku*.

Peter Dickinson is married, with four children, and divides his time between London and Hampshire.

Some other Puffins for older readers

ONE MORE RIVER
Lynne Reid Banks

The conflict of personal and political loyalties, explored through the friendship of a Jewish girl with an Arab boy. By the author of *The L-Shaped Room*.

THE SUMMER AFTER THE FUNERAL
Jane Gardam

A brilliant, painful book about the grievous experience of breaking away from the security of family life to develop a workable and complex personality.

THE ENNEAD
Jan Mark

A vivid and compelling story about Euterpe, the third planet in a system of nine known as the Ennead, where scheming and bribery are needed to survive.

MISCHLING, SECOND DEGREE
Ilse Koehn

Ilse was a 'Mischling', a child of mixed race, a dangerous birthright in Nazi Germany. The perils of an outsider in the Hitler Youth Movement and in girls' military camps makes this a vivid and fascinating true story.

NOAH'S CASTLE
John Rowe Townsend

Set in a lawless, hungry Britain, this provocative book paints a chilling picture of a family under stress, revealing their strengths and their weaknesses. Recently filmed for television.

THE TWELFTH DAY OF JULY
ACROSS THE BARRICADES
INTO EXILE
A PROPER PLACE
HOSTAGES TO FORTUNE

Joan Lingard

A series of novels about modern Belfast which highlight the problems of the troubles there in the story of Protestant Sadie and Catholic Kevin which even an 'escape' to England fails to solve.

THE ENDLESS STEPPE

Esther Hautzig

The exile of a young child and her family to Siberia and their subsequent life there. This magnificent and moving book is a true story which will live long in the memory of any reader.

PROVE YOURSELF A HERO

K. M. Peyton

Kidnapping is a terrifying enough experience itself, but Jonathan finds that his eventual release causes him even greater problems!

THE KING OF THE BARBAREENS

Janet Hitchman

True story of an orphan, a plain, intelligent girl who is passed from one foster-home to another. She longs for love but ruins her chances by her defiant attitude.

A VERY LONG WAY FROM ANYWHERE ELSE

Ursula Le Guin

A very contemporary problem. Owen has difficulty coming to terms with a real relationship because of the teenage media's concentration on sex.